My Man's Best Friend

My Man's Best Friend

Tresser Henderson

www.urbanbooks.net

Urban Books, LLC
78 East Industry Court
Deer Park, NY 11729

ISBN 13: 978-1-60162-350-8
ISBN 10: 1-60162-350-X

First Trade Paperback Printing June 2012
Printed in the United States of America

10 9 8 7 6 5 4 3 2 1

Distributed by Kensington Publishing Corp.
Submit Wholesale Orders to:
Kensington Publishing Corp.
C/O Penguin Group (USA) Inc.
Attention: Order Processing
405 Murray Hill Parkway
East Rutherford, NJ 07073-2316
Phone: 1-800-526-0275
Fax: 1-800-227-9604

My Man's Best Friend

A Novel by
Tresser Henderson

Acknowledgment

First and foremost, I want to give all honor and praises to my Lord and Savior Jesus Christ. Without Him, none of this would be possible. He has blessed me with so many gifts in my life, and I can't thank Him enough for what He has done, what He is doing, and what He will do in my life.

To my high school sweetheart and husband, Wil, you are my support. Wow, look how far we have come, babe. People are shocked we are still together. We make it look easy, but we both know it's been a roller coaster of emotions. I'm happy we have matured together. Thank you for being a wonderful father to our children. Thank you for loving me and walking this road with me, even when our road gets bumpy. Still, we always find a way to smooth things out. I love you dearly and pray our union as one will remain unbroken. With God anchoring our way, we will be okay.

To my children, you are the joys of my life. It's funny how kids can teach you a thing or two, and you all have taught me many things, especially patience. Even though you are adding gray hairs to my head as we speak, you are my blessings, and I love you.

To my mother, Rebecca, you are my rock and my voice of reason. You have been the one who tells me to never give up on my dreams. You are the woman I hope to be some day. There isn't a day that goes by that I don't think of you and remember your encouraging words. You have the spirit of uplifting and have taught me to "Put God First." I love you so very much. I am blessed to have you as *my* mama.

To my daddy, Clarence. How blessed am I to have my dad who's helped make me into who I am. We've had some difficult times and tend to bump heads often, but it's okay. You are a great example of how God can bring an individual through difficult times. Never stop telling your story of triumph. I'm thankful I have you in my life. I love you, Daddy.

To my sister, Sabrina, and brother, Clarence, I love you guys. Clarence aka Duddy, LOL, know that there is so much more to life. You are a kind and genuine man. Never change that humble spirit about yourself.

And to Brina, thank you for reading this book first, even though you called me yelling about it. LOL! You are straight up about everything (*too* straight up), but I can count on you to always tell it like it is, even if it does come out harsh at times. But you know what? That's what I love about you. I'm so blessed to have you and Duddy as my siblings.

To Kenneth Greene. I know I haven't seen you in years, but I pray you see my book and read this. You are the reason why I started writing. You asked me in my lowest of days, "What is something you have always wanted to do?" I told you I always wanted to be a writer. You told me to write something so you could read it. I thought you were crazy, but I did what you asked, and I had a few pages to you the next day. You read it. Then you looked at me and told me this was my "gift." They say God places people in the right places at the right time if only for a season, and He did that by placing you in my life when I wanted to give up on so much.

Kenneth, I didn't give up. Thank you so much for being a blessing in my life and for giving me the courage to do my God-given talent.

Acknowledgments

To Minister Patricia Liggon, I want to thank you for listening and being there for me. You are so much fun, and I love talking with you. I know many might not think ministers can be fun, but God has truly shown me through you. Don't let anyone tell you different, for you are a woman of God and the spirit of joy constantly flows from you. Thanks for being so open and honest with me and sharing your words of wisdom.

To Crystal Townes, we have gone from cousins to best friends. I think I talk to you as much as I talk to Mom. It's pretty tight between you and Rochelle. LOL. My husband knows when I'm on the phone I'm talking to either you, Mama, or Rochelle, which is funny. You have survived what many may see as defeat. Don't lose that spirit of endurance. God has blessed you and will continue to rain down His goodness and mercy upon you.

To Rochelle Cicero, we started out on shaky ground years ago, but unusual circumstances brought us closer. Now we can't stop venting to each other. Our talks go from serious and tearjerking to gut-busting laughter. I'm glad we have become great friends. Thanks for reading my work and pushing me even when I didn't want to be pushed. Now it's your turn. Follow your dreams, girl. Step out on faith and do you! You have a story to tell, so tell it.

To Melissa Terry, girl, you have read every book I have written. You have been my sounding board, and I thank you for believing in me enough to take time out of your life to do this for me. Thanks for all your encouragement. I appreciate what you have done for me. I miss our girls' night out. We really need to get back to doing that again for sanity's sake. LOL.

To Andre Price, you have been such a blessing to me. I thank you for everything you have done for me when

Acknowledgments

I tried to self-publish my book. You have such a patient and kind spirit, and I know God is going to continue to bless you. I appreciate you so very much.

There are so many family members and friends I could name who have supported my dream. To all my aunties, uncles, nieces, nephews, sisters- and brothers-in-law, and many cousins, I want to thank you. My family has played a huge part in my life. I wish I could name all of you, but I know if I tried I would forget somebody, and I don't want to hurt anybody's feelings, so I'm going to say I love you all. I also would like to thank my friends. A lot of you are like my family. Thanks for your support.

Last, but not least, I want to thank all the individuals who took a chance in purchasing my book. My dream can't come true without you. Thank you so much and may God continue to be a blessing to you.

"Believe it! Claim it! Trust in the Lord!
And watch how your dreams will come true!"
~ Tresser Henderson

Derrick

As soon as I walked up on the porch of my parents' house I knew this was not going to be a good visit. I made the mistake of bringing Zacariah with me. I don't know what I was thinking, especially since she looked like she was going to a strip club to perform in her barely-there cotton top and short denim shorts clipping her butt cheeks. I knew it was warm, but damn, did she have to dress as close to naked as she could get?

She whined, "It's too hot. Why did we have to stop by anyway? It ain't like you don't talk to her on the phone," saying it like it stung her tongue.

I finally turned and looked at her, thinking, *Will you please just shut the hell up for five minutes?*

She rolled her eyes saying, "Don't be looking at me all crazy. You know I don't like coming over here anyway. Your mama doesn't like me, so I don't know why you insist on bringing me with you. I'm not going to pretend everything is cool between the two of us because you know that ain't me."

"Would you please be quiet? Like I told you in the car, we were in the neighborhood, and I wanted to see how my mother was doing. If you want to go back and sit in the hot car, go right ahead," I said, pointing in the direction of my automobile.

"Fine! Give me the keys," she said holding her hand out.

"For what?"

"Because I'm going to turn the air conditioner on. It's hot, and I'm not about to sweat these curls out on my head," she said, pointing to the spirals brushing her shoulders that she just had done at the beauty shop.

To avoid anything else with her, I reached in my pocket and handed her my keys. She popped her chewing gum and stepped off the porch.

"And hurry up because I don't have all day."

I shook my head watching her strut away. With her I knew I couldn't say anything because it would just lead to an argument. I wanted so bad to tell her, "You can sit under the tree until I get back," because I didn't want her burning my gas up. Was she not aware of the price of gas these days? Come to think about it, she probably didn't know since I was always filling her ride up for her.

I don't know how our relationship ended up here. It's been four years, and we're going at each other's throat about every little thing. In the beginning, things between us were good. That was, until I found out she cheated on me. I've had a hard time trusting anything she did and anything that came out of her mouth after that. She told me it would never happen again, but somehow, I couldn't bring myself to believe her. Zacariah only cares about herself.

How I fell for her still astounds me. We met at church. I was attending morning service with Mama, and she was with her best friend Essence. I know that sounds crazy, but Zacariah did attend church. Her smile captivated me, but her body called out to me. My mama raised me to treat women with respect, and I try to, but I'm still a man.

When I saw Zacariah looking the picture of beauty standing five foot three with her coffee-colored skin and a body that made men whip their heads around, I had to speak. Once I got up close and personal, I saw her small waist and a bootie that made you want to smack your mama. Not that I would ever smack my mama because she was the woman I loved most in my life. Plus, I wanted to live. But Zacariah was slammin'. I must have been blinded by her smile. No. I think it was her hips that hypnotized me. Those hips are what got me hooked as they rocked back and forth on my Johnson the first time we ever had sex, and I have been addicted to her ever since.

It only took a couple of months to find out Zacariah's true colors. They say opposites attract, and it couldn't be truer in our case. I'm more of the laid-back, reserved type of guy, where Zacariah is loud and disingenuous. Her attitude kicked in like a tornado dropping down on a sleeping town. She turned into the most snobbish person I had ever met. I still can't understand how I didn't see this sooner.

Zacariah turned her nose up at so many people, especially the ones who do not fit into her category of slim, lovely, stylish, and established. By established, I mean having money. And I didn't mean her own money. I mean somebody else's hard earned cash. Who else was going to keep her nails and hair done all the time? She never pays her bills on time, but she always looks like a million dollars wherever she goes. She chooses getting her hair done over keeping the electricity on in our home. Selfish, which is what describes the woman I fell in love with, and stupid is what you can call me.

Shaking my head in frustration, I opened the screen door to my parents' home and walked in. Cigarette smoke hit me in the face as soon as I stepped in. I waved my hand hoping I could bring some fresh air to my nostrils, but it didn't work.

"Daddy, you need to quit that bad habit," I said looking at him playing chess with one of his old buddies.

"And you need to stop telling me what I need to be doing, son. I'm a grown man in case you forgot."

"I know, Pops, but in case you forgot, cigarettes kill. Secondhand smoke is just as bad, and Mama doesn't need to be inhaling this toxic smoke."

He looked up at me, peeking over the black-rimmed glasses hanging on the tip of his nose. Steadily puffing on his cancer stick he said, "Your mama isn't complaining."

"Pops, Mama has been trying to get you to quit for over twenty years."

"And she still with me. She must not have too much of a problem with it, or maybe it's the way I put it down on her," he said, eyeing me again with a devilish grin.

That was my cue to leave the room. Pops knew what to say to get me out of his face. I held up both hands, smiled knowing there was no reason to argue with him, and went looking for Mama.

I went into the kitchen where I knew she would be. That short walk brought back great memories of me growing up in this house. I pictured dinner around the table with home cooked meals, and holidays when family would come over to celebrate the season, and nights when Mama snuggled next to me when I was little, talking to me about how I could be anything I wanted to be as my eyelids got heavy with sleep. I smiled as I remembered my wonderful upbringing as I moved closer to the sweet smell of Mama baking something.

When I entered, she was washing up some dishes. I felt like every time I came here she was doing something. She never stopped, and her house was proof of her impeccable efforts. Lucky for me, she instilled those same cleanliness habits in me too.

"Hey, Ma," I said giving her a peck on the cheek.

"Well, hey, baby. What brings you over this way?"

"I was in the neighborhood and thought I would stop by to see how you and Pops were doing."

"Well, it's a nice surprise," she smiled, drying her hands off on her apron. She came over to me and wrapped her arms around me.

"What was that for?"

"Is there something wrong with wanting to hug my only son?"

"Never," I said smiling. "I see you cut your hair." Her short cut took off at least five years from her age. Not that Mama needed time removed. For fifty-two, Mama looked great. Her skin was flawless, her smile was bright, and her energetic spirit made people think she was in her thirties.

Bringing her hand to her head, she rubbed her hair saying, "I like it too. It's so easy to maintain. I thought about coloring it because I got some gray coming in, but I decided to let the gray show."

"It looks good."

"Thank you, baby. Go ahead and sit down at the table and let me fix you a glass of tea. Are you hungry? I got some leftover meatloaf from last night and a cake in the oven. It should be ready in a few minutes."

"No, I'm good, Mama. I just had something to eat with Zacariah."

"Um," she said in that motherly way, letting me know she didn't like her. "Is she with you now?"

"She's outside."

"I guess she too scared to come in."

"Mama, she knows you don't like her."

"And she ain't lying."

"Mama."

"Son, I told you before I don't care too much for that girl. She's disrespectful, loud, and sometimes just straight up ghetto."

"Mama."

"And I know you're with her, but I wish you would leave her alone. You should've left her when she cheated on you the first time, and I say *first time* because there's going to be a second, that's if she hasn't cheated on you again already. She proved then she's not to be trusted," Mama said, setting the glass of ice tea in front of me.

"But that's for us to work out. I appreciate you trying to look out for me, but I know what I'm doing. Plus, I love her."

"Right now, you are lusting over that girl with all them breasts and tail hanging out all the time. I can tell she's a freak."

Sipping on my tea, Mama's words caught me off guard, and I almost spit the tea halfway across the kitchen.

"You okay, baby?"

"I'm fine. I'm just wondering what you know about freaks?"

Her eyebrows arched, and I knew then I had put my foot in my mouth. I should have left the subject alone.

"Son, I may be old. Let me rephrase that. I'm not old. I'm mature, and I know a whole lot about freaking, which is why I can recognize a freak when I see one."

I wanted to rip my ears off my head and stuff them somewhere deep so I wouldn't have to hear about my mother being a freak. No son ever wanted the words "freak" and "Mama" in the same sentence. It is hard enough when my parents get all lovey-dovey with each other. Of course, I'd frown, and they would laugh and say, "How do you think you got here?" Everything in my stomach would want to come back up. No child wanted to know their parents had a love life of any sorts. Especially the type where freaking was involved.

"Okay, enough about that, Mama," I said laughing as did she.

"Look at my baby boy getting uncomfortable with his mother."

"It's just the topic of conversation, Mama. Can we change the subject? Let's talk about how you and Pop have been doing. Are the two of you making it okay?"

"We're doing good. Your father is working some, and I'm still getting my disability, so we're making it. It's just the two of us, so we don't need much."

"If you need any money, Mama, you know I got you."

"I know, baby, but we're doing fine. God is taking really good care of us."

I nodded in agreement. That's when I heard a knock at the door and Pops said, "Come in."

I knew it was Zacariah. Mama gave me that look, and then went over to the oven to check her cake. Zacariah spoke to Pops, and then came into the kitchen where Mama and I were.

"Hello, Ms. Shirley."

"Hello, Zacariah," my mother said not looking in her direction as she took the cake out of the oven. Zacariah looked like she wanted to roll her eyes, but she decided against it when she saw me glowering at her. She knew when it came to my mother, I didn't play.

"Are you ready to go, Derrick?" she asked, sounding impatient.

"I was just about to come out."

"It doesn't look that way to me with you sitting here drinking a nice cold glass of tea," she said sounding aggravated. "I wish I had a sip of something to quench my thirst."

Zacariah looked in Mama's direction and was ignored like I knew she would be.

"I guess I can't have any tea, huh? I guess I'll continue to swallow my spit and hope that will satisfy me."

I gripped the glass with both hands trying not to lay her out in my Mama's house, so I pressed my lips together trying to think of something to say, but Mama beat me to the punch.

She came back over to the table with me and sat down eyeing Zacariah's barely-there attire. Clearing her throat Mama said, "He'll be out when he's finished drinking his tea, okay?"

"Well, hurry up, Derrick, because I'm tired of sitting in the car. You know I got somewhere to go later, and I need to start getting ready."

Mama looked at the clock on the wall which showed 6:48 P.M. She then looked at me, and her face told the story. Mama was doing well by maintaining herself, but I knew in a matter of seconds she was going to be all over Zacariah.

I stood and said, "Give me a few more minutes and I'll be out, okay?"

"Just hurry up," she said walking out of the kitchen. I didn't want to look back at Mama because I knew I was going to hear it.

"That girl needs to learn some respect. Coming up in my house almost naked. Your daddy and his friend got an eye full of her goods. And you know she dressed like that so men can drool all over her."

I sipped my tea.

"And if she comes up in my house one more time acting like I'm bothering her, I'm going to lay her behind out. It's been a long time since I've been around a person who makes me want to lose my religion, but that child right there is aching for a tongue-lashing from me."

I nodded, knowing better than to say anything to defend Zacariah because Mama was right.

"The nerve of her marching herself in here like you were suppose to jump when she wants you to," she said getting up from the table and wiping the spot where my glass was sitting.

"Mama, I'll talk to her."

"And say what? You should have got her straight right where she stood."

"I was trying not to disrespect your house, Mama."

"Well, she didn't mind disrespecting it. This house is more yours than hers."

"But you are my mother who I respect and love."

She smiled, letting some of the anger residing within her subside a bit. I wanted a moment of peace, and I didn't appreciate the way Zacariah acted, but I couldn't deal with her now. I came to see my mother and no one, not even Zacariah, was going to interfere with that.

"Well, I'm glad you came by to see me."

Standing, I said, "You're my mother, and I love you," wrapping my arms around her.

"I love you too, baby. But I don't want you to leave yet. I'm going to cut you a slice of this cake."

"Mama."

"I don't want to hear it. The Lord must have known you were coming by today for me to make this cake. Now give me a few minutes and I'll cut you some."

"Okay," I said smiling at her reaching into her white custom cabinet and pulling out a container to put the cake in. I looked around the kitchen thanking God for me being born to such a great woman. With my hands in my pocket, I pulled out five one-hundred-dollar bills. I knew Mama wasn't going to take it, but I always found ways to leave it with her.

"Here you go. I cut you three pieces," Mama said, handing over the lemon pound cake that smelled delectable. I leaned in and kissed her on the cheek again, slyly slipping the money into her apron pocket.

She felt my hand and said, "Boy, I told you I don't need any money."

"Love you, Mama," I said, jogging out of the kitchen smiling.

Kea

Too many nights I have sat alone, on this couch, in this room, looking at the ivory-colored walls wondering, "Where the hell is Jaquon?" The television played while my heart was jumping out of my chest in anticipation of his arrival. Running to the door, I wondered if the footsteps in the hallway outside of our apartment door were his. I peered through the peephole trying to see who it was. Again, it was not him. It was some guys going to the apartment right across the hall from me. They were laughing, giving each other dap. One was a white boy, and the other was black. Both were dressed in jeans and a white tee. Soon as Sheila, my whore of a neighbor whom I also named Freak-a-Leak, opened the door, some sensual music scurried past her. She had the music blasting. I was surprised no one had called the cops to complain.

She stood there scantily dressed with a matching bright red bra and panty set covered by an opened silk robe hanging from her shoulders. Her long micro braids swooped over her left shoulder as her bright red lips smiled at the men, welcoming them. You could clearly see she didn't bother to close her robe, exposing her entire body. Her size triple D breasts damn near toppled out of her bra, almost knocking at my door, and the G-string screamed to be freed from her substantial behind.

"Come in, boys," she said smiling, stepping back to let them enter. I knew then it was going to be a freak fest over in her living quarters. Probably why she had the music so loud, to drown out the screams of passion they were about to utter. At least somebody was getting some.

I walked back to the sofa and slumped down into the plush cushions. With each minute passing, my anxiety level increased. I had already called Jaquon several times just for it to go to his voice mail. Voice mail, that evil contraption set up for individuals just like him. For individuals who said, "I don't feel like talking to her right now," leaving your voice floating in a cell phone message nightmare.

I knew he was screening his calls. He had to be. What other reason would he have to not call me back? How dare he see my name pop up and not answer the phone, like I wasn't important to him. He had been gone all day without so much as a phone call. Granted, he worked, but he got off over five hours ago. He didn't call to see if I needed anything or just to let me know he'd be home later. I wasn't adequate enough for that. I guess that's what I got for being his at-home bootie. You know, that bootie at home that you know is going to always be there no matter what he does. I will never matter as long as Jaquon stayed in the streets playing Casanova. Bastard!

This was getting old, and I was mad at myself for crying my man's blues because he was out doing every-thing under the moon with whoever was willing to play a part in sexually pleasing him. And I knew there were enough playthings to go around. You got your freaks, bobble heads, and spread eagles. Those who will try anything, those who like to suck anything, and those who will do anything with you and your crew.

In my mind, I pictured the different faces of women who could turn his head, give him head, and make him bury his manhood deep inside them. Breasts large and lips softly glossed over sucking him as he whispered, "Suck it, baby. Daddy likes it when you suck it like that."

I was going crazy with my thoughts, but these thoughts were images demonstrated to me firsthand. I saw it with my own eyes.

Over a year ago, I followed him because I got tired of him telling me he was hanging out with the guys. As much time as he spent hanging with the guys almost made me think he was gay. I mean, a few of his friends were fine. Maybe he enjoyed being with them for sexual purposes.

I quickly disregarded this assumption because I knew Jaquon loved women. Maybe he loved them enough to be cheating. So one night I decided to follow him. To my dismay, he led me to some female's house. She opened the door with a smile plastered on her face as she welcomed him with an embrace and a kiss. I knew then I should have kept my behind at home, but like most females in this situation, I had to see more. I honestly started to convince myself that what he was doing wasn't that serious and Jaquon wouldn't hurt me like this. So I needed more proof.

I got out of my car and began to snoop. I searched every window of her house until I found them in her bedroom.

Homegirl didn't waste any time as she lay him down and began to strip for him. The lust on his face let me know he was enjoying every minute of it. I wanted to break the trick's window, but my eyes told my body to wait. I had to see more.

When bobble head whipped out his manhood and choked herself with it, I was done. Jaquon moaned and gripped her head as she sucked him long and deep. He pumped his hips up and down as she swallowed as much as she could of him. The look Jaquon was giving her was the same look he gave me when we made love, and that was the straw that made me lose all common sense.

I searched until I found a brick that was decorating her flower bed. I went back to that window before she could mount him and threw the brick through it. Glass shattered everywhere. Both of them jumped up trying to get away from the flying shards of glass, and that's when Jaquon saw me. I told him, "It's over," and walked away.

That window cost a nice piece of change that I wasn't ready to give up, but the court told me I had to. So I paid it, or rather, Jaquon paid it for me because he felt so guilty about what he had done to me. Needless to say, like a dummy, I took him back. I decided never to follow this man again because I didn't know what my next reaction would be.

Temptation had devoured Jaquon up and literally spit him out. He enjoyed the attention from women, and it wasn't like they didn't know he was my man. This area wasn't that big for tricks to not know Jaquon and I were in a relationship. I dressed him, caressed him, put blood, sweat, and tears into him. Now, trifling women were coming out of the woodwork to get worked by his wood, leaving me at home trying not to get any splinters.

Looking over at the socket to make sure the phone was plugged in, I clicked the phone on making sure a dial tone greeted me. It did. The sound of the constant buzz sent more anger through me because it just proved Jaquon wasn't thinking about me. Did he not see the sun had disappeared from the horizon and stars lit up the sky to indicate another day ending? Soon, morning would emerge, and I wondered if he would beat the sun home this time.

I picked up the phone and dialed his number again.

"Yo, what up? This Jaquon. Leave me a message and I'll get back to you when I get a chance. Holla."

"Jaquon, this is the tenth time I've called you. Where the hell are you? Why haven't you found the time to call me back? What is so damn important that you can't answer your damn cell phone? If you are not going to answer the damn thing, then why do you have it or are you screening your calls? I know that's what you're doing. You better not be messing around on me, Jaquon, or I will make your life a living hell! You better call me back soon," I threatened, slamming the phone down into the base.

Picking up the remote, I flicked through many channels which didn't have anything interesting to capture my attention until I came across the Oxygen station. One of my favorite shows was on, *"Snapped."* Bouncing my foot trying to release my anger, I knew I could be one of these women. I knew I could have a story told on me about how I killed my man. Some women did it for money. Some did it because they were in an abusive relationship. And some did it because it was easier to get rid of their partner than divorcing them. In my case, and like a lot of other women, I would be doing it because he cheated. I would be the woman who had had enough of her man's adulterous ways and decided to take revenge into my own hands.

I pictured myself taking him into our bed one last time as an act of getting my last groove on. I know it sounds crazy, but the man got skills when it came to having sex. After, I would make him a dinner to die for. Then this man would die from it. Arsenic poisoning would do.

I would smile at him sitting across the table from me and ask, "Baby, are you enjoying dinner?"

He would say, "I don't know what I did to deserve this. You sexed me, you are not arguing with me, and you cook like it's Thanksgiving. I'm in heaven right now."

"Baby, I'm doing this because you deserve it."

Next thing you know, we would go to bed, fall asleep, and the next day, I'm the only one to wake up to see the sun's rays shine bright.

The only thing stopping me from going through with this is the fact that I knew karma would catch up to me. Picturing myself in handcuffs as the police led me to the mug shot section, my mind would be a mixed slate of emotions. No tears would fall. Just a sense of relief that this man was out of my life for good and he could no longer inflict pain on my heart.

"Turn to the side," the officer would say as I held up my ID number that would represent me as I began to complete a sentence of life in prison without the possibility of parole. County-issued jumpsuits would now be my gear of choice, and a roommate would accompany me for the next lifetime. This could easily be me. And it scared me because I knew I was capable of hurting this man to the point of having to pull jail time. But I knew he wasn't worth it.

The phone rang, drawing me out of my deep thoughts, and I fumbled with it as I quickly grabbed it.

"Hello."

"What you doing, girl?" my best friend asked happily.

"Dammit."

"If I knew I was going to get all that, I wouldn't have called you," Terry responded.

"I thought you were Jaquon."

"What has Jaquon done this time?" she said, saying his name like it burned her lips.

"That's it. I don't know what he's doing right now. He hasn't called me since he got off of work. I'm sitting here now trying not to contemplate premeditated murder."

"Girl, you need to get a grip. You know he isn't worth any time in prison."

"I know, but it would make me feel so much better."

"So would leaving him, taking all his possessions, cleaning out his bank account, and stepping. You can do that without a prison uniform having to be involved," she said.

Terry couldn't stand him, because she was also aware of all the turmoil Jaquon had put me through. She had been my friend since ninth grade and has always had the confidence that says, "I can do anything that a man can do." She was single with no children and didn't want any until she met the right man to have them with. She was smart and beautiful, and this was why she's an excellent attorney. Who knows, I might need her services one day.

"It's not that easy," I told her.

"But killing him is?"

"At least if he's gone, I wouldn't have to see him, especially with another woman."

"That bastard would haunt you in your dreams if you took him out, and you still wouldn't get the peace of mind you're searching for. Now I know you don't want to leave him, but if you want to keep your sanity, then I would advise you to find another place to stay," Terry suggested.

"Why do I need to uproot myself?"

"Uproot him. Kick his behind out then."

"I can try, but he's not going to go anywhere. This apartment's in his name," I sighed, immediately wishing I hadn't let those words escape my lips. I knew Terry was going to go off.

"What do you mean in his name? Didn't I tell you to get your name on that lease too?"

"Yes, but I hadn't got around—"

"All that time you spend moping couldn't have been spent on getting your name on the lease, Kea? You have been there for how long?"

"Three, four years. I don't know. I can't think."

"I know it's been long enough to make that happen. I do know that. You never should have moved in together without your signature, giving you a claim to the place. I schooled you better than that."

"I know," I replied, regretting that I brought it up.

"Big mistake, and so was he. I told you that man was no good," she said proudly.

"I *know*. Please don't rub it in."

"Great looks and a big Johnson don't mean anything in a relationship. Whoa! Did I just say that?" Terry paused rethinking what she said.

"Yes, you did," I confirmed her mishap.

"Let me step back and reexamine that thing again. I mean Jaquon wouldn't be good in a relationship. Looks and a big Johnson are like Porterhouse is to a steak. It's almost like hitting the lotto. A good job and faithful to go along with those two things would be richly appreciated. I'm talking Oprah-rich too."

"You are not helping," I said.

"I'm just saying."

"I'm not thinking about his Johnson right now."

"That's a lie because you thinking about his manhood being buried between the legs of some hoochie," Terry said. "That's why you stressing now."

"Why can't he just be faithful?"

"Why can't I be a billionaire? Why can't you use the common sense God gave you? Remind me again why you are with him."

"I don't know, Terry."

"Okay. Let's recap. How many times has he cheated on you?"

"Too many times to count."

"And you have gotten how many infections from his philandering?"

"Okay. I get it."

"Do you really? Because I swear we have had this conversation way too many times. And I shouldn't have to remind you AIDS is spreading rapidly among African American women."

"I know this," I said in frustration. Terry's education session did not need to be spoken to me every time Jaquon was the topic of conversation.

"And you are still playing stupid. You're risking your life for what? But I don't know why I'm wasting my breath talking to a brick wall. You're going to give that bastard another chance, and he's going to show you he's still a trifling whore."

"But, Terry, I love him."

"And I love chocolate. I love butter almond ice cream. I love myself some Denzel too, but you don't see me losing my damn mind over these things."

"You know it's not the same. You don't have a man, so you can't understand where I'm coming from."

"Hold up. Wait a minute, girlfriend. Just because I don't have a man doesn't mean I don't have sense enough to know a dog when I see one. I saw Jaquon's trifling demeanor from a mile away. I'm here for you when you are soaking in misery because he hasn't thought about you all day. I was here for you when you went to the doctor. I was here for you all those other times he cheated on you. So don't you go there on me not having a man because if having a man consisted of dealing with the bull you've been putting up with, I don't want one," Terry said angrily in one breath.

"I'm sorry, Terry. I didn't mean to—"

"You damn right you sorry. You have ticked me off. I almost hung the damn phone up on you, but you need a friend right now, and I'm trying to be that person."

"I know, and I'm sorry, okay? I shouldn't be taking my frustrations out on you."

"Just think about what I said. And if you don't want to listen to that advice, then take this one. Cheat on him. Tit for tat."

"I can't do that."

"As long as that man knows you're going to sit home, argue once he gets in, and you still take him back, he's going to keep doing it. Give him some of his own medicine to swallow."

"Girl, I hear you, but I got to go," Kea said, rushing her off. "I got a beep. And it might be Jaquon."

Essence

I was walking downtown going to this restaurant to get some drinks with my friend Zacariah, trying not to step on the lines in the sidewalk since it broke your mama's back, when I heard this masculine voice within my proximity. Walking in his direction, I immediately slowed my pace taking in some of his conversation.

"I told you my cell phone is dead, which is the reason why I haven't called you . . . I'm talking to you from a pay phone . . . If you don't believe me, come downtown . . . Get dressed then. I'll be here . . . If you aren't coming then stop flapping your lips . . . Girl, you are ticking me off. You lucky I even called you . . . You need to let go of your paranoid behavior . . . I told you I'm not doing anything . . . Damn, it's been six months and you still trippin' . . . Fine!"

I continued to step slowly, acting like I was looking for something in my purse. I sized him up in a matter of seconds checking off my list of criteria a man has to meet for me to even speak to him. Tall, check. Dark, check. Fine, check, check, check. He was just the way I liked them and built to withstand what I could put down. He had on jeans, a blue collar shirt, and white sneakers on a size extra large foot. He had cornrows to the back and a face that was nicely edged up. The closer I got, the more I smelled the scent of his cologne that sent wetness between my thighs.

"I'm getting off the phone . . . I'm done talking to you . . .

"No, *you* go to hell," he stated, slamming the receiver down.

Soon as he hung up and turned to walk away from the pay phone, he ran directly into me. Rather, I made sure he bumped into me, dropping my purse to the ground for dramatic effect and everything.

"Excuse me," he said backing up.

"I'm sorry. I wasn't looking where I was going," I said, squatting to pick up my purse and some spilled items, hoping he would help me. And that's exactly what he did.

"I didn't see you coming," he stated.

"It's okay. I wasn't watching where I was going either, trying to locate my cell phone."

"I guess we both had other things on our minds besides walking, huh?" he said smiling. "Bad enough I had to use that nasty pay phone."

"Nasty is right."

"My cell died on me earlier and guess where my charger is?"

"Uh, I'm going to guess at home," I said as we laughed. "If I can locate my phone, you can use it if you want," I told him, looking at how big his hands were as he picked up my tube of lipstick and handed it to me.

"No, I called who I needed to talk to but thanks anyway."

"Thanks for helping me pick up my stuff."

"It wasn't a problem," he said as we rose to our feet.

Still pretending to look for my phone I said, "I guess I left it at home on my dresser. Dammit. And I needed to make a call myself. I don't have change to call my friend and tell her I'm running late. Do you have any?"

He reached in his pocket pulling out quarters.

"Here you go."

"Thank you. I really appreciate this. I can give you a dollar to make up for this."

"A dollar won't break me," he laughed.

"Are you sure, because I can give it to you?" *I really could give it to you.*

"Go ahead and call your friend. It's cool."

"I'm sorry for my manners. My name is Essence Clemmons." I held out my hand to shake his.

"Essence, like the magazine, huh?"

"Yes," I said feeling his warm strong hands grip mine.

"My name is Jaquon Mason."

"It's nice to meet you, Jaquon."

"Well, I better get home," he said.

"So soon? The night hasn't begun yet."

"True, but my girl is trippin' because I didn't come home after work."

"She should know it's Friday. A man needs to unwind after pulling eight hours," I said, telling him what he wanted to hear.

"Try twelve hours."

"Then you really need a drink."

"Tell me about it. I had a week from hell on my job. Maybe drowning my stress in the bottom of a bottle of liquor will help me."

"What do you do?"

"I work for the electric company."

"Oh? So you hook people up," I teased.

"You could say that," he smiled.

"I bet you were busy after that storm we had on Tuesday. It knocked out the power at my house."

"Yeah. That's why it's been a bad week. Everybody wanted their power on at the same time, not realizing it takes some time."

"Which is more reason to unwind. Why don't you relax and have a drink with me?" I asked.

"I don't think that's a good idea," he protested.

"It's just a drink, in a public place. You can leave after one. My treat," I smiled, making the deal sweeter.

"Just one," he said holding up one finger.

"Yes, just one."

"Only if you will let me pay. A man can't have a woman paying for him."

One drink led to two, which led to several more. We were so twisted when we left the restaurant we were holding each other up. My friend Zacariah was at the bar getting her talk on with some middle-aged gentleman. We had a code. If either of us ran our fingers through our hair, that meant prospect, don't bother me. That's exactly the signal she gave me, only I didn't return the signal. Jaquon was fun tonight so I didn't bother thinking of him as another score. And I'm glad I met him because I would have been drinking by myself tonight because the men in here were whack.

Jaquon ended up driving me home. I was too drunk to drive my own car so I had to leave it. I would get Zacariah to take me to pick it up tomorrow.

How he made it to my house, I don't know. Talk about the blind leading the blind. Both of us were intoxicated, but we made it without any problems. He was a gentleman and helped me to my door. I acted like I was too drunk to walk, but that was not the case at all. I was buzzed but not to the point that I didn't know what I wanted from Jaquon. He didn't know I could drink the average man under the table.

Soon as the key was in the lock, he said, "I had a nice time with you, Essence, but I better be getting home," backing away slowly.

I swung my door opened and told him, "Come on, Jaquon. Chill for a bit."

"But . . ."

"Please, just stay a bit. You're already in a load of trouble with your girl, so you might as well have fun because you know when you get home, it's going to be on."

I could see the wheels in his head turning as he put his hands in his pockets and swayed back and forth. Holding my hands out like I was weighing his options I said, "Fun. Arguing. Which one would you rather do?" holding up the hand for fun.

He smiled and said, "You're persistent, aren't you?"

"Only when I want something," I replied, looking at him seductively. "And you know your girl is not going to let you go anywhere without her. Not even to pick up a soda. So chill."

My plea worked, and Jaquon entered with me. He walked in and stood at the door like he was scared to come into my place any farther.

"Relax. Make yourself at home," I said walking to the console table behind my couch. Kicking off my four-inch heels, I stumbled a bit. Jaquon came up behind me and caught me before my behind hit the floor.

"Oops. I guess I'm tipsier than I thought," I laughed. He let go of my waist making sure my equilibrium was back. "I'm good now thanks to you. Please, have a seat," I said, gesturing toward the sofa. He walked over to my brown leather couch and sat down.

"I'm going to get us something to drink."

"Don't you think we've had enough?"

"No alcohol. Just some juice," I said exiting.

I went into the kitchen retrieving two glasses out of the cabinet to pour us some juice. Placing the glasses on the counter, I tried to think of a way I could better capture his attention. I had already determined I had to have him when I saw him talking on the pay phone. One-night stands usually ended with me robbing them, but this man robbed me of my breath. He was fine as hell. A cross between Tyrese and Denzel. He has swagger with a touch of thug and a smile to die for. I knew what I had to do.

I unzipped my dress, letting it fall to the floor getting my heel caught. Again, my behind almost hit the floor. I laughed to myself as I picked up the garment and placed it over the back of a chair. Pouring the drinks, I picked up the glasses and headed to the living room.

Entering, I saw Jaquon was looking through my picture album I had left on the coffee table. I stood as he concentrated on the pictures of my parents and cousins back home. He looked so damn cute and my body instantly started to ignite.

Walking closer to him until I was standing over him I said, "Here's your drink."

His eyes slowly moved up my legs, to my thighs, to my hips, my stomach, my breasts, and then my smiling face. His look was one of surprise and one of a man who wanted me just as bad as I wanted him. Just the way he licked his lips made me want to drop the drinks to the floor and hop on his face.

"Thank you," he said softly, not able to take his eyes off my unclothed body.

"I hope you like mango juice," I smiled, handing him the glass as he slowly took it. "It's all I had in my fridge. But I think I can offer you some other juice you might want to consume," I said, smiling at him devilishly.

"Essence, I . . ." he said as he stood up, letting the album fall to the floor, "need to go." He set his drink on the coffee table.

"You don't like what you see?" I asked, walking so close to him there was no space left between our bodies. We stared at each other for a long moment, and then I leaned in and kissed him deeply. Instinctively, Jaquon's mouth opened, welcoming my tongue. He tasted like peppermint, and I gripped the back of his head with my free hand, pulling him into me. My hormones were racing. Caught up in the moment, I let the glass of juice I was holding slip from my hand, falling to my couch. But I didn't stop consuming him. I would clean the mess later.

Now I had my other hand free to grip his Johnson, which had grown tremendously from the stimulation. I couldn't wait to have him inside me. He tried to push me away, but I wouldn't let him. The power of my persuasion was too intense for any man to refute. I made him want me.

Jaquon's hands started to tour the avenues leading to our sexual destination. One minute he was trying to resist me, and the next, he was taking full control, acting as though he had known my body forever. His hands gripped my butt cheeks with dynamism, forcing my body to collide with his. He was handling me rough, and I loved it. He was a man who took control, which only heightened my bliss. He picked me up, using my bootie as a handle to hold on to as my legs draped around his waist. Jaquon carried me to the kitchen table, which I thought was unusual. Usually the bed was the area of choice for these exploits.

He sat me on it and swiped everything that adorned it to the floor. My placemats, napkin ring holders, and floral arrangement went crashing to the hardwood floor. Pushing me back, he laid me down, lifting my legs into the air. Then he stood over me saying, "I bet you never been feasted on like this."

Feasted, I thought. The man was about to get down for real. I responded by saying, "I can't say I have."

"I like to bring things to the table, if you know what I mean," he grinned. "I'm going to let you know I'm a brother who can handle his business."

"Then handle it, baby," I urged.

Sitting in one of the chairs, Jaquon pulled me to the edge of the table, pushing his face deep into me. First, contact sent my body into indescribable pleasure. Damn, he knew what he was doing. I couldn't hold back what I was feeling and pulled his head deeper into me. Back-to-back explosions erupted from my body as my juices were offered to quench his sexual thirst.

"Don't stop," I begged him as he flicked in and out of me. "Please don't stop," I pleaded, knowing I was moments away from climaxing again.

Jaquon sat back in the chair smiling at me.

"No. Not yet," I said looking down at him. "What are you doing? I told you not to stop," I practically begged.

"It's not over yet, sweetie," he said standing. He reached to unbutton his pants and proudly released the beast raging to escape its restraints. The brother was hung two times over, and I wondered for a split second if I would be able to handle what he was going to put down on me. As a woman, I couldn't tell him, "hell to the nawh." Me, being a master of this craft, I had to prove I could handle all of him. And if going to my OB-GYN the next day was what I would have to do to make sure everything was okay, then so be it.

Instead of entering me, Jaquon walked around the table until he was standing over me. I turned to see his extension angling toward me. *Could my mouth even wrap around it?* I thought. This was definitely not a one-handed blow job.

He smiled down at me before stepping forward until the tip of his manhood was touching my lips. I licked it, trying to size its girth before opening my mouth to consume him. I couldn't take him all, but I worked what I could using both of my hands to stroke him. His moans let me know he was enjoying what I was doing and it only made me want to please him more.

After I lubricated him for a few minutes, he pulled away saying, "Not yet." I could tell by the way the head was swelling he was getting close to climaxing.

He moved back down to my womanhood looking down at my moist opening. Then he grabbed his extension, shaking it at me, and asked, "Are you ready?"

Hell, nawh, was what my mind screamed, but I nodded yes.

He climbed atop the table like a carnivore attacking its prey. I looked at him. Then I looked at his massive Johnson angling its way to my entrance. I wanted it, but I'm not going to lie, I was fearful too. My curiosity wanted to know what it felt like. I wanted to know how deep he would penetrate my inner walls. Jaquon let me know in a matter of seconds, pushing his way deep as his Johnson split me open. Deeper and deeper he went until I didn't think he could go any farther.

Suddenly, he pushed my legs up to my shoulders and I began to tremble. You would have thought I was lying on a block of ice the way my body was shaking. I didn't know if it was my body trying to reject its invader or my nervousness at such a monstrosity penetrating me. Either way, I continued to tremble.

Trying to accept his pleasure was a task that made it hard to enjoy his strokes. If pain was pleasure, I had a hell of a lot of it. After a little while, my body started to get used to its invader. As I relaxed, my walls gently accepted him deeper, so deep that this man hit something within me making water run as if I was pregnant and my water had just broke. I had no clue what the hell was going on, but he smiled and kept stroking his way to a climax.

This man had me feeling things I had never felt before. I don't know if it was his ruggedness or the sensual way he gazed at me, but something about him tantalized me. Maybe it was the way he licked his lips and enticed these hips. Whatever it was, I had fallen hard. Maybe the beast went deeper than I thought, tapping at the core of my brain, telling it to worship him. Whatever this feeling was, I didn't like it. I wasn't supposed to fall for the one-night stand. In this case, he was supposed to be my score.

As soon as we were done, Jaquon climbed off of me and began to get dressed. He never spoke a word, sliding his clothes on as I watched silently. I wanted to speak but exhaustion and soreness had me. I lay on my side, holding my stomach, wanting to pretend to be asleep, but how could I? I was still on top of a kitchen table lying in a puddle of my own juices. What could I say anyway? The sex was amazing. Maybe we could hook up some other time.

I could see guilt had started to creep upon his face. For a moment I felt bad that I contributed to his failing relationship. I hoped he would be able to work through explaining his infidelity to his girl. If it was any comfort to him, he did make me suffer having to deal with his immensity. My insides hurt like hell. I couldn't wait until he left so I could crawl into a warm bath and soak the pain away.

Jaquon walked to the door and looked at me one last time before exiting. I closed my eyes thinking how lucky I was to have had him for one night and the only score I had attained tonight was getting the biggest Johnson I had ever experienced.

Zacariah

Of all the people Essence had to show up with, she had to be with Jaquon. Talk about irony since he was my man's best friend. Thousands of men walking around in the area and she picks the one person who I disliked most. Here I was trying to get my game on and she shuts it down at halftime being with him. I hoped he didn't see me, especially with me trying to push up on this guy.

I stroked my hair turning my head quickly hoping Jaquon didn't see me with Red Bone. It would make his day to see me with this man, just so he could go back and inform Derrick about my little rendezvous.

Cooper was Red Bone's real name, and he swore up and down he was the Mack Daddy of smooth brothers. He looked as though his brotherhood was in question due to his light skin, curly hair, and green eyes acting as kryptonite to the ladies. And, yes, he lured me in nicely, but not with his hair or his eyes. He had me when I saw him sporting a Rolex and a Dolce and Gabbana velvet blazer with a crisp white shirt and black leather and suede moccasin-style Penny Loafers. He screamed *money*.

Of course, I couldn't act like I was taken by him. That's why I walked by him in my Asian-style printed dress accentuating my exposed back. The Jimmy Choo's lengthened my legs, making them sparkle like a trickling river on a sunny day. Soon as I passed him, he eyed me, just like I knew he would. I caught the eye of several other prospects also, but none of them interested me. That's because they were screaming, "I'm broke. Can you buy me a drink?"

Sitting down at an empty stool at the bar, I beckoned the bartender and asked for an apple martini. When he brought me my drink, he pointed at Red Bone and said it was taken care of. I lifted my glass and nodded in his direction. He smiled, and I said, "Gotcha!" to myself.

Moments later, he came over and introduced himself to me.

"My name is Zacariah."

"Zachariah?" he questioned.

"No, it's Zacariah. Za . . . car, as in car . . . rhea, like diarrhea. Zacariah."

"Okay, I got it now. It's a beautiful name for such a beautiful woman," he said, looking at me lustfully.

This was the only part I hated about telling anybody my name. Every time anyone saw it, they thought I was a guy called Zachariah. I loved my name because it was sort of unique. I didn't hear many individuals with it, but sometimes it did become a burden with so many pronouncing it incorrectly.

Red Bone was a prosecuting attorney, which explained his pricey attire. He bragged on himself like he was giving a bio on how fabulous it was to be him. He told me about his forty-four hundred square foot home in the Hills, his Porsche coupe that he paid $83,000 for, and his collection of vintage cars. He had looks and money, but nothing else of interest to talk about. He bored me beyond belief. It was all about him, him, and please, let's talk about him some more. I had to sip my drink frequently to keep from yawning in his face and playing narcoleptic to his tiresome banter. Laughing when he laughed not knowing what the hell he was talking about, I acted like what he was saying was law itself. I really wanted him to shut the hell up and invite me to a nice, luxurious suite for a quick nightcap.

I snapped back to attention when I saw Essence and Jaquon walking in my direction. I couldn't let him catch me so I quickly excused myself and proceeded to the ladies' room. Maneuvering my way there, I cussed at myself, hoping Jaquon didn't see me. I didn't want to get busted, but I damn sure wasn't ready to leave without doing what I came here to do. I would not be a happy woman if I couldn't jack this man for some of this money he'd been talking about most of the night, but I would sit in this restroom until the place shut down so Jaquon wouldn't see me with him. I knew if I tried to exit, Red Bone would see me and make a scene somehow without even trying. Maybe if I wished hard enough, Essence would follow me in here. But hell, if I could make wishes come true, then I would wish for my own damn money and wouldn't need a man to give it to me.

Most people would wish for peace on earth and some other crap I'm not interested in. Me, I would wish for wealth beyond my wildest dreams. I mean, wealth that could afford me a big house with servants and a pool in the backyard. I would want a closet full of designer clothes and another full of pricy shoes. I would have cars, jewelry, and a plane to fly me anywhere my heart desired. Forget peace on earth. Call me selfish. Now, if I had unlimited wishes, maybe, but from the cartoons and fairy tales, you usually only got three and I wasn't about to waste them on a world that didn't give a damn about me.

Snapping back to the here and now, I wondered why Essence didn't come after me. This way I could tell her the deal and she could get Jaquon out of here. But no, that was too easy and nothing ever seems to come easy for me.

My entire life consisted of hard work. My mother and father were alcoholics who fought all the time over who drank the last can of beer or emptied the liquor bottle and put it back in the cabinet empty. I went without food sometimes due to their drinking. I went to school with dirty clothes and an uncombed head, which caused me to get picked on as a child. The only reason I got to eat lunch at school was because it was free due to our financial shortcomings and I was lucky then that Mama had sense enough to complete the needed forms. Funny how I never had food in the house, but my parents could find some change to scrap up to go pick up a pint of this and a can of that.

When I hit my teen years, I had basically learned how to survive on my own. Family turned their nose up at me because I wasn't worth the time or trouble. I was the nappy-headed child created by the alcoholic twosome. So that left me on my own. I stole. I schemed. I even robbed to keep my head afloat. That was, until I learned that men could take care of me if I took care of them. I used my body to get what I wanted. I had to do what I had to do to survive. By the age of twenty, I had lost my father. All that drinking caught up with him, and he died of cirrhosis of the liver. Even when the doctors told him he had to stop drinking or he would die, he let their words fall on deaf ears.

I guess Mama was still living. I didn't really know since I moved away from her and most of my family right after my dad passed away. His death only sent her spiraling further into the bottom of bottles. What reason did I have to stay, and I have never looked back. They didn't give a damn about me then, so why should they care about me now? I needed them when I was child, but I was not worth receiving the love I knew I deserved. So here I stand. Yes, I have a good man at home, but our relationship could end whenever. So I had to keep the money coming in to be able to take care of myself. I loved Derrick, but I loved money more.

Zacariah

Pacing the mushroom-colored tile floor, I noticed I was not alone. I was so deep in my thoughts that I didn't notice a pair of legs behind the white stall door. Homegirl was either doing the number two or drunk as hell and couldn't find her way out. As long as I had been standing here, I should have heard something, but there were no sounds coming from the other side of the door. Some toilet paper should have been pulled or some flushing should have been happening by now, but nothing.

"Hello, are you okay in there?" I asked.

The chick didn't say anything.

"Hello in there, are you okay?"

The stall door clicked, but the door never opened. I wanted to push it open, but my mind led me to all of the horror movies I had seen. Soon as I pushed this door open, a maniac would jump out and bludgeon me to death.

"Get it together, girl," I whispered to myself. Then I started to wonder, was I the crazy one here? I'm the one talking to myself out loud.

When I got ready to step forward, the stall door eased open. Out stepped this short, skinny female with mascara running down her face. It was clearly evident she had been crying. The mascara made her eyes resemble a raccoon's. Her appearance scared me for a minute because she stood there looking bewildered and not saying anything. She was not an ugly chick. She was actually a very pretty woman. And for me to say that in her state of disarray, you knew she was nice looking. She was just having a moment taking her to a not-too-good-looking status. She looked at me, but it was like her spirit had disappeared from her body.

"Are you okay?" I asked wanting to reach out to her but thought better of it.

She stepped out of the stall, shaking her head no. Her arms started to hug herself tightly as more tears streamed down her cheeks. Even though she was cute, her body was that of a crackhead. She had no curves at all, and her breasts looked like those of a girl just starting puberty. I started to run out and go pick her up a Southern dinner with mash potatoes and gravy, macaroni and cheese, and a nice slice of lemon pound cake to help put some weight on her. Then again, maybe her eyes were watering because she just finished throwing up all the food she ate. You never know these days. Women were doing whatever it took to get skinny.

The woman was dressed in a short black slip dress with a Chanel bag hanging from her shoulder. Her hair was jet black and bone straight sweeping her shoulders. I wanted to snatch her bag and tug on her hair to see if it was all hers because it looked too pretty to be real. Her nails were done. Diamonds dangled from her earlobes and despite her anorexic state, her skin was flawless. The only thing throwing me off was the fact she had kicked her shoes off in the nasty bathroom. Disgusting, I thought because I knew there were a lot of different germs eating away at the bottom of her feet, mainly urine and fecal matter.

"Are you here alone tonight?" I asked.

She didn't respond, walking to the sink, looking at the lights above the mirror.

"Do you want me to call a friend for you?"

She shook her head no.

"What about your man?"

She immediately made eye contact with me, and I wanted to run away. Her stare was so frigid I thought ice daggers were going to start shooting out of her eyes.

"Why do men cheat?" she asked with a slow, sorrowful voice. "Can you answer that question for me?"

Finally something, I thought. "I don't know. It's in their nature," I offered.

"I'm a good woman. Why does he not love me enough to be faithful to me? I'm really a good woman."

"Honey, I don't know. All I can say is drop him and move to the next man."

"I tried to leave him, but he begs me to come back to him and I . . . and I . . .," she said with tears streaming down her cheeks again. Her quiet demeanor soon changed into uncontrollable crying. Through her weeping she continued to try to talk saying, "I believed him, and I know I'm grasping at straws, but the love I have for him makes me take him back. He professes his love to me all the time, and I . . . I . . ."

"Believe him," I said completing what I think she was trying to say.

She nodded. "I can't take it anymore. I really can't. He's killing me, and he doesn't even know it."

"Look, give me the number of a friend of yours and I'll call them to come pick you up. I think you really need someone right now," I said trying to convince her.

"It doesn't matter because they can't save me now."

"Save you?" I said looking at her with a questioning gaze.

She dropped her eyes to the floor and said, "Nobody can help me now."

Homegirl reached in her purse and pulled out the biggest butcher knife I had ever seen. I maybe exaggerating, but it was gigantic. I thought she was reaching for some foundation or eyeliner to get her face spruced back up—but a knife! I thought she was going to come at me with it so I jumped back. My instincts were to run out of there, but I realized she was closer to the door and I was too damn far from it. I wanted to scream, but nothing came out. Only dry air entered as my mouth remained opened sucking in air at the sight of that butcher knife. I was coming close to hyperventilating. I wanted out of there, and I was on the other side of the restroom trying to make myself disappear into the painted brick walls. Didn't women have to pee anymore?

Usually this door was a revolving source of women's reactions to consuming way too many drinks or the need to freshen up their makeup. If I wanted to be in here by myself, the space would be full to capacity.

I tried to play it cool, like I wasn't afraid of her holding this weapon, but I didn't know if it came across that way since I could hear myself panting like I had run a marathon. That alone confirmed my panic state.

"It doesn't matter anymore," she said twirling the blade, looking at it as the light hit it. Her mind had left the building, and I was looking for a window to push her out of.

"Just put the knife down. What is that weapon going to solve?"

"Peace. Revenge. Satisfaction," she said with a voice so eerie I truly feared for my own safety. She seemed like the type that would take other people's lives before she took her own.

Dropping her purse to the floor she turned to look at me. Was she about to stab me with the knife? Fear had me glued in place, and all I could say was, "Just put the knife down. It's not worth it."

"I'll teach him to cheat on me," she said serenely. She began to raise the knife in the air. I wanted to scream, but still nothing would come past my lips. Was she coming closer to me or was it my imagination working overtime?

I managed to mumble the words, "Put the knife down," hoping she would comply, but she just looked at me with that same blank stare she had when she walked out of the bathroom stall.

Closing her eyes, she lifted the knife above her head. I backed away some more until I was against the wall. She then placed her other hand on the handle and whispered, "Please forgive me for what I'm about to do," and plunged the blade.

Zacariah

I had never seen so much blood in my life. How could so much blood come out of one skinny person? I couldn't move. I was paralyzed in a state of panic. To see this woman plunge that enormous butcher knife into her stomach instantly made my stomach throb.

The door opened at the time she wounded herself so another woman witnessed the attempted suicide. She did what I couldn't do and screamed. Moments later, herds of people came scampering in and around the bathroom door while the body of the skinny chick lay on the cold tile floor. Her eyes were bulging, and she was making a gurgling sound, like she was trying to catch her breath. Blood oozed from her mouth as she continued to try to breathe. Each breath taken was a struggle, sounding like it was her last. Then she stopped moving or saying anything. Her body lay still as her hands fell from her wounded abdomen unto the floor. Her eyes were still open. *Is she dead?* I thought, and *Why would she do something like this to herself?*

Several bouncers pushed their way through the crowd to get to what everybody was looking at. Once they saw her lying on the floor, one of them kneeled down beside her to feel her neck for a pulse, but he said he couldn't feel anything. Another came over wanting to remove the knife from her abdomen, but the bigger bouncer pushed him away, telling him he could not remove it. He didn't want to risk any more damage being done, just in case she did have a faint pulse he couldn't feel.

My feet were rooted to this spot. I was watching as they frantically tried to stop the bleeding. Then I heard sirens in the distance, hoping they would get here soon to save her. Three other bouncers began to clear the area to let the paramedics through.

That's when I felt a warm hand on my bare shoulders. It was the woman who walked in and saw the incident with me. She was trying to get me to leave the scene. She pulled me into her and escorted me out of the area. With all eyes on us as we both exited, people were whispering and some were loudly asking what happened over and over again. Neither the woman nor I said a word.

Red Bone was in the crowd, and he came over to me, putting his arms around me, also asking, "What happened?" I scanned the crowd to see if I saw Essence, but neither she nor Jaquon were in sight. *Good,* I thought.

After answering Red Bone's questions, I got another hundred asked by the bouncers, the manager, EMT, and the police. I had nothing else in me and wanted to tell them all, "You should have all stood together so I could have explained the incident once." They could've at least tape-recorded my story so I wouldn't have to keep repeating the same thing. Or maybe that was their way of interrogating me. Ask the same question several times to see if they got several different answers. But the only story they were going to get from me was, "She plunged that blade in her own stomach."

By the look on a couple of the officers' faces, I could tell they thought I was responsible. I was the only one in the restroom with the victim. Salt and Pepper they were. One was white and the other black. Both were of burly stature, and both had pen and paper out scribbling my feedback. Maybe they thought I did it and made it look like she did. Maybe I was one of those females trying to get rid of the competition ruining her relationship with her man. Or maybe it was because I was black. Whatever, I was not happy with them scrutinizing me with suspicion like a criminal. If it wasn't for the other woman walking in at the time of skinny girl's stabbing, they'd probably be putting handcuffs on me reading me my rights.

But I had Red Bone by my side. Plus, the lawyer in me watched enough court cases to know I could talk my way out of this. Where was the blood on my hands? Why wasn't any blood on my clothes? Why were my fingerprints not on the weapon? If I wiped my hands off, where was the evidence? Check the toilet, my purse, the pipes of the sinks and the stalls. I was innocent, and this was a crime that was not going to be pinned on me. Open-and-shut case it was. Just the thought of them thinking I did this ticked me off.

After the police questioning, they did their jobs keeping the area secure. When the paramedics wheeled the wounded woman on the gurney past everyone, Red Bone gasped, making me jump.

"Angela," he said loudly attempting to run over to the wounded woman.

"Stand back," the police officer said grabbing him.

"But that's my wife! That's my wife," he said hysterically. The officer looked at him, and then at me. I knew what he was thinking as more doubt registered on Salt and Pepper's faces. Damn, I would think the same thing too. In that moment, I was guilty until proven innocent in their minds. I was the other woman with the victim's husband.

In shock myself I kept saying, "His wife?" *You mean to tell me the man I was hanging out with was the husband of the suicidal woman holding the knife who I was alone with in the bathroom? She had to have seen the two of us together, which explained her tears. No wonder she was staring at me like she was. She could have stabbed me, then herself. Lucky for me, she didn't. This could have been a murder-suicide case due to a jealous woman who had finally had enough from her cheating husband.*

Unfortunately for her, she succeeded in showing him because later I found out she was pronounced dead at the scene. The news shook me up. I knew in that moment the paramedics could have been saying those same words over my body but fate stepped in and saved my behind.

Needless to say, it was a night I would never forget. Red Bone didn't have to worry about me again, even though I was pretty sure he wasn't thinking about me anyway. He now had to plan his wife's funeral. I guess she really did show him, by proving that she loved him 'til death do them part.

Derrick

Picking up Zacariah was the last thing I wanted to do tonight. She found her way here. Why couldn't she find her way home? Soon as I pulled up, I could tell something was wrong. The many police cars were a clear indication. I saw Zacariah standing at the curb and pulled up for her to enter. She jumped in without saying a word. I mean I didn't even get a hello or thank you for coming to pick her up. She sat in the passenger seat with her arms crossed looking straight out the window not acknowledging me at all like I was her mortal enemy or something.

"So you are just going to get in here without saying a word?"

"I called you over thirty minutes ago," she said rudely.

"And I'm here."

"But you took too long getting here."

"Did you forget where we live? It's not like I was around the corner, you know," I said defensively. "And I couldn't fly through every stoplight or pass every car to get here for the almighty Zacariah. You're lucky I even came to pick you up. You want to run your mouth about me taking too long? It could have been all night," I said, driving off, hoping my slight squealing of the tires wouldn't cause a cop to come after me.

"And what is *that* supposed to mean?" she asked.

"It means I could have stayed in my bed instead of coming to get you."

"You know what? Can you just shut up and get me home?"

"Not until I find out why I'm picking you up in the first place."

"Because I asked you to, that's why. Is that a good enough reason?"

"Zacariah, I don't need your attitude."

"And I don't need your questioning me either. Can't you just take me home and shut the hell up? Damn."

"Hold up. You better watch how you talk to me. Just because you're having a bad night doesn't mean you're going to take it out on me. I'm doing you a favor. I could have left your stank behind still standing on the curb."

Still looking out of the window Zacariah said, "Derrick, I'm in a bad mood because a woman took her life in front of me tonight, okay?"

"Whoa," is all I could say.

"You see now."

"Baby, what happened?"

"Just a few minutes ago my name was stank behind. Now it's baby," she said looking at me.

"I'm sorry. I just didn't appreciate your attitude when you got in the car."

"Now you know the reason for my mood. And to be honest, I really don't feel like talking about it right now. Maybe I can tell you about it in the morning. I've had to explain this same story too many times tonight. I really don't feel like repeating myself again."

"Maybe this will stop you from going out now. Maybe this is a sign for you to slow your roll and stay home with your man," I said.

"I guess you want me to become Susie Homemaker and stay under your ass all the time," she said looking over at me.

"I'm not saying that. My point is it doesn't look good for you to be out at all times of the night every weekend. And please let me state, you can never be Ms. Susie Homemaker."

"First of all, I don't see anything wrong with me going out," she said with the folds in her forehead coming together for a meeting on frustration. "Second, don't ever say what I can't be because I can be anything I damn well please, okay? I just don't choose to be waiting on no man hand and foot, cleaning house and cooking dinner all the time. That ain't me."

"Which is why I said you can never be Susie Homemaker. Plus, you can't cook."

"Yes, I can," she squealed.

"Boiling water doesn't count. You have to actually stand by the stove and put something into the water and tend to it for it to be considered cooking. How many pots have you burnt up boiling water?"

"I walked away for a few minutes."

"That few minutes nearly burned the house down. Face it, Zacariah, you can't even heat a microwavable dinner."

She smacked her lips, tightening her demeanor, not wanting to deal with the facts presented.

"Baby, I'm just saying, you don't have to get upset."

"I'm not upset," she said sternly.

"Yes, you are. And maybe that's because you know I'm telling the truth."

She rolled her eyes, sighing.

"Not many men would put up with your diva behavior. Not to your extreme anyway. I'm a good man who sits home waiting for his woman to get home after she flirts, shakes her ass, and consumes as many drinks as men will buy her."

"How do you know—" she attempted to speak.

"Don't even say it. I know men buy you drinks because you have never purchased one on your own for as long as I've known you."

"Derrick, enough knocking me tonight. You don't have to be with me if you don't want to. I'm not forcing you to stay with me. And if you have such a problem with me going out, why don't you go yourself?"

"So you saying you wouldn't mind me going out with Jaquon?" I said laughing. Zacariah didn't reply because I knew she couldn't stand him. "You wouldn't mind me going out with him, having a woman buy me a drink, and having her grind all up on me all night?" I asked approaching a green light.

"You damn right I would mind because don't no woman need to be putting her hands, breasts, or ass on you. And as for Jaquon, he's a bad influence," she said.

"And all your friends are a great influence."

"Essence is," she retorted.

"She's a liar."

"No, she's not."

"Well, she lied to me to protect you. You cheated on me before, remember, and I know she knew about it," I countered pulling up to a red light.

Zacariah didn't answer. I sighed looking at the light which was still red. I noticed a white coupe pull up to my left side and admired the rims. In the car sat two females who were very attractive. Both looked over at me and smiled. Neither broke their stare, that was, until Zacariah leaned forward and started screaming at them.

"Who the hell are you looking at?"

"We're checking out your man," the one in the passenger seat said with long hair sweeping her shoulders.

"He's cute. Maybe he should drop you off and follow us so we can get to know him a little better."

The woman turned her attention to me and asked, "Have you ever been with two women at the same time before?"

I wanted to say never but Zacariah yelled, "Don't make me get out of this car and snatch that weave outta your head."

Both women's facial expressions changed from smiles to straight up wanting to beat Zacariah down.

"Get out of the car then, trick," the girl snapped back.

Zacariah reached for the door handle, but it was locked. The light turned green, and I sped off, eliminating her possibly catching a beat down.

"You should have let me check those whores."

"And catch a charge? I don't think so," I said minutes away from pulling up at my house. I looked in my rearview mirror making sure the coupe wasn't following us. It wasn't. It was just some girls wanting to start trouble.

The garage door opened, and I pulled in. Zacariah had already taken her seat belt off and didn't let me stop the ride completely before she jumped out. I, on the other hand, took my time. By the time I made it up to our bedroom, Zacariah had gotten undressed. She screamed, "I'm going to take a shower."

"Do you want me to join you?"

"No! I don't need you crowding me. Go back to bed or watch television," she yelled, slamming the bath room door.

On cue, the doorbell rang and I knew who it was. I swear he stalked my house.

Wishing this night would end with some peace, I opened the door saying, "Not again, Jaquon."

"Just tonight, man," he said walking pass me.

"When are you going to learn that you can't come here every time you do your dirt?"

"Come on, Derrick. I haven't been over here in weeks."

"Who was she tonight?" I asked shutting the door.

Jaquon ignored the question, walking toward my basement entryway. He proceeded down the stairs like I didn't say anything. He took it upon himself to make himself at home, as usual. My basement was completely finished and looked like a second apartment with a living room, bathroom, small kitchen area, bar, and pool table. He walked over to the coffee table, picked up the remote control, and turned on the fifty-two-inch flat panel TV. He then went to the fridge and pulled out a beer, kicking off his shoes, and plopped down on the sofa.

"You know you are making this too much of a habit. You barge in my place, taking over like you pay bills here."

"Derrick, this is my second home."

"Then contribute to the mortgage, my light bill, cable, and food."

"I don't have any money today," Jaquon said with his eyes fixed on the score to the ball game that was on earlier.

"Who was she tonight?"

He laughed saying, "She was tight. Body was like," moving his hands in the air to represent her having a big round bootie and nice-size breasts. "Shorty was hot, and she had me on fire."

"If you keep this up, you're going to be on fire, burning," I said chuckling.

"If I'm burning, I swear tonight was worth it because homegirl had it going on."

"I thought you weren't going to cheat on Kea anymore."

"I wasn't, Derrick, but this chick came on to me. We had a couple of drinks. Then we had some more drinks, and then I took her home."

"And you just had to tuck her into bed," I said.

"We never made it that far," he said reminiscing on the evening. "She started hitting me off. My mic enjoyed the sounds she played with her lips."

"TMI, Jaquon. TMI."

"We did it right there on her kitchen table. Shorty had some skills, and she was straightforward with what she wanted. I couldn't deny her."

"Yes, you could have. You could have walked out that door and took your ass home to Kea."

"Oh, my baby, Kea."

"I guess you forgot about her in the midst of you blowing this chick's back out."

"I did think of her and tried to resist, but, oh, girl was persuasive," he said.

"Your trifling ways are going to catch up with you."

"Maybe, but for now, I'm going to enjoy myself."

"You need to go home to your girl."

"Where's your girl at?"

"She's taking a shower," I said.

"Washing off her trick's cum?"

"Man, don't be talking about her like that," I said with irritation. "Would you like it if I called Kea a trick?"

"You couldn't. Kea is a good girl. Zacariah, well, we know what she's done in the past. I still can't figure out why you took her back," he said, taking another sip of his drink.

"The fact is we are still together. If you keep doing what you are doing, Kea is going to get smart and leave you," I said.

"She's not going anywhere," Jaquon said arrogantly.

"Keep thinking that. Eventually, sweet, innocent Kea is going to retire you and find herself someone to take your position, if you get my drift."

"No one can fill my position, if you get what *I'm* saying."

"Funny, but please believe there is always another brother who will work harder at filling Kea up since you never seem to have time to do it yourself."

Kea

The sun did beat Jaquon home. When I got up to get dressed for the day, he was not in bed next to me. My stomach felt like bees were buzzing around in it, stinging me every time I took a breath, but I couldn't cry. My tear ducts had dried up. I had been crying so much my eyes were swollen. I really couldn't open them much. They felt like weights were pressing down on them. Looking in the mirror in the bathroom, I stared at my reflection thinking, *What is wrong with you? You are a beautiful woman and can do better than Jaquon. Why do you feel you have to stay with him?*

I answered my own question speaking, "It's because I love him."

I watched my lips move, repeating those words over and over again. "It's because I love him." I didn't know why I loved him so much. All he did was hurt me. What did I do for him not to want to be with me? I really couldn't see myself without him. And I knew once those keys jingle in the door, I was going to be so happy he was finally home, thinking, *He chose to come home to me. Whoever she was, it didn't matter because he still came home to me.* However, it was the next day, and whoever she was, she had him all night while I slept alone.

Still staring at my reflection, I shook my head at my excuses. *It's because I love him.* The voice inside me said, *When are you going to start loving yourself?*

I shrugged, watching my shoulders almost touch my earlobes. I started to run some warm water in the white porcelain sink. I had to wash the residue of salty tears off my face which was incased by it, like I slept with a facial mask on all night. With pores tight, I dipped the washcloth in the soothing water and gently rubbed it across my face. With each stroke, I felt renewed. Afterward, I ran cold water over the cloth and placed it over my eyes to help with the swelling. I couldn't go meet my sister looking like this.

I didn't feel like being around my sister today. I was supposed to meet her at the bridal shop to try on my bridesmaid dress one last time before her wedding next Saturday. Instead, I wanted to crawl back under my blue cotton sheets and relax all day. I was in no mood to feel happy about her getting married to a great guy who owned his own home and had lots of money. Every time I went around her, she talked about how happy she was and how this had to be the wedding of her dreams. I knew I was supposed to be happy for her, but my life was not a cakewalk like hers. We lived totally different lives. I had issues going on and to see her breeze through life like things were peaches and cream disgusted me.

After showering, doing my hair, and eating a bowl of cereal, I began to get dressed. Soon as I snapped on my last bracelet, the phone rang.

"Hello."

"Hey, Kea, this is Derrick."

"I guess you calling to tell me Jaquon was with you all night."

"Yeah, he stayed with me. If you don't believe me, ask Zacariah when you see her next time. You know she will not lie for Jaquon. She can't stand him."

"That's all well and good, Derrick, but he stayed out all night long again and I could care less if he was sleeping at your house or in an alley somewhere. Jaquon should have came home."

"Kea—" Derrick called out, but I continued to take my frustration out on him.

"I'm tired of his crap. He like's sleeping over there so much, then maybe he should move over there permanently."

"I know he needs to get himself together," he said before I cut him off again.

"Why are you calling for him anyway? Why couldn't he be man enough to call me himself? Is he trying to get a feel on the type of mood I'm in? Well, you can tell him I'm pissed the hell off."

"I just called to tell you he was on his way home. I don't know why he didn't call you himself. He told me to give you a ring, so I did."

"Well, thank you for calling me, Derrick."

"Anytime. And Kea?"

"Yes, Derrick?"

"Don't hurt my boy too bad," he said laughing.

A few minutes later those keys I had been longing to hear jingled in the door lock. My heart kicked up some beats, and I almost ran to him, but I didn't. I wasn't going to be nipping at his heels like I always did, wrapping my arms around his neck, then arguing with him about where he's been all night.

Hearing the screeching of the door hinges, the door opened, and then closed. I heard Jaquon call out to me.

"Baby, where are you?"

I didn't answer.

"Kea, baby, are you here? You got to be here because your car is still outside."

The more he spoke, the closer I could tell he was getting to me.

"There you are," he said, coming over to me with one hand behind his back. He tried to kiss me on the cheek, but I stepped back before his lips could touch me. He paused, looking at the side of my face before backing away. I didn't say anything.

"Damn, you look good," he said with his eyes roving up and down my body. "You smell good too. What's that fragrance again?" he asked in his joking manner, and I continued to ignore him.

"I brought you some flowers," he said bringing his hand from around his back, holding a dozen yellow-stemmed roses. He held them out to me, but I didn't bother to take them.

"Baby, I know you're mad at me."

I paused and looked at him like, "Duh," still saying nothing.

"So you're going to give me the silent treatment now?"

Still nothing.

"I'm getting scared because this is unusual for you. Your mouth should be running a mile a minute by this time."

Still I said nothing, rolling lip gloss on my lips.

"Baby, say something," he pleaded putting the flowers on the bed and trying to pull me toward him. I pushed his hands off of me and went to the closet to get my shoes.

"Where are you going?"

"Out," I said, finally speaking.

"But I just got here."

"And?"

"Baby, I'm sorry for not coming home last night. I got drunk with the fellas and . . ."

". . . you stayed with Derrick because you couldn't drive. He called me like you told him to. It still doesn't explain you not being in our bed last night and how your fingers couldn't pick up the phone to dial our number."

"I did call, but you started arguing with me."

"Because you weren't here with me," I snapped. "I'm sick and tired of you getting off of work every Friday and not showing your face until the next day. I'm also tired of you getting your boy to do your dirty work. And to be honest, I'm starting to get sick and tired of your cheating ass."

"I'm not cheating. I was trying to get here as soon as possible."

"Soon as possible should have been last night," I stated, "with me."

"You're right, baby, and I'm apologizing."

"Jaquon, I have heard it all before, remember? I have numerous lines logged into my memory, along with all the hurtful things you have ever done to me. And right now, my gut is telling me you are lying yet again, and that you were with a woman last night. You probably did stay with Derrick, but at some point last night you had your dick buried deep in some trick."

"Baby, come on. I know I hurt you in the past, and I promised you I wouldn't do that again," he said actually sounding like he meant it.

"And if you think calling me from a pay phone was supposed to smooth things over, you must have fallen and bumped your damn head because I don't believe your cell phone went dead."

"My phone did go dead," he said. "That's another reason why I couldn't call you."

I looked at him like he was stupid. Walking over to the nightstand, I picked up my phone and dialed his number. His cell phone rang. I looked at him, and his face fell to the floor. His chin was deeply tucked in his chest while he tried to think of another lie.

"Dead, huh?"

"It was, until I charged it. Derrick has the same phone I do."

"And you used his cord to charge your phone, right?"

"Yes."

"You were too drunk to drive home. You were too drunk to call me. But I'm supposed to believe you were sober enough to remember to plug your damn phone in and charge it?"

"Yes. No. I mean . . . Baby, you're confusing me," he said.

"People who lie get confused, Jaquon, and you are a straight up liar," I stated, getting madder each second that passed that he was near me.

"Kea, I know you think I was cheating."

"Did you?" I asked with arms crossed.

"No, I didn't. I was with the guys."

"Sure you were. You know what? I'm too pissed to talk to you right now. You come strolling up in here like things between us is all good, but they aren't. If you want me to be wooed by your flowers and want me to throw my arms around your neck, happy you finally came home to me, it's not going to happen this time. What I should have done was wait at the door to issue you a can of Whoop Ass before I gave you your walking papers."

"Don't do this."

"I'm furious, but I'm not going to trip. I'm not going to mess up my makeup fighting with you. I got somewhere to be."

"Baby, where you going?"

"If you were here like a man should be with his woman at night, then you would know. But since you're acting like my *roommate*, you'll get no information from me." I picked up my keys, tossed my purse over my shoulder, and left him standing there bewildered.

Kea

Pulling in front of the bridal shop, I practically jumped out of my vehicle before it stopped moving. I rushed into the place, yanking open the double glass doors to get in. Looking around, I saw my sister Emory talking with one of her bridesmaids.

"Sorry I'm late. I got held up," I said.

"You're almost an hour late, Kea. You barely caught me."

"I know, Emory, but I told you I got held up."

"It must have been Jaquon," she said turning her lips up at me.

I looked at her not wanting to explain anything. I guess from the expression on my face she knew to leave it alone.

"Okay, I will not go there with you today. It's about me now. So let's get started," she said pulling me by the arm, taking me to the woman handling the order.

"Now you know each of you have chosen a different style of gown, but all of them are the same color."

"I remember," wishing I could forget.

"I can't wait for you to try yours on because it is gorgeous. I saw it when she took out the other dresses."

Looking around at the many women smiling as they tried on their dresses, I followed Emory to our section where we had our own salesperson to help us. Three other bridesmaids were there already trying on their dresses, happy with the selection they had chosen.

I was late that day too when we came here to pick out our gowns. Again, everybody was there trying on dresses and it looked like all the best ones had been chosen. I was mad because each of them had on gowns that were my style. If I would've gotten there earlier, I would have beaten them to the punch in choosing the dress I wanted. Instead I had to search for one that was not old-fashioned. I didn't want any puffs, lace, and bows on my bootie. I wanted sleek and elegant. I searched the rows of gowns and found one that was to die for. I took it down, happy it was in my size, nine. No bows and no frilly chiffon. Putting the gown up against me looking in the mirror, I knew this was the one. Checking my color choices, it did come in lilac.

Having this be my final time to try on this dress before the wedding next Saturday, I went into the rather large dressing stall. I proceeded to undress and slipped on my garment. Emory kept peeping in at me like I didn't know how to dress myself. I told her to stay out. Zipping the side, it fit like a glove. I turned to see the bootie I was blessed with sit high on my back and hips with enough curves to see them from the back and the front. I came out of the dressing room, and Emory's mouth fell open.

"That dress looks fabulous on you," she said beaming. "I wish you didn't have all that ghetto bootie though," she said looking at it like it made her sick.

"I don't know why you trippin' because you got the same ghetto butt," I struck back.

Everybody around us laughed.

"I do, but not like the one you got on your back. You've been getting way too much protein."

"And it does the body good," I said, slowly descending my hands down my body.

"You are *so* nasty," Emory threw out.

"You said it, I didn't."

"Turn around and let me get a full view," she said twirling me around.

I took off walking like I was modeling designer clothing at fashion week. When I turned, I snapped my fingers and said, "Diva is here." Laughter filled the air, and it felt good to not think about my problems for a little while.

"I'm so glad you picked this one," Emory said to me.

A pair of rhinestone-studded strapped shoes made the garment complete. They were cute, yet sexy, with three-inch heels. I had to walk around in them to make sure they were comfortable. I didn't want to be standing at the front of the church mad because my feet hurt. They were comfortable.

We finished after an hour of dresses, shoes, flower girl, and Emory also picked up her veil and tiara with her gown. Now, we were finally on our way. Each of the bridesmaids kissed Emory on the cheek, telling her they would see her at the bachelorette party which they were having in a couple of days. I tried to leave like everybody else, but Emory called out to me.

"Wait a minute, Kea. I want to talk to you."

What is it now? I thought.

"You know I love you and . . ."

Oh boy, here we go. This can't be good.

". . . and I don't mean to get all up in your Kool-Aid, but I got to ask you something."

"Ask away," I said smiling sheepishly.

"Where did you get those scars on your back from? I noticed them when I walked in on you dressing."

"What are you talking about?"

"You know exactly what I'm talking about, Kea. Is Jaquon putting his hands on you, because if he is, we need to call—"

"Jaquon isn't crazy, Emory! I may put up with him cheating on me, but I be damn if I let a man put his hands on me," I exclaimed, getting angry at the thought.

"Then how did you get them?" she asked sincerely.

"I don't know. Maybe I fell into something," I replied, looking at her like she didn't know.

"Sounds like you making excuses for that man of yours."

"He didn't do this," I protested.

"I don't believe you, but there's nothing I can do about it since you're denying it. But I tell you one thing. If that man is putting his hands on you, you need to leave him."

"Did you not hear what I just said or are you just playing stupid?"

Here she was trying to be this caring sister that she never was to me. I was trying to figure out when we lost that sister bond, and then it occurred to me. Childhood. We were siblings, but only by blood and not by emotions. We loved each other, but it was this unspoken pain between us that neither of us ever wanted to discuss. Especially Emory. Ms. Goody Two-shoes knew exactly where these bruises came from, but she must have blocked remembering all the abuse. Yes, she was above my level in intelligence, beauty, importance, and I can name a few more, but that was because Mother put her there.

Emory was the favorite one, and she knew this. Sometimes it bothered her, but sometimes she acted just like our mother with that better-than attitude. I never knew which sister would show up when I got with her. It used to be she would at least try to salvage the closeness Mother tried so hard to separate between us, but lately, each day that passed revealed

Emory following in Mother's footsteps more and more. Everything had to be in place with her and her home. Everything had to be expensive. Everything had to represent money. Those were the qualities of Mother. I just prayed she wouldn't pick up some of Mother's other demeaning ways.

If we wanted to talk about looking rich, my dear mother's picture would pop up if you googled her. She always looked exquisite on the outside. But her spirit was that of the devil. She was pure evil, and I was the demon-child she never wanted, and she never hid the fact that she hated me. Sometimes I wished she'd aborted me. Every time she spoke to me, something negative spewed from her mouth.

You have to get good grades, Kea.

Don't have sex before marriage, Kea.

Sit up straight, Kea.

Smile like you mean it, Kea.

Why can't you be more like your sister, Kea?

I wish you were never born, Kea.

You are never going to be anything, Kea.

Every word out of that woman's mouth seemed like a critique to be this vision of perfection that she never would see me as anyway. Why else would every word that came out of her mouth be used to destroy me? The only thing missing to make us abide by her rules were the wire hangers, and even then, she found other objects to get results.

Every time I saw Mother, she would brush my clothes, removing invisible lint from them. She would brush my hair away from my face, push her open hand into my back to straighten it up, and put her finger under my chin to lift my head higher.

"You need to be more like your sister," she would say. "Do you see how fabulous she is? She's getting married to a wonderful man and has a rewarding career. All you have to show for yourself is a degree, a thug, and an inkling of your sister's beauty."

Talk about uplifting the spirits of a daughter. She might as well have been screaming *ugly, stupid, fat,* and *worthless* to me. I knew I was none of these things, but having to deal with my mother's unattainable standards was too much for me to deal with. After the last time visiting her, I told myself I would never make an effort to see her again. That was the last time she thought I needed lashes across my body like a slave from the past as she tried to make me into this person I knew I could never be in her eyes because she hated me. I think she enjoyed humiliating me. And every time she demeaned me, I swore I could see a smirk on her face, like she enjoyed inflicting pain upon me.

The only thing positive about going to her house of horrors was my father. He was there, and I loved him dearly. If it wasn't for him, I wouldn't bother to see Mother at all. But since he was still her husband, I had no choice but to continue to visit the mother from hell.

Looking at my sister Emory, I just smiled. She knew deep down where my bruises came from. Maybe Emory was waiting for me to tell her. But this was something she already knew of. Even if I told her, what could she do about it? All Emory knew how to do was walk the straight and narrow playing little Ms. Goody Two-shoes, pretending the things in her life were majestic. I loved her with all my heart, but I knew one day her perfect little world would come crashing down. I just hoped Emory would be strong enough to handle the devastation after her collapse.

Essence

"Urrrrhhhh," my body jerked as my knees dug into the tile of my bathroom floor. The toilet was calling my name, and I answered with heaves. My morning breakfast came up with a force that made my body tremble. Coughing, I tried to pull my hair back so puke wouldn't coat the strands of my long auburn-colored locks. At this point, I wished I had pulled back my hair in a clip so I wouldn't have to fight with it, the toilet, and my puke.

Finally happy that my upchucking was over, I sat on the cold floor, leaning against the wall wondering why I did this to myself. Why was it every time I ate, I felt like I needed to get rid of the food within me? Oh, that's right. I didn't want to be fat. Fat was not an option for me. Fat was my enemy combined with the fear of cellulite, rolls, and public humiliation.

Growing up a chunky kid, I was ridiculed for the way I looked. I was always the big girl with the cute face that my grandparents loved to grip in the palms of their hands.

"You have such a cute face," they would say like that was the only part which existed of me. I had a body attached to this face, but I guess it wasn't cute by society's standards, nor by my family's.

I didn't see myself as beautiful, which is why I made a promise to myself that as soon as I found a way to get the weight off, I was going to keep it off in order to fall into

the category of beautiful. Diets didn't work for me because I loved to eat. Portion control and salads weren't
doing it for me. I refused to go on the crack diet. It did
seem to work for some family members of mine though.
I heard the drug made people skinny, but maybe it was
all that running around they did stealing and selling
merchandise that keeps their weight down too. Still, I
didn't want to resort to such drastic measures.

Back when I was growing up, they didn't have weight-
loss surgeries, so I had to suffer through it. And suffer
I did. I wanted the weight to simply vanish without me
really putting too much effort into it. We all wished for
that magic potion that would make you lose pounds in
days or even weeks. And it didn't help that I was unlucky
enough to inherit the genes of my parents who were
considered big boned. Both sides of my family were considered big boned. We were what you called Southern,
which meant everything was fried and cooked in a lot of
fat and butter. Even corn bread was made to taste like
soft slices of cake, and Kool-Aid had enough sugar in it
to make two gallons off of one pitcher. Southern was a
heritage I loathed, but now I could embrace it with love
since I was skinny. I could eat whatever I wanted by just
sticking my finger down my throat to make those same
delectable calories come shooting back up and not land
on my thighs.

I was enjoying fitting into a size five/six jean. My stomach was flat, my tits sat up, and my inner thighs were not
rubbing together, ready to catch fire and have everything
around me go up in a blaze. I loved myself now, despite
the stigma around bulimia. That's why it remained my
best friend and also my little secret.

Getting up off the floor, I washed my face and
brushed the rancid taste of digested pancakes, bacon,
eggs, and fried potatoes out of my mouth. Gargling

with mouthwash, I went to my room to get ready to go to the gym to work out.

Laying out my workout clothes, I picked up my cell to see if anyone had called. Four missed calls appeared and three saved messages. Two calls were from Zacariah and two from my mother. Dialing my voice mail, I listened to the messages.

First saved message.

"I don't know why you aren't answering your phone. I guess it's because you got you some last night. I'm coming by anyway so you better clean you coochie and kick him to the curb because I will be there soon. And I know you got gym but wait for me. You better wait too, Essence, because I will come down to that gym and embarrass you. I got some juicy info to dish to you. Later girl." Beep.

I didn't feel like fooling with Zacariah this early in the morning. She always seemed to get me vamped up for some reason. I could tell by the urgency in her voice she had some information to tell me even before she said anything.

Second saved message.

"Essence, this here is yo' mother, jus' in case you forgots my voice. I haven't heard from yah in quite some time now. I am glad to see yah circular phone number . . ."

Circular phone? I thought.

". . . hasn't changed since the last time I spoke to yah. You know it wouldn't hurt for you to pick up a phone and call to see how yo' parents are doing. Better yet, come see us. We still live in the same place, baby. I know you don't likes the country, but this here is where you from and yah shouldn't never forget that 'cause we still here. Just 'cause you city now living hundreds of miles . . ." Beep.

Mama's message was cut off midsentence. I was wondering how long it was going to let her talk. I was happy to hear from her, but at the same time, I cringed at the Southern tone she used. Her words were slow and drawn out, which is why she probably got cut off. But still, that was Mama's style, slow and steady.

Third saved message.

"Yo' machine cut me off so I had to call back. I don't know why it did that to me . . ." with me hoping this time she would get out what she wanted to say in this message. *". . . but anyway, all I was trying to say is yah living so far away don't mean you can just forget about your dear parents. Baby, we miss you. Give us a call so we can hear your voice and know yah still alive. Baby, life too short so pick up that phone as soon as yah get this message. Call me. I love you. Bye."* *Beep.*

I decided now was not a good time and I would have to call her later. I knew if I got on the phone with them, I would be talking for at least an hour. And that would be because I would have to speak with each of them and anyone else who was in the house this day. And it was Saturday. Everybody and their mama were perched up somewhere in Mama's house, and I didn't feel like answering the same questions over and over again.

"What you been up to?"

"How's city life?"

"What's the temperature today?"

"Where you going?"

"You met any celebrity people?"

"You got any sexy friends you can hook me up with?"

"When you coming home?"

I was not trying to go through that right now so I decided to take my shower and get ready to leave so I could work out some of this stress that was building.

After taking my shower and getting dressed, I grabbed my duffle bag to leave. I picked my keys up and headed out the door. Zacariah wasn't here yet, and I wasn't about to wait for her slow behind to show up. Zacariah saying, "I'm coming right over," meant three hours later.

Walking down the sidewalk, I looked at my keys in my hand to unlock the car when I was taken aback at the sight before my eyes. My mouth fell open and right at that moment an insect saw this as an opportunity to fly into my mouth. I choked, gagging as I tried to cough up the bug and get it out of me. Staring at my car, I looked at it in disbelief. Somebody had covered my car in what looked like petroleum jelly. Hair grease? Who in the hell would do this to me and how in the hell did they manage to come up with so much of it?

Walking closer to my ride, I could see it was smeared on the hood, the door panels, the roof, lights, trunk, and all the windows. A quick blast of water was *not* going to get this off my car. Under the wiper blade sat a white piece of paper. I pulled it out, holding it with the tips of my fingers, trying not to get the substance on my hand.

"Since you like screwing people over, I thought I would give you some lubricant to help you with that. Watch your back, trick."

What was this all about, and who did this? I hadn't screwed anybody over. Maybe Zacariah, but not me. Maybe this person got me confused with her or somebody else. I was hoping so, but if they did get it right, I didn't have any clue about who could have done this to me.

Kea

What better way to find out about Jaquon's goings-on than to talk to the main person he claimed to be with all the time? After arriving home, I couldn't stand being in the same place with him. He was acting like things were cool with us. His "I don't give a damn" attitude ticked me off a lot, and I refused to live like this. If he wanted somebody other than me, than he needed to go. But today, I chose to leave.

I knew Derrick didn't want to meet me because like any man, he didn't want to get involved. I called and practically begged him to meet me at a local donut shop. Derrick stuttered over his words, looking for every reason not to meet me, but I knew my tear-filled voice persuaded him.

Entering the facility, the sweet smell of the donuts engulfed me. I instantly became high with excitement about eating one of these warm pastries. For a second, I almost forgot why I was here. Looking around, I saw Derrick sitting toward the back of the establishment. I went to the counter and ordered two glazed donuts and a cup of hot chocolate before going over to him.

Looking at Derrick's dark mocha skin and neat close cut tapered to perfection made my heart flutter a bit. I had never had this reaction to him before, but seeing him looking more handsome than ever flipped a switch within me that I didn't think could be turned on by another man.

"Have some," I said, trying to break the awkwardness of our meeting. I didn't know why it was awkward. I had known Derrick for a long time, so this shouldn't have been as uncomfortable as it felt.

"No, thank you. I just ate two myself."

"I was really hoping you were going to say no anyway," I said smiling.

He smiled back saying, "You know those things are addictive."

"I know, right? Especially when they're warm. These just came out too," I said looking down at the glazed bread. I picked one up and bit into it. The taste made me close my eyes in tantalizing delight.

"Good, isn't it?" he asked.

"Too good. I think I could eat a dozen of these things, but I know I don't need the extra pounds."

"A little weight won't hurt you," he said watching me lick the glaze off my fingers. Just the thought of him watching me made me wonder what he was thinking. Then I thought I knew what he was thinking as I removed my wet index finger from my mouth. This was too much like . . . like . . . Well, you know.

I picked up a napkin wiping my hands.

"Derrick, I'm glad you came to meet me."

"Well, you really didn't give me a choice in the matter."

"Sorry for the tears, but I really needed to talk to you."

"I know this has to do with my man, so what do you want to talk about?" he asked getting to the point.

I lowered my head trying to build up the courage to ask him these questions I had to know the answers to.

"You have known me for quite a while now, and I hope we have become good friends."

I looked to him for confirmation, and he said nothing, but his nod gave me the answer I wanted. So I continued.

"I know we are not close as you and Jaquon, but I hope you know I'm not a bad person."

"I know this, Kea," he said leaning with his elbows on the table.

"I need to know one thing. Is Jaquon cheating on me again?"

Derrick lowered his head shaking it.

"I know he's your best friend, and you don't want to betray his trust, but I have to know. Please tell me," I said with pleading eyes, which he was trying to avoid.

"Did you ask him?" Derrick questioned.

"You know I have, and he denies it. He denied it when he was cheating before so why would he start telling the truth now? To be honest, I don't know if I can bring myself to believe anything coming out of his mouth."

"Kea, I don't want to be involved in this," he said genuinely.

"Just tell me. Shake your head yes or no, anything to help me decide what I need to do."

"What does your gut tell you? Deep down, I know your womanly instinct has already given you the answer you're seeking."

"I'm scared that my paranoid state could have a lot to do with my gut, Derrick."

"Is that what Jaquon is telling you?"

I nodded.

"Kea, you know the answer already. I don't have to be the one to confirm or deny this. What do you feel?"

"I feel he is cheating on me again. What are you going to tell me?"

"You are putting me in a bad situation. I can't believe you expect me to help destroy what you all have."

"So are you saying he is?" I asked.

"That's not what I said, Kea," he replied nervously.

"Derrick, you are not helping in the destruction of what Jaquon and I have. He's doing a good job of that all by himself."

"So why do you need me? I can't betray my friend."

"I'm going to take this as you having something terrible to tell me," I said complacently.

"Again, I say, go with your gut. You're a smart, beautiful woman. You know what you need to do."

"Was he at your house last night?" I asked like he didn't say anything.

"Yes," Derrick said nodding.

"What time did he get there?"

"I'm not sure."

"Was it late?"

"Yes," he said.

"Were you out with him?" I asked not wanting to give him the opportunity to think of a lie.

"No."

"I knew it. He told me he was with you all night."

"He was, but it was earlier, so he's not lying about that."

"Don't lie for him, Derrick. That's not your style."

He nodded.

"He's lying again. I know it, and I'm sick and tired of dealing with his games," I said getting upset. I covered my face with my hands trying to calm my nerves and will the tears back into their ducts. Dropping my hands to my lap I said, "Why does it have to be like this, Derrick? Why can't he just love me and be true to me?"

"I don't know. But what I do know is you deserve to be happy."

"But I'm not. I'm miserable."

"So put yourself first for once in your life."

"But it's so hard," I said with my voice cracking.

"I've been where you are. Zacariah stepped out on me, but I gave her another chance," he said.

"And you trust her?"

He looked around as if the answer were going to fall out of the sky.

"Not fully," he said turning back to look at me.

"So why are you with her?" I asked finally taking a sip of my now-warm cocoa.

"I'm with her the same reason you're with Jaquon."

"Love," I said nodding.

"We've been through a lot together, and I guess another reason I might stay with her is fear. I've been with her for so long now, I don't know how to be by myself. I don't feel like getting back into the dating scene."

"That's how I feel."

"Kea, you don't need me to help you with this. Regardless of what I say, you're still going to be with Jaquon. You've proven this already when you caught him before."

"You're right," I said, looking down at my half-eaten donut.

"Jaquon has done some trifling things in his past, but one thing I do know is that he loves you. He may not show it like he should, but I know he does care for you deeply. You're the best thing that has happened to him."

"Derrick, I'm really not feeling the love right now."

"Talk to him. Hear him out and go from there."

I finally got the courage to look Derrick in his face after looking at everything but him during our conversation. Most of the time I spent twirling my fingers and looking out the window or at my donuts, but this time, I wanted to look into his eyes which represented a genuine spirit I wished Jaquon had.

"Why us?" I asked.

"What do you mean?"

"Why did we choose individuals who cheat on us? Why couldn't we find each other since the two of us are the ones remaining true?"

He smiled saying, "Jaquon lucked out and got to you before I did."

"I wish I would've met you first, Derrick. I know I wouldn't be going through what I'm going through now."

We stared at each other a few seconds too long before Derrick broke the connection.

"Okay. I think it's time for me to go, that's if you don't have anything else you want to talk to me about."

"Nawh. We're good. I appreciate you speaking with me."

"It's all good. I hope things work out for you. Remember what I said. Try making yourself happy first and everything else will come together."

Zacariah

Essence was no fun this evening. Each time a nice-looking guy came up to her, she turned him away with her face all frowned up telling them she was gay.

"What the hell is your problem tonight? You're turning away perfectly good prospects."

"Did you forget what happened to me? My car was put into the shop due to somebody trying to destroy it. You think I want to smile up in a man's face?"

"Forget about your car. You got the mess being clean up. It's time to have some fun," I said moving in my seat to the beat of the music.

"I'm not feeling it tonight, Zacariah."

"I bet you if Jaquon was here, you would be feeling him."

"How did you know his name?" she asked curiously.

Between her frantic state of mind about her car and my near-death experience, I never got a chance to bring Jaquon up. "Because he's Derrick's best friend."

"Are you serious?" she asked surprised.

"Girl, when you walked up in here with him the other night, I thought I was going to fall off my bar stool."

"Why didn't you tell me?"

"Duh, you were occupied with him and your car situation."

Essence said nothing, twirling the beverage with the stir stick.

"I wish you would stop looking depressed. What you need to do is catch you a score. Making money always makes a girl feel good."

"Don't you mean taking."

"Making. Taking. Whatever; it's still money."

"Did you ever stop to think maybe I'm tired of this game? Hell, it's probably the reason why my car got greased up."

"Girl, I think your car getting greased is hilarious," I laughed.

"Ha-ha. I can't believe you're laughing at your best friend's misfortune."

"Come on, Essence. You don't find it funny?"

"Hell, no! My car is in the shop. I'm driving a rental."

"Oooh, you got a point there. But why did you get that compact box anyway? It looks like a child should be driving it. They didn't have an Explorer or Suburban?"

"I had to get what the insurance claim could afford me."

"You couldn't sweet-talk the person filing your claim?"

"It was a woman."

"And?"

Essence shook her head and said, "Something is wrong with you."

"But you love me though," I said looking at this guy who sat next to me.

"I'm just tired of all of this. In the beginning, I was doing this for the money, but I have a great job and can take care of myself without scheming all the time."

I put the back of my hand to her forehead to feel if she was running a high temperature. She pushed my hand away.

"Maybe you're sick. That's what it is because you can't be telling me you tired of getting paid."

"I'm not saying I'm completely done with this, Zacariah. Then again, I could be. I don't know right now. All I know is tonight is not the night. I need time to step back and think about things," she said sipping her drink. "I should be home talking to my mother right now, letting her know I'm still alive. I can't believe I've let so much time pass without seeing her or my father."

"How long has it been?"

"A little over a year I think."

"Do you know how lucky you are to have both of your parents alive and still together?"

"I know. And here I am not appreciating them. Too busy trying to get paid," she said glumly.

"Go home and call them. Better yet, go home and mark a date on your calendar to go visit them. Then call them with the news of you coming to visit. If you want, I'll go with you."

"You would do that for me?" Essence asked.

"Girl, a free trip to Georgia? Hell, yeah, I'd go," I said laughing, bringing a smile to Essence's face. "Now leave before it gets really late. Maybe you can still catch your mama up. I know old people like to go to bed early, but I think she'll wake up to talk to her long-lost daughter."

In saying that, Essence gathered her purse, hugged me, and left to go home, leaving me to do this thing on my own. It wasn't the first time, and I hoped it wouldn't be the last. Essence really did sound like she was ready to give this game up. It just helped when she was with me in case I came across a fool not knowing how to act. In those situations, we would pretend to be together. You know, girlfriend and girlfriend. Many guys got turned on by that and wanted to join, making it a trio.

If he looked as though he had money, then that worked because the two of us worked together to get paid, but in other instances, we would totally dismiss the guy.

Maybe I should have thought about quitting this myself. I mean, a woman ended her life in front of me. I'm fearless but going into that restroom had me on edge. Not to mention the argument I had with Derrick about me going out afterward. Maybe one day I would stop, but that was a big maybe. Tonight, I was determined to have my fun even if it was by myself.

After about an hour of mingling and getting my drink on, I found myself another prospect. He was tall and sexy with dark skin, a clean shaven face, and neatly locked dreads tied up. He noticed me immediately. When I smiled at him, I felt my cell phone vibrate. It was Essence.

"Yeah, girl, what do you want?" I asked staring at the chocolate brother.

"Will you call Derrick?" Essence shouted not saying hello.

"Why are you screaming at me?"

"Because your man wouldn't let me get in my place good before he was ringing my cell phone off the hook. I was in the bathroom trying to handle some business and couldn't concentrate from him calling me every few minutes. I guess he couldn't get in touch with you, so I was the next best thing."

"What did he say?"

"He wanted to talk to you, and I told him you had gone to the restroom and I would have you call as soon as you got back."

"Thanks, girl. I'll call him."

"Do it now, please, so I can have a peaceful, uninterrupted night."

I didn't want anyone around me to hear my conversation in case I had to lay Derrick out, so I went to the hallway leading to the restrooms. I was not about to go into the ladies' room. Tonight, if I had to use the bathroom, I was going to use the men's bathroom. Before I could dial his number, though, Derrick buzzed me. I answered.

"Hey, baby, I'm sorry I missed your call," I said, sounding sweet. "I was just getting ready to call you back."

As soon as I heard his voice assault my ears, I knew I had to hurry up and get him off my line.

"Derrick, I'm not having this conversation with you right now."

"The other night wasn't enough for you. You still itching to be seen."

"I'm just hanging out, and there's nothing wrong with that."

"You have a man, Zacariah. Why are you there?"

"I'm chillin' with my girl."

"Why don't you chill with me?"

"I live with you. Why do I need to chill?"

Derrick was ticking me off, and I didn't want my mood to be altered over the same old mess. Finally I just told him, "I'll be home later after I drop Essence off." I hung up the phone and turned it off so I wouldn't be interrupted again. I didn't feel like dealing with his crap. Tonight was about having fun, and I was going to make sure I did.

Needless to say, I didn't waste any time getting to know Dark and Sexy. Looking at his body made mine heat up. Most prospects didn't turn me on, but there was something about this man that had me ready to rip his clothes off. The brother actually had a lot of things in common with me too. We both liked watching baseball. We both enjoyed butterscotch candy, and both of us loved ourselves some black cherry ice cream. The night flew by as we danced, drank, laughed, and talked about so many things. Next thing I knew, the club was closing.

Agreeing to go to a hotel room with me, Dark and Sexy escorted me to our room for the next few hours. We bought a bottle of bubbly before leaving the last establishment and took it up to the room.

He popped the cork and poured two tall glasses of champagne. I sipped slowly while Dark and Sexy gulped his. I think he was excited about getting some. Little did he know I slipped a little something in his drink that would have him out cold very soon, but I didn't mind working him over before he passed out. After all, he was fine. I almost hated to do this to him.

Dark and Sexy ended up being small and dwarflike. His dick was so small I felt like I wanted to laugh at him when he exposed his Vienna sausage to me. His thing was like threading a needle. A donut would be my hole while the pencil would represent him entering me. I felt like I was sitting on a flat surface grinding myself into an orgasm. I think a flat surface would have given me more pleasure than his needle-size Johnson.

Still I worked him upside down and right side up. I was waiting for that pill to kick in. Usually when adrenaline got pumping, the pill worked faster, but Dark and Sexy must have had a slow system. He moved until he couldn't move anymore. His last few strokes did bring him to his climax, knocking him out cold.

I got out of the bed and got dressed, looking back at Dark and Sexy snore with his mouth wide open. Usually I took a shower, but it was getting late. I had to get home before Derrick filed a missing person report.

Picking up his slacks off the chair, I reached into his back pocket but nothing was there. Squeezing his pants, I felt nothing. Where could it be? Picking up his jacket I did the same, finally feeling something in his inner left pocket. There was his wallet. Opening it I looked for cash first.

"Jackpot!"

He had eight hundred and sixty-four dollars in cash, four platinum credit cards, three gas cards, and some other credit cards to major department stores. I almost screamed with joy. I loved when a scheme came together. Also in his wallet were pictures of what looked like his wife and kids. They were smiling, looking like the happy little family. And he was here with me. Goes to show happiness does not take you far these days. If you got a good man, you needed to keep him, but they came few and far between.

I snatched most of his money leaving a few bills. I also took one credit card and one gas card. As high as gas was these days, I should have taken all three. The reason why I only took one of each was because most times, it would take them awhile to realize one was missing. If I always walked out of here with everything, I felt it would draw more suspicion to me.

Snatching the score out of his wallet, I put it back in his pocket, blew a kiss to his sleeping body, and left him there to find out about my cost for his pleasure later.

Derrick

It's funny how the tables turned. I was just talking to Kea about trust, and here I was suspecting Zacariah of cheating on me again. Why else would she stay in the clubs? Why else would she come stepping foot up in our home so late at night? I mean, the next morning.

It took everything in me not to go off and break her neck, but I restrained myself as much as I could. She came strolling in after four. I waited in our room in the dark. She thought I was in bed sleeping, but I watched her every move. I could tell she looked disheveled and wondered how in the hell she got that way if she wasn't sleeping with another man.

Never turning on the light, she went into our walk-in closet and clicked the light on in it. She undressed, and I waited for her to put on her robe and head for the bathroom. She started to do just that, but my voice bellowed through the darkness, startling her. She jumped, grabbing her robe shut like it was going to shield her from the evil presence lying in wait for her.

"Where have you been, Zacariah?" I asked with a calm, serious voice. With the lights still off, I knew she couldn't see my hands digging into the arm of the chair, close to ripping it to shreds.

"Boy, you scared me half to death," she said, trying to sound innocent.

"Where have you been?"

"I was out with Essence."

"And the two of you have been together all night?"

"Yes, Derrick, we partied, and then decided to get a bite to eat before we came home. What's with all the questions?"

"And you went to a restaurant looking like that?"

Zacariah put her hand to her frizzy hair and said, "I know I look ruff but if you danced all night and sweated your hair out, you would look like this too. I mean, damn, you can't expect me to come out looking like I did when I got there."

I laughed thinking this woman was good. I rubbed my chin contemplating the next thing I wanted to say.

"Why are you lying?" I asked her sternly.

"Oh, here we go again. You with your accusations. Derrick, I'm not lying. Call her. She'll confirm we were together."

I laughed again, rubbing the back of my head thinking maybe that would relieve some of the pressure that was building up within me.

"I know Essence would confirm y'all being together. That's your girl, and that's what friends do."

"Like you do for Jaquon?"

"Yeah, you can say that."

"So why are you questioning me?" she said irritably crossing her arms. "Spit it out already."

"I know you were with Essence at some point tonight, but you weren't with her all night."

"Derrick, I don't have time for this again," she said starting to walk away.

"Hold up for a minute. I want to tell you the funny part."

"What funny part?" she said heatedly.

"I know for a fact Essence has been home for a while now."

"And how do you know this?" she said still trying to play me like an idiot.

"I know this because I sat outside her place waiting for you to drop her off at home. How surprised was I to see her pulling up in her own damn car—alone. Your car, the one I bought you, was nowhere to be found," I said with a chuckle.

Zacariah looked uneasy but didn't say anything.

"You're not laughing? You look a bit stunned. Why would that be, baby?"

She still said nothing, looking more uneasy at the fact I was still laughing.

"So what I did was call Essence after I gave her time to get in her place. I gave you the benefit of the doubt that maybe you snuck in from the back or the side or maybe you were in her place already. I came up with all kinds of scenarios that would explain where my baby was."

Zacariah remained quiet.

"So when I called, do you know what she told me?" I asked looking at Zacariah inquisitively. "She said you two were laughing it up together. I asked her to put you on the phone, but she said you had gone to the bathroom and she would have you call me back."

By now, Zacariah moved from one leg to the other, not saying anything.

I moved up and positioned myself on the edge of the chair, put my elbows on my knees and clasped my hands together.

"Let me lay down the scenario for you, even though you know how everything went down, but I want to remind you just in case it slipped your memory. I hang up with her. She calls you to warn you what she told me, and then you attempt to call me, but I called first. You played the whole thing off like she was still with you. But she wasn't, Zacariah. Essence was at home alone."

Zacariah said nothing. For a woman with a lot of mouth, she was silent.

"And I know you couldn't have been in the house because both of you confirmed you two were partying it up."

Zacariah now shifted from foot to foot, clasping her robe like she was afraid somebody was going to pull it off of her.

"Now I know that's your girl and you should be proud that she covered for you like she did, but the two of you were not smart enough to not get caught in lies. I don't give a damn about Essence. You are my woman, and now I'm left wondering why my woman lied to me."

"Derrick—"

"And before you speak another word, let me warn you that you better tell me the truth, Zacariah, or I swear—"

"I was out," she said sanctimoniously.

"I know that. With whom? Who the hell have you been with all damn night?"

"I wasn't with anybody. I was by myself. I lied because I knew if you knew Essence had left, you would want to know why I still wanted to hang out without her. You know how suspicious you get."

"And I wouldn't be that way if you never would have cheated on me."

"I've apologized about that so many times. It was one little indiscretion that's in the past. Why can't you trust me?"

"Little indiscretion? Trust you?" I questioned. "There was nothing *little* about you ripping my heart out."

"You know I didn't mean it that way."

I laughed and got up out of the chair. I walked over to Zacariah, and she took small steps backward like she was trying to get away from me. I was not a violent man and had never put my hands on a woman. Well, maybe a couple of times, but that was because one spit on me and I smacked her in her mouth, and another slapped me and I gave that slap right back to her. But seeing Zacariah standing before me blatantly lying to my face, I wanted to choke the hell out of her. I wanted to wrap my fingers around her neck and squeeze until she confessed the truth to me, but I had to maintain. I hoped I would maintain because I was getting angrier by the second. I had to talk to myself in my head, begging myself to please not hurt this girl.

Don't hurt her.
Don't hurt her.
Don't hurt her.
Don't hurt her.

This replayed over and over in my mind. She was a female. I could go to jail for hitting her. I was a black man so that meant I would go to jail *just because* with no questions asked.

So I rubbed my hand over my closed fist, squeezing tightly, trying to release some of my rage. This girl was cheating, and I wanted her to admit it to me. Knowing Zacariah, she would take it to her grave.

I walked up on her with about a sneaker length of space between us. She leaned against the wall, still clutching her robe. I positioned my hands on the wall on each side of her, closing her in. Then I leaned in closer and asked her, "Did you cheat on me, Zacariah?"

"Derrick, you are too close. You need to step back up off of me."

I lifted my hands in the air in surrender and stepped back two times. I folded my large arms across my chest and asked again, "Did you cheat on me, Zacariah? It's a simple question that requires a yes or a no answer."

"No, I didn't," she said assertively, but I could hear the nervousness in her voice.

I shook my head at her defiance as I moved close to her again and reached down, lifting her robe, exposing her womanhood.

"What are you doing, Derrick?"

I didn't answer her. I put my hand between her legs, rubbing it against her exposure and slid a couple of fingers inside her. She gasped with the entrance and for a moment I think she enjoyed it. I stroked my fingers around in her damp mound before pulling my saturated fingers free. I stared at her the entire time my examination was going on. Then I brought my hand to my face and sniffed. Her eyes became as large as saucers. I looked at my fingers, and then rubbed her wet juices in her face, across her nose, sticking my fingers into her mouth.

Just like I suspected, she *did* cheat on me.

Zacariah

Derrick went into a tirade. Trying to wipe the residue off my face and out of my mouth, I watched in horror as he started flipping over things in the room. He picked up the bench in front of our bed like it was made of feathers and threw it across the room.

"You let another man cum inside you," he stated, throwing a glass vase against the wall. It was filled with flowers he brought me days ago because we celebrated four years together. It shattered, like our relationship, and the flowers flew everywhere. I didn't move. I was too scared to move. I stood and watched him lose his mind. I was still trying to get over him putting his hands between my legs and rubbing the slimy aftermath in my face. He caught me off guard with this one. I never thought he would do anything like this. Coming home dirty ended up being one of the biggest mistakes ever.

"How could you do this to me again?" he screamed.

"I'm sorry, Derrick."

"You damn right you're sorry. You're a nasty whore. I loved you, and you treat me like a punk. I never cheated on you."

I couldn't say anything. I believed him. I had never heard anything in all these years about Derrick stepping out on me.

"Awwwwwwhhhhhhhh," he screamed. "I trusted you, and you do this again!"

"Derrick," I called out, but he turned to me with so much fury, I jumped back, hoping he was not going to turn his rage on me next.

"I work. I cook. I clean. I come home to you. I buy you gifts. I have provided you with a great life, nice clothes, a nice house, jewelry, and you do this."

"Baby, we can work through this."

"You think I'm going to try again with you?" he asked stunned.

"Don't give up on us," I pleaded.

"*You* gave up on us. You gave up the first time you cheated, and here you go again with your whoring around. I can't trust you. Hell, I think it's been more than just two times you've been screwing somebody else. This just happened to be the time you got caught."

I was hoping my face didn't confirm his suspicion. Of course, I had cheated on him more than once. There's been too many times to count. I'm addicted to the hunt. I'm addicted to the feeling I get when a man shows interest in me. I didn't get that coming up. I was the ugly stick-figured girl in school who blossomed into a bodacious hottie. I loved the attention.

"I can't do this anymore, Zacariah. We're done."

"Derrick, please don't leave me," I pleaded, really wanting him to stay with me. Even though I loved the attention, I loved his companionship more. He was good to me, and right now I wished I could get help just so I could keep him.

"Too late for all that, you whore. We're done. Now pack your things and get the hell out of my house."

"You're kicking me out?"

"Do you think I would give you the satisfaction of living here after what you did?" he asked resentfully. "I want you gone."

"Where am I going to go?"

"I don't care. You can sleep in the streets as far as I'm concerned," he said taking off his shirt.

"You know I don't have any family here."

"Then call you girl Essence. She *always* has your back. Let her back your ass up now."

"But it's after four in the morning. How am I supposed to gather all of my belongings?"

"Maybe you should call that guy you were with and let him rent you a truck. Hell, you don't have much to take anyway. I bought every freaking thing up in here. You're lucky I'm not making you leave with only the clothes on your back."

"I picked this out," I said pointing at the mahogany bedroom set.

"And what job did you have to pay for it?"

"Do you remember the first night we spent in it?"

"I don't want to remember. As soon as you leave, I'm going to have it hauled away. I don't want to lie in a bed that a whore slept in."

I said nothing.

"You're getting exactly what you deserve—nothing. Your name isn't on my mortgage. You have no stake in this place. Get the hell out."

"If that's what you want," I said sadly.

I called Essence up to come get me, packed a couple of suitcases, and put them in her car. I couldn't put any of my things in the car I drove because Derrick's name was on that too. A 2009 Lexus IS250, black with tinted windows—gone.

By 5:30 A.M., I was getting into Essence's ride and pulling away from what I called home. I messed up. All this time I had been jacking men for their dough and here I was jacking myself with losing the best man that I had ever had in my entire life.

Kea

Who in the hell was knocking at my door like they lost their damn mind? It was too early in the morning for all this. Walking like a zombie awakened from the dead, I scooted across the carpet, turning the lights on as I got closer to the door.

"I'm coming!" I screamed as the knocks persisted with urgency. My heart was still in my stomach. I didn't like to be woken up like this. Either somebody better be hurt really bad or dead. Pulling my robe shut, I peeped through the hole to see Derrick standing there. I clicked the locks and opened the door.

"Is Jaquon here?" he asked, looking like he had lost a battle in war or something.

"What's wrong with you, and why are you over here this time of the morning, Derrick? Your banging has probably wakened the neighbors."

"Kea, I just need to talk to Jaquon," he said with nothing but a gray tank top on with black jeans and sneakers. "Is he here?"

"I thought he was with you."

Jaquon lied to me again, not expecting Derrick to show up at our place, but I was not about to worry about that now. I had to see what was going on with Derrick.

"Dammit," he said loudly, rubbing the back of his head, pacing back and forth like he had consumed twenty cups of cappuccino.

"Derrick, please come in and talk to me," I said grabbing him by the arm and pulling him inside before somebody came out to see what was going on.

Shutting the door I asked, "What's got you so rattled?"

"Kea . . . I . . . I . . ."

He took deep breaths, not able to speak.

"Calm down and tell me what's wrong. Did something happen?"

He nodded yes.

"Is your family okay?"

Another nod.

"Are you hurt?"

He gave me a long glance and his eyes spoke volumes to me. "Does this have to do with Zacariah?"

He walked over to the sliding glass door and peered out into the darkness. The chaise lounge chair was positioned there, and Derrick plopped down on the edge. He lowered his head into the palm of his hands and said nothing. I didn't know whether to leave him alone or try to comfort him, but I decided to continue to talk to him.

"What did she do, Derrick?" I asked walking over to him.

He looked up at me. His eyes were red, but I couldn't figure out if it was from him crying or the rage consuming him.

"She slept with somebody else tonight."

"What?" I said sitting down beside him.

"Did she confess?"

He frowned his face and said, "Hell, no!"

"Then how did you find out?"

"I caught her in lie after lie so this time, I did my own examination which concluded another man had . . . had . . ."

"I get it. You don't have to say it," I told him not wanting to know the details.

"The whore didn't even bother to take a shower before she came home to me. His cum was still running out of her."

"Where is she now?"

"I kicked her ass out. She with her girl Essence now."

I sat there not knowing what to say. I just watched as a man who loved this woman crumbled right in front of me.

"Would you like something to drink? I got some beer or soda. Just tell me anything I can do to help."

"You're doing it," he said looking at me. "And I'm sorry I came over here like this. I had to get out of that house. Every time I turned around, I saw her. I smelled her perfume on our sheets and envisioned her lying in the bed waiting for me. I ran to the bathroom and tried to wash the stench of her away. I tried to cleanse the memory of her away, but she was everywhere I turned. She even chose the paint color on the walls. She helped me pick out the furniture. She . . . She helped my home become what it is, and I . . ."

He then stood up rubbing the crinkles in his jeans.

"I'm going to go now. I've disturbed you long enough," he said abruptly.

"Derrick, you don't have to go."

"I should have called before I came over," he said, moving toward the door.

Grabbing his forearm gently I said, "It's okay. You can stay." I placed my hand on his chest to stop him from leaving.

As soon as I touched him, I could feel the ripples beneath his shirt. My thoughts quickly imagined for a second how he would feel next to me. The tank top had his body looking desirable. I hadn't looked at Derrick like this before, but I was up, close, and personal, and I saw that the brother was fine as hell. I always thought he was cute, but now, sex exuded from him.

Standing over me, he walked backward, releasing the connection my hand had on him.

"Let me fix us something to drink, okay? I don't want you driving in your condition. And I know that sounds crazy with me offering you alcohol, so I'll fix you some punch or something."

"You don't have to—"

"It's my turn to be there for you, Derrick. Please let me," I said softly.

"Thank you, Kea."

"For what?" I asked.

"For this," he said just before grabbing my face and kissing me deeply.

Derrick's anger erupted into a passion I was more than willing to receive from him. Sexual currents shot through me as his intensity inundated me. Coming up for air, we both looked at each other as our lips disconnected.

"I'm sorry," he said. "I didn't mean to—"

"You didn't mean to do this?" I said kissing him again. I began tugging at his belt buckle. I pulled him in my direction as I walked backward until we were standing in my bedroom.

"Kea, this isn't right."

I shushed him with my finger against his soft lips. Then I sat on the bed with him still standing in front of me. I unhooked the belt buckle, eager to see the muscle that was going to bring my body intense satisfaction. His Johnson nearly smacked me in the face when it became free. The rage had transported to his dick, and its target was aimed at me.

Jaquon was the only guy I had ever given oral to, but something about Derrick made me drop my guard fully and let the freak within me come to surface. I engulfed him with my mouth and watched the muscles in his rippled stomach heave in and out as I sucked him to maximum growth.

"This isn't right," he struggled to say as his hands gripped my hair sending me another message. I worked him until I couldn't anymore. Standing, I kissed him again, and that's when Derrick laid me back on the bed.

He ripped the robe off of me and tore my panties off. He dove into me, giving me the best tongue-lashing I had ever experienced. Derrick didn't have a problem returning the favor as a craving mixed with ferociousness united into a sexual synchronization that sent my body into numerous eruptions.

Reaching into his pocket, he pulled out a condom, ripping it open with his teeth. He put it on with one swift move. When Derrick entered me, my back arched from the impression his manhood made within my walls. Another stroke sent shockwaves through me as I felt him hit areas within me that made me twinge in pain. I thought Jaquon was gifted, but Derrick was running in first place over him right now. Once his momentum was established and my body adjusted to his immensity, our bodies became one in motion. He lay on top of me and kissed my breasts, paying attention to each of my nipples. I caressed his back, pulling him into me.

In the back of my mind I knew this was wrong, but I didn't care because it felt so right. Jaquon wasn't here. His best friend was, so I wanted to give him what Jaquon had been neglecting. I did hope Jaquon wouldn't come home while we were in the throes of heated passion. Even though he had hurt me so many times in the past, I didn't want to crush him by having him see me sexing his best friend.

Essence

If Zacariah thought I was going to sit up under her and watch her mope about losing Derrick, she had another thing coming. I still had a life and just because she was staying here didn't mean my life was going to stop and revolve around her. I decided to still keep my date with Jaquon. I really wasn't in the mood to play friend to her tonight since she brought the entire situation on herself.

For some reason, I couldn't keep my mind off of Jaquon. There was something about him, and I couldn't put my finger on it. Was it his smile, his body, or his conversation? I didn't know. Or maybe it was the way this man worked me over. No man had ever rocked my body the way he did, and I guess my body was having withdrawals from wanting more of him.

I knew I didn't have his number, but what I had was his name. And I knew he worked for the electric company, so I took a chance and called his job. Sure enough, I found him. A message had to be taken since he was out in the field, but I hoped he would call me back. He did, and I was like a young girl happy a guy she had a crush on called.

"I hear you called me," he said arrogantly.

"So, you remembered me."

"Of course, I do. I can't eat at a table now without thinking about you."

Me too, I thought smiling at his smooth words.

"You're funny."

"Nawh, I'm just being serious. So what's up with you? Are you calling me because you want to get together again?"

"Wow. You don't waste time, do you?"

"Not when it comes to something I'm interested in."

"So, you interested in me?" I questioned.

"I'll tell you like this. Why don't I come over to your place later and we can grab something to eat. Do you like seafood?"

"I love seafood."

"So it's a date."

"See you at seven."

Dinner was the last thing on our minds as Jaquon took a detour to a secluded spot in the woods. Without hesitation, we both threw ourselves at each other. Deep kisses led to clothes being torn off, and the next thing I knew, my body was going into conniptions as Jaquon rode it like waves crashing into the surface. Nature was our music as the crickets chirped loudly, and I could have sworn I heard Luther serenading in the background. The cool air gently touched our hot bodies as we stood buck naked in the deserted area with nothing but darkness surrounding us. The only light we had was from the moon trickling down like sparkles highlighting our pleasure.

The brake lights on his ride were the only thing on as I envisioned it to be like candles lit for this romantic session. This must have been a spot he was familiar with because I didn't know it existed. I wasn't trying to have sex in the woods, outside, leaning against a car, but this was an exhilarating experience for me.

Bending me over, the palms of my sweaty hands held on to the hood of the car as he grinded into me. Each stroke drove him deeper. His pound was a force to be reckoned with. I hoped my spine wouldn't shatter with the strength of him pulverizing my essential womanhood.

Eagerness wouldn't allow me to take off my G-string as Jaquon pulled it to the side and slid his manhood in and out. He started entering me in the right orifice, massaging my exit which only sent shivers up my back. Little did I know he was trying to get me ready for what he wanted to do to me. He kept playing around that area, which turned me on, but at the same time, I was scared his next stroke was going to miss my essential and enter my exit, ripping me beyond repair. My heart pounded with the anticipation of what I knew was coming. Fear and excitement bombarded me simultaneously. I kept thinking this man was so good that I was willing to do whatever he wanted, but I would regret it later.

Entering me with the ease of a python slithering into a hole in the ground, Jaquon entered my anal area. At first, I wanted to push him off me and scream out in pain, but once he kept going, the pain eased up a bit as he went back and forth slowly and pleasure entered.

"Do you want this, baby?" he asked.

"Yes," I said softly.

"Tell me you want this," he demanded.

"I want this, Jaquon. I want this so bad. Baby, give it to me."

I loved when a man talked to me when he was handling his business, and Jaquon was a talker.

"You feel so good, baby."

"I want to savor this sweetness, baby."

"Throw it back to me, baby."

Each word sent me closer to reaching my zenith. The closer I got, the more I became light-headed. The more I moaned, the more he gave me what I asked for.

"I'm cumin', baby," I said to him as his speed increased. "I'm cumin'," I yelled. My climax was too much for me to handle and I . . . I . . . I . . .

Essence

I squinted as the bright lights blinded me. I looked around disoriented because I didn't know where I was and what was going on. I lifted my hand to my eyes to feel a tiny sting atop my hand. Squinting, I saw an IV hooked up to me. My sense of smell kicked in as I inhaled the aroma of what seemed like alcohol, Pine-Sol, medicine, and other things letting me know I was in a hospital. With my vision coming into focus, I tried sitting up in the bed. A hand touched mine, and I jerked it back, not knowing who was touching me. Turning to the source I saw it was Jaquon.

"What's going on? Why am I here?"

"I brought you here because you passed out on me."

"Passed out?" I questioned. "I don't pass out."

"Well, you did tonight. We were doing our thing," he said with a little smile, "and the next thing I know, I was standing there with my dick exposed, looking at you lying on the ground. You scared the hell out of me, Essence."

The expression on his face was so cute.

"I scooped you up and rushed you here. Lucky for me you were wearing a dress because I don't think I could have put your pants back on to bring you here. I might've rolled you outta my ride, letting you hit the asphalt and kept going because me walking in here with a half-naked woman and me being a black man, they would have had my behind under the jail."

I smiled at him, saying, "I'm sorry. I don't know why I fainted like that."

"Maybe I was just that good and you couldn't handle what I was putting down."

I swiped at him before looking around for a nurse or a doctor.

"Did they tell you the reason why I passed out?"

"Nope. I tried to find out, pretending like you were my wife, but one look at my left hand told them different. By law, they can't disclose any of your medical information to me. They were at least nice enough to let me sit by your side."

"I can't believe you stayed."

"I couldn't leave you like this. That would make me a bad guy, and I'm not a bad guy," he said.

"You're just one who likes to cheat all the time, huh?"

Holding his chest he said, "That hurts me right *here*."

"It should."

"But you don't mind being the other woman," he protested.

"Just call me settling for less," I said.

"Why do you keep coming at me with your dagger-like comments? I'm not the enemy."

"My comments weren't meant to hurt your feelings," I said smiling. "I thought I was just stating facts."

"Well, you damn sure are not making me feel good right now. I feel bad enough that you're in here."

"Jaquon, I haven't been able to find a man who makes me happy. Either he's gay, got kids, or committed to another love," I said, pointing at him.

"Hey, I'm not gay."

I laughed. "You know what I mean. I'm just saying my experiences have proven love doesn't matter. That's why I'm not in a relationship now."

"But love does exist," he said.

"And what does love mean to you? You're cheating on a girl who loves you, and you claim to love her. If it's love you claim you have, then why cheat?"

"I don't know, Essence. You have a point. I'm a man who loves to have sex. The idea of being with only one woman for the rest of my life scares me. What if I get bored?"

"Are you bored now?"

"No. Kea excites me."

"And yet you slept with me."

"I see where you're coming from," he said defeated.

The nurse came in with the doctor holding a laptop instead of a file.

"Good morning, Ms. Clemmons."

"Good morning, Doctor. Now, tell me what's wrong with me."

"You are straight and to the point, aren't you?"

"I want to know what's going on," I said.

The doctor looked at Jaquon and looking at the door said, "Can you please excuse us for a minute."

"No, Doctor, he can stay."

"Okay. Suit yourself."

I looked at a now-standing Jaquon who paused as I smiled, hoping he would stay with me. He put his hands in his pocket and waited to hear what the doctor was going to say.

"Ms. Clemmons, I hate to ask you this, but are you bulimic?"

I looked at Jaquon, and he looked at me waiting on the answer.

"No," I answered, denying the accusation.

"Are you sure? Your examination revealed you were dehydrated and suffering from malnutrition. Your teeth are weak, and your throat has small ulcers indicating you have been throwing up for quite some time."

I wished I had listened to the doctor and had Jaquon leave the room. This was the last thing I wanted him to hear about me. No one knew my dirty little secret but me and my toilet bowl. Now it was out, and I didn't know what I was going to do to maintain it. I was a bulimic, and I didn't think anything this physician was about to tell me was going to change that fact. I wondered how Jaquon would look at me now. Did he see me as sick, disturbed, or just plain crazy? Anyway, I wanted to rip this IV out of my arm and run away. But I couldn't. This was my reality that I knew would come out one day. That day was today. I just didn't think it would be around someone like Jaquon, the guy for the moment who I was into and the only person who knew my secret eating disorder.

Kea

This morning, I woke up alone yet again, but Jaquon not being next to me didn't bother me one bit. Today, I felt like a new woman, and this new woman wanted to start her day off with some coffee. With two cups of coffee in hand, I tried to click the deadbolt lock to my apartment and stuffed the keys in my pocket. I was taking my neighbor a cup of coffee. As soon as I heard music, I knew Freak-a-Leak from across the way had opened her door. I turned to see her standing there leaning against her door eating an apple. I pictured her consuming things like bananas and hot dogs but not anything healthy like an apple.

"Who was that good-looking man leaving your place this morning?" she asked.

"What business is it of yours?"

"I'm just asking because if you weren't getting down with him, I was going to get with him myself because the brother was fine."

I wanted to push her ghetto behind down the stairs but thought better of it, knowing she was the type of person quick to file a lawsuit.

"He's taken," I said callously.

"My bad. I didn't know you were cheating on Jaquon."

"I'm not. That guy was his best friend."

"Even better. They say good-looking people travel together. Damn, I'm jealous of you. You got the best of both worlds."

"It's not like that," I said argumentatively.

"Don't get your panties in a bunch. I believe you," she said winking her eye, smiling. "Whenever you are done with either of them brothers, send them my way because I would be more than happy to sample those pieces of chocolate."

I walked downstairs to get away from her before I really did push her down the stairs.

Mr. Hanks was sitting in his usual spot outside the apartment complex near the steps. He lived on the bottom level and always sat outside in his green yard chair with a pack of cigarettes and ashtray in hand. He was puffing on one when I walked up.

"Good morning, Mr. Hanks. How are you doing this morning?"

"I'm doing fine. I'm enjoying another day blessed to me."

"I brought you some coffee," I said passing him the cup of dark liquid.

"Well, thank you, Kea."

"I put two tablespoons of sugar in it just the way you like it. I'll be cooking in a little bit too. When I get done, I'll bring you down a plate."

"You need to stop spoiling me," he said, trying to take a sip of his coffee but his cough halted him.

His cough was terrible. It sounded like he had enough mucus in his chest to be diagnosed with emphysema. Still, he puffed on those cancer sticks, not giving his cough a second thought.

Short with a round belly, Mr. Hanks looked like a man who had been through a lot in his time. The years had not been good to him, but he never let that stop him from enjoying another day. He had a bunch of kids and none had anything to do with him. Back in the day, he was a playa. He went through his share of

women, and all his kids were confirmation of his sleeping around. I think he had more kids than he was aware
of, but no one wanted to claim him as their dad.

I didn't know why, because Mr. Hanks was a decent
old man. I felt sorry for him because he lived alone. No
one ever visited him. I couldn't imagine going through
my elderly years with not one person calling or dropping by to see how I was doing.

Living on money he won from the lottery, Mr. Hanks
had some cash. He looked like he was broke, but I was
told his bank account proved different. Rumor was he
won over a million dollars, but you would never know
it from his demeanor and the fact that he lived in an
apartment complex which was not in the best of neigh-
borhoods.

On a few occasions when I found myself in a bind,
he offered to help me. Of course, I declined, but he
insisted, getting me out of a couple of jams. I always
paid him back. With gratitude for helping me, I started
taking him food when I cooked dinner some nights and
breakfast some mornings. Mr. Hanks didn't have anybody cooking for him. He may have had money, but he
didn't get a home cooked meal often. So I tried to bring
him something. It was the least I could do and with
time, both of us had become really good friends.

"You know you don't have to go through any trouble
cooking for me, Kea."

"I know, but I'm going to fix me something too, so
it's not a problem. Are you going to church today, Mr.
Hanks?"

"Nawh, I don't think so. I haven't been feeling too
good lately. This cough got my chest hurting something
terrible."

"You know I'm going to fuss, don't you?" I said.

"I know. I know."

"Then why haven't you been to the doctor yet, and why are you still smoking?"

"Honey, I don't have much longer here on this earth. I done lived the life I was supposed to, and I'm going to enjoy smoking until it kills me."

"And it is killing you," I stated, sitting down on the third step of the building.

"What are you doing up so early anyway?" he asked.

"I got a lot on my mind."

"I know it has to do with that no-good man of yours. Where is he at anyway?"

"He hasn't gotten home yet."

"You see what I'm talking about? The man got a good woman at home, and he still finds the need to stay out all night. Bastard."

"Leave him alone," I said defensively, knowing Mr. Hanks was right.

"Alone he needs to be. I don't know why you insist on wasting your life with that no-good son of a—"

"Okay," I stopped him. "Remember that you were trying to stop cursing. Especially on Sundays," I said smiling.

"Jackie, Jookie, Jomo, or whatever that punk's name gets under my skin."

"His name is Jaquon, Mr. Hanks. And does he get under your skin because he reminds you of your younger self, maybe?"

"That could be it. I do see a lot of myself in him, and if he keeps it up, he's going to be just like me. Alone with no one who wants to deal with him. He's lucky to have you. You're a beautiful woman, and he's messing up. He doesn't even realize you can have any man out here you want."

"I know," I said, not knowing how to respond to the truth which had been told to me several times already recently. "You really don't like him, do you, Mr. Hanks? What has Jaquon ever done to you?"

"He looked at me. I wanted to smack the bastard soon as we made eye contact."

I laughed.

"That boy ain't nothing but trouble, just like that gal living across the way from you."

"You mean Freak-a-Leak?"

"You mean freak nasty. Her legs open twenty-four hours a day. I'm surprised she can walk as many men she keeps stuck up in her."

"Let her do her thing," I said laughing.

"I'm letting her do it, just as long as she doesn't do it to me. Don't you know she asked me if she could hook me up with some of her gushy stuff? I told her hell to the nawh. That gushy stuff probably has some type of infection aching to get out of her."

"You are so nasty, Mr. Hanks."

"Why would she want to sleep with somebody as old as me anyway?"

"She's probably heard about your lottery winnings."

"Kea, I'm sixty-two years old. She told me she got some Viagra for me. Trick trying to kill me. If I even look at one of them pills, my heart might stop beating."

"Maybe she likes you."

"She thinks I got money. If I would have agreed to her offer, I'd be broke now because that trick would have got me for everything I own. I don't want her in my place, much less on my dick."

I laughed, enjoying his antics. He never failed in making me laugh.

"If I never told you before, Mr. Hanks, I enjoy these talks," I said looking at the blue sky with white fluffy clouds moving.

"Same here, Kea. You have made these past few months worth me living another day."

I got up off the step, wiping the dirt particles off the back of my jogging pants and embraced him.

"I'll be back in a few with your breakfast."

"I'm looking forward to it," he said taking another puff off his cigarette and a sip of his coffee.

Kea

After filling my and Mr. Hanks's belly with bacon, eggs, and biscuits filled with grape jelly, I snuggled beneath the covers of my bed with a good book by Brandon Massey. I sipped on a cup of hot cocoa because for some reason I was cold.

Taking the opportunity to enjoy the peaceful moment, I knew later it would change once I went to work. I was a waitress and had to go in at five o'clock. I didn't care too much for the job, but it helped pay the bills. Plus the tips were awesome. That was the only reason why I was still there.

Soon as I got engrossed in the pages of the book I was reading, Jaquon walked in looking like he was worn out. He probably was, but this morning I didn't care. I sipped my cocoa and proceeded with reading my book.

He noticed I wasn't paying attention to him and stood waiting for me to say something, but I ignored him. Walking into the bathroom in our room, he came out like he had seen a ghost.

"Kea," he called out to me.

I didn't say anything.

"Kea!"

"What, Jaquon?"

"Why is the toilet seat up?"

As soon as he said that, I remembered Derrick going to use the bathroom after our tryst. I thought I had everything covered. I changed the sheets. I took a shower, and I made sure the condom wrapper was put in the bottom of the trash can in the kitchen, even taking the initiative to dump food on top of it. I could have dumped the trash, but that was the one chore Jaquon did manage to do. Me doing that would have thrown red flags up for sure since I never dumped the trash. When he asked me again why the toilet seat was up, I tried to play it off like he did it.

"You must've left it up."

"I know I put it down. It's a habit since you used to complain so much about me leaving it up," he said looking at me with a frown.

"You don't do anything around this house to help me, but you can remember you put a toilet seat down? Please," I said smacking my lips and returning my eyes to the words on the pages, hoping he would let this go.

"So you mean to tell me you haven't used this bathroom since I've been gone?"

Damn. He had a point there. We did have two bathrooms in the place, but I hardly used the other bathroom. I always used this one. Come to think about it, had I used the bathroom today? I had too. I always go to the bathroom when I wake up in the morning, but I went before Derrick left. The other time I did use the guest restroom. Damn, Jaquon was coming at me too fast with all these questions, and in my panic state, I felt like I couldn't think of a good enough answer. *Think, Kea, think.*

"Why are you tripping over a toilet seat, Jaquon?" I asked trying to throw his suspicion off of me. "Why are you trying to start with me? Can't you let me read this book in peace?"

"Something doesn't feel right, Kea."

"I see you're letting your paranoia get the best of you."

"Are you cheating on me?" he asked bluntly.

The slight soreness between my legs said yes, but I told him, "No, are you?" I said smugly, knowing he was not going to confess anything.

"Baby, you know I'm not," he said with a straight face and everything.

"You have said that before, and I got burned, remember? In more ways than one."

"I told you I wouldn't step out on you again."

"And I'm supposed to believe you? Have you looked at the time lately, Jaquon? Forget about the time. Look outside and see the sun. You didn't beat it home this time either. That makes two times in a few days. Looks like you are up to your old tricks again, and I would be a fool to believe anything coming out of your mouth," I said, placing the book on my chest.

He leaned against the doorway, crossing his arms, looking at me. I know he was trying to think of something and probably was wondering how this conversation got turned around so quickly.

"The nerve of you to come in here asking me about a damn toilet seat. If I were you, I would be trying to think about how I was going to explain where the hell you been all night."

"I hope you know I wasn't out cheating, Kea. I was with Derrick."

My eyes shot to him, and I smiled. "You were with Derrick, huh?"

No, he didn't step foot in another lie. If I were a land mine, I would blow up in his face right now. Look at him. He's serious with his dishonesty. I'm supposed to believe him more because he's swinging his hands around to explain how sincere he is in his faithfulness. Probably the same hands he used to please whoever he was with before he came home to me. Jaquon was good. Before, I was too stupid to see past the love I had for him. One look into his eyes and I would melt like butter, hoping he wouldn't hurt me again. But now that my mind is clear and I'm sleeping with his best friend, I see right through him.

His eyes let me know no matter how much he claimed to love me, he would still continue to be the dog he is and get a piece on the side. It's in his nature to be a playa. As many fish as there are in the sea, I thought I had the prize catch. If I knew he was going to turn out rotten, I would have thrown his ass back and let somebody else get sick of him.

I wished I could get words to come out of my mouth and say, "You're a bald-faced liar." As soon as he asked why, I would reveal, "Because your boy was over here screwing me last night. That's why the toilet seat was up. Your boy was giving it to me like you should've been giving it to me, but you were too busy juggling your little whores to pay attention to the fact it's been three weeks since you thought about touching me in an intimate way." Oh, how I wanted to destroy him with what I had done to him. But not now. I wanted to mess with his mind a little more so I said, "What if I told you Derrick called here looking for you?"

Essence

I could hear Zacariah before she got to my room. Evidently she brushed past some nurse or the nurse was in her way or something because all I heard was, "Don't be looking at me all crazy. You are in MY way."

"You don't know how to say excuse me?" the nurse retorted.

"Excuse you," Zacariah screeched. "You shouldn't have been in my way. You need to pick up your pace or go help some sick people. That's your job, isn't it?"

Moments later, Zacariah entered my room. I did have my eyes shut before I heard her loud voice wake me. I was almost asleep. The television was showing some game show I wasn't watching when she stood over me popping her chewing gum.

"Why do you have it so hot in here?" Zacariah asked loudly.

"Why do you have to be yelling all the time?"

"I'm not yelling," she replied, raising her voice another octave.

"Bring your voice down, Zacariah. This is a hospital."

"And? If they don't like the way I'm talking, then they need to get out of earshot of my conversation."

I sat up in the bed and sighed deeply.

"What's wrong? Are you still feeling bad?"

"No, I'm fine. I'm getting a headache from you screaming. Plus, I'm ready to go."

"Well, let's go then," Zacariah said tossing her purse on my bed.

"I'm waiting for the nurse to bring my paperwork for me to complete."

"Well, they need to hurry up."

"Why are you in a hurry?"

"Girl, I got a dinner date."

"You don't waste any time. I thought you would be over at Derrick's house trying to get him back."

"I'm not worried about him. He's easy. I'll get him back later, but for now, I'm trying to get my eat on."

"So where did you meet this one?" I asked, getting out of the bed to stretch my legs.

Zacariah ignored my question as she took her jean jacket off and fanned herself saying, "It feels like an oven in here. Do they think we're turkeys since they're trying to bake us like one? I don't want circles under my arms from damn near sweating to death."

I had to laugh at her. To me the room felt good, but I was in a thin hospital gown with my back out, and it didn't help that I was cold natured.

"Girl, you're crazy," I said.

"And, oh, I appreciate all you're doing for me, Essence. You're a good friend to me."

"Girl, you know I would do anything for you," I said, watching her pull out a pack of cigarettes and hitting the unopened pack in the palm of her hand. I looked at her like she had lost her mind.

"What? Why are you looking at me like that?"

"What do you think you're doing?"

"I'm getting ready to light me up a cigarette. Why?"

"Did you forget where you were?"

"No, and?"

"And we are in a nonsmoking facility. This is a hospital. You know, the place people go when they get sick, have operations, and give birth. Smoking is not allowed."

"You can't open a window?" she said seriously, and I really was hoping she was joking, but deep down, I knew she was for real.

"We're on the thirteenth floor, Zacariah. Windows don't open."

"So I got to wait until I get outside?"

I nodded, and she put the pack back in her massive purse huffing loudly.

"Do you want me to go get somebody to release you? I'm getting tired of waiting."

"No, Zacariah. It's only been a few minutes," I said.

At that moment, the door opened, and my nurse finally walked in with my papers.

Zacariah smacked her lips and said, "No wonder you aren't ready. Run you over with a cart isn't doing her damn job," she said looking the nurse up and down with her face frowned up.

"Zacariah," I called out, wanting her to act like she had some home training. Come to think about it, with a mother who was hardly around, she didn't have anyone to really show her how to act with some dignity.

"It's okay, ma'am. I'm use to all kinds of rude individuals who don't know how to conduct themselves in public. That comes with this job."

"Trick, I'll show you how rude I can get when I beat that ass."

I jumped in front of Zacariah, who was now standing and waving her arms like she was in the streets ready to throw down.

"Will you cool it?" I asked, trying to push her back down in her seat.

"That ho ain't going to disrespect me and get away with it," she said, pointing at the nurse who didn't budge. She just stood there smiling at Zacariah.

Then the nurse shook her head in amazement and said, "Here are your papers, Ms. Clemmons. Sign here, here, and here," she instructed me, pointing to the different sections releasing me.

"I ought to beat your ass for looking at me," Zacariah shouted with neither of us wanting to recognize her ranting.

Signing a few more sections, I passed the nurse my papers. I looked at her, and she looked as though she knew what I was thinking. "I'm sorry for my friend acting like a damn fool."

The nurse smiled and nodded, saying, "It's okay."

"Ain't nothing okay with me, you trifling whore."

"Zacariah, this is uncalled for," I finally yelled. "Shut up before security escorts you outta here."

"Escort me because I'm ready to go anyway."

"Ms. Clemmons, you are free to leave," the nurse said moving with confidence, letting Zacariah know she wasn't afraid of her. And maybe that confidence was her knowing she could whoop Zacariah's behind. Either way, the nurse never fell into Zacariah's ignorance, and I admired her for that.

When I got home, I got settled in my bed and decided to rest for the remainder of the day. I crawled beneath the covers, clicking the television on to see what shows I could get enthralled in. While clicking, I came across *The Cosby Show*. It was my favorite show to watch when I was growing up, and seeing Clair made me miss my own mother.

I turned to look at the phone. Picking it up, I dialed a number that took me a minute to remember. Only because I always got two numbers turned around.

Instead of dialing 912-555-5252, I would dial 912-555-2525. Hearing the ringing made my heart flutter as I anticipated hearing someone's voice.

"Hello," a soft tone spoke bringing bliss to my ear.

"Hi, Mama, it's me, Essence."

Kea

It was Emory's wedding day, and she looked stunning walking down the middle of the church. Smiling from ear to ear, she looked like the princess she always dreamed to be. Scanning the audience, I saw Jaquon gazing at me smiling. He whispered the words, "I love you," and I frowned, knowing he was nothing but an impostor. I turned my attention to the reverend who prayed over Emory and her soon-to-be husband before having them say their vows.

The ceremony seemed to whiz by with me being the maid of honor, holding her flowers while she put the ring on his finger and his on hers. They lit the unity candle while I made sure her four-foot train was beautifully laid for the audience to admire. And finally, the reverend said, "You may now kiss your bride." Emory's husband lifted the veil from her face and planted a nice, gentle kiss upon her lips with the preacher saying, "Church, I give you Mr. and Mrs. Aaron Coburn."

The church stood clapping, and we grabbed the arm of the groomsmen following the bride and groom out of the church.

The next hour or so consisted of pictures taken in many different poses. I wanted to say enough already because my feet were killing me, despite me thinking these were going to be comfortable shoes. Mother was beaming with joy. She finally got one of her daughters married off to a nice, respectable, and wealthy gentleman. It was all about the money with mother and how we were represented in front of people. We were the perfect family. After all, we were supposed to have been mothered by the best.

At the reception, things kicked off with dinner, the first dance with Daddy, and then the cake cutting. I couldn't spend any of this time with Jaquon, which suited me fine. Not that I wanted to, but he was supposedly my significant other. Needless to say, mother did not like him. I should say she didn't like the fact I was living in sin with a thug who couldn't afford to put a ring around my fourth finger on my left hand.

"Kea, darling, doesn't this make you want to find a decent man so you too can get married?" she asked sitting beside me in her nine-hundred-dollar gown. I have to say my mother was a beautiful woman with flawless skin, each hair in place, and a smile that lit up a room. Little did people know that beneath her elegance was an evil woman.

"I'm not ready to get married, Mother," I responded looking around at people passing who said, "This was a fabulous wedding," to my mother who beamed with glee. But just as fast as her smile appeared, her controlling manner reared its ugly head back at me.

"Honey, I really think you should move out until you two decide to make it official. That's *if* he can make it official."

"Mother, if I move out, it will be because I no longer want to be with him."

"Trouble in paradise?" she asked with raised eyebrows. "Are you finally wising up to this man's tawdry behavior? I mean, he has been cheating on you for quite some time now. I don't understand why you've put up with him this long."

"Maybe I'm wising up now. Maybe I have found someone else to take his place," I said taking a sip of my champagne to ease the pain of talking with her.

Mother almost choked on the tea she was sipping, placing her hand on her chest, trying to cough without looking graceless.

"Kea, do you mean to tell me you have someone else? I thought I saw you come here with Jaquon."

"I'm just saying maybe I have found interest elsewhere, Mother."

"So when do I get to meet this man that is brazen enough to get you away from *him?*" she asked pointing with her eyes in the direction where Jaquon sat.

"Mother, get a grip. You would be the last person I would introduce to anyone. You should understand why. I mean, you are the shrewdest, most unloving, self-centered, insensitive mother there is. And did I mention abusive?" I said with a smile.

She whirled her head looking at me like she could bash my head in. "You ungrateful little twit," she said speaking through her teeth, continuing to fake a smile at everyone around us.

"There is my mother. I was waiting for her to show up. Do you want me to go get the rubber hose you used to punish me into behaving like a respectable woman or are you just going to backhand me right here in front of everyone?"

"Not here. Not now," she hissed. "You will not ruin this day for us."

"By 'us,' I guess you mean you and Emory. I thought this was *her* day," I said sarcastically.

"This is her day. Emory has done something you will never do, and that's find a good man who's worthy. And since you are worthless, you will only get men who will use you, abuse you, ruin you, and leave you, because they can see how insignificant you are too."

"How about I ruin you?" I said standing and hitting my champagne glass with my fork.

She looked up at me in shock saying, "You wouldn't."

I smiled and cleared my throat, "Can I have your attention, please, everyone?" The loud chatter turned into whispers.

"I want to toast the bride and groom. Emory, I love you with all my heart. We are both so different, like night and day, but still, we stand here today as young, vibrant women who have triumphed through many misfortunes. I'm so happy you have found a man who can take good care of you. Aaron is a great guy, and I know he will love you through the lifetime you two will spend together. Many blessings to you both," I said lifting my glass to them and everyone did the same.

Emory looked at me with eyes filled with tears as she blew me a kiss. I acknowledged by doing the same. Looking down at Mother who smiled proudly yet nervously, I looked back at Emory long enough for her to know where I was going with this. She nodded.

"Today is the first day your life can finally begin. I hope your days are filled with genuine love. For us, the only love we have ever experienced was from our father," I said, looking over at Dad who seemed to look proud but also sad.

"Mother, dear," I said solemnly, looking down at her smiling fake face, "only loves herself. She loves her appearance, she loves money, she loves men with money, and she loves to pretend to be this stylish, prominent woman. But how can she be this when another one of her loves is to see her child suffer as she takes a rubber hose to her daughters' backs to turn them into something she thinks is worthy of her vision of perfection."

The guests gasped. Heads turned as I looked at Mother, Daddy, and then at Emory, who didn't seem to be bothered by my little outburst, which surprised everyone but us. Last night, I took it upon myself to talk with my sister about her accusation. I told her it was Mother who was still beating me. Emory began to cry and apologize, but I told her I knew it wasn't her fault. From there, our conversation entered territory we'd never visited before. For the first time ever, our sister connection was being established. With this breakthrough, I also let her know it was time to stop Mother from treating us like she did. So I kept going.

"Mother does not deserve to be called Mother at all. I should call her Frances. Though she gave birth to me and my sister, she has never loved us to the level of us believing it. Her form of discipline was to strip us down to our undergarments, making us turn our backs to her while she gave us twenty lashes like we were slaves who had defied our master. I guess in a way we were her slaves. Especially me, the child she never wanted. And she made sure to let me know this every chance she got."

I turned to her and said, "What was that you said, Mother? Oh, I remember. I was worthless, and that I will only get men who will use, abuse me, ruin me, and leave me because they can see how insignificant I am too. That's what you just said to me not even ten minutes ago, Mother. Yet, you sit and put on your fake smile all the while demeaning the daughter you pretend to love."

Mother looked like she was smelling something foul. She stood suddenly and said, "You ungrateful little tramp," slapping me across the face.

The crowd gasped again. I smiled, knowing Mother was showing these people who she really was. Daddy stood, telling her, "You better not put your hands on her again."

I rubbed my cheek and said, "Ladies and gentlemen, here is the *real* Frances Fields."

She looked into the faces of the many stunned individuals.

"She is spewing nothing but lies," she said to everyone listening.

"What reason would I have to lie, Mother?"

"Because you insist on making my life a living hell. I did everything for you and your sister. You think you can embarrass me like this?" she said with hands thrashing.

"I only told the truth, Mother," I said calmly.

"Lies. All lies," she retorted.

"They are not lying," Daddy said, finally coming to our defense. "You have beaten those girls for as long as I can remember. I wanted to do something, but I didn't. I just sat back and watched you torture my babies their entire lives, and I will never forgive myself for allowing you to do what you did to them."

"Shut up, Joseph!" Mother shrieked.

"No, you shut up, Mother," I said.

"My life revolved around making sure you girls had everything at your fingertips," she said defending herself.

"But everything came with a price," Emory retorted.

"That's life, and if it wasn't for me doing what I did for the two of you, Emory would never be marrying Aaron. And you. You—"

"Do you not understand that with love from a real mother I could have walked a path of greatness without feeling worthless, unloved, and full of anger? All you had to do was wrap your arms around me and tell me, 'Baby, it's okay. I will love you regardless of any situation.'"

"How can I love you? You—"

"Don't do it!" Daddy yelled at her interrupting her flow.

Emory sucked in air before saying, "Mother, I'm moving to California with Aaron." She touched her stomach and said, "We are expecting our first child, and I don't want my child to grow up with a grandmother like you."

"Expecting? Moving? What? When? Why didn't you tell me?" Mother asked taken aback.

"I didn't tell you because I didn't want you telling me how much of a screwup I was for getting pregnant before we got married. And I didn't want you to convince me that being near family was the proper way to live my life just so you could dictate how I should raise my child."

"Well, we are an important part of you, Emory," Mother stated.

"Kea is right in everything she's saying, Mother. Even in the fact we are not as close as we should be, and that's only because you have always treated me like I was better than she was. We were supposed to be raised with the same type of love. I never should have been your favorite. The only reason I was spared much of your wrath was because I saw how bad it could be with Kea being the example you used to try to mold me."

Mother stood firm not responding.

"All I can do now is pray that Kea and I can mend this relationship between us," she said smiling at me.

"We will," I acknowledged.

Mother sat back down in her seat, brushing the wrinkles out of her clothing once again.

"Well, I guess everything is settled and this conversation is over. There is nothing more to discuss. Band, can you play some music, please. This is my daughter's wedding," Mother said, picking up her glass of champagne and acting like nothing was wrong.

Derrick

There she stood looking the vision of beauty near the rail of the balcony overlooking the grounds of the reception area. The full moon seemed to be shimmering down sparks igniting my heart. Its size was much larger than usual and represented the extent of what Kea had just done in front of a crowd of people awhile ago. I walked beside her and looked at the moon with her.

"Beautiful, isn't it? Kinda gives you a soothing feeling."

"What are you doing here, Derrick?" she asked with surprise evident on her face.

"I'm a guest at this wedding."

"Who invited you?"

I laughed saying, "I can't be invited to a wedding?"

"I didn't mean it like that. What I meant to say is, how do you know my sister?"

"I don't. I know the groom. He's my brother."

Her mouth fell open.

"A bug is going to fly in if you keep it open like that."

"I didn't know you had a brother," she finally said.

"Oh, he's not my real brother. We're fraternity brothers. I'm an only child by my mother, but I probably have many siblings. Daddy did his thing back in the day. My mother wasn't the only woman he was sleeping with."

"Wow. So, you don't know if you have any other siblings?"

"Nope. And that's scary too, when you meet a young lady and got to ask her what her daddy's name is."

She laughed. "You're so crazy."

"You know I'm telling the truth. People are sleeping around too much these days. You might actually end up dating your sister. It gives me chills just thinking about it."

"You didn't ask me who my father was," she said.

"That's because I knew who your daddy was. Remember, I met him that time your parents celebrated their wedding anniversary, and Zacariah and I tagged along with you and Jaquon."

Just the mention of that name started to change my mood. I hoped Kea didn't see it.

"I remember. Daddy was more than welcoming, but my mother was cold as ice. And now you can see why," she said giggling, and her smile hypnotized me. I stopped and peered into her eyes.

"No disrespect, but I'm glad you're nothing like your mother. You have risen beyond any stigma she has tried to place on you, and I'm proud of you for standing up for yourself this evening."

"It was long overdue. I hate I had to do it here, but I figured this was as good a time as any to expose her evil ways."

"I'm sorry you had to go through everything you went through."

"What doesn't kill you makes you stronger. I'm a living testimony to that," Kea said.

Both of us stared deeply at each other and for a moment the conversation ceased until Kea began to speak again.

"Look, Derrick, about the other night," she said shifting uncomfortably.

"Maybe now is not a good time," I said looking at another couple who walked onto the balcony admiring the huge moon illuminating the serenity.

"So when is a good time?" she asked.

"You tell me."

"Jaquon will not be home until late. Why don't you swing by our place?"

"No, why don't you come by mine? Zacariah no longer lives with me, and this way, we don't have to worry about any interruptions during our 'discussion.'"

She smiled saying, "Sounds like a plan. What time do you want me to come over?"

"The sooner the better," I said looking at her sultrily.

She looked intensely at me and turned her attention back to the full moon, hugging herself as both hands gripped each of her shoulders. I loved the way the light cascaded off of her skin. And then I remembered how Kea felt when she was in my arms. I wanted so badly to pull her into my arms this instant, but I thought better of it. It was a good thing I didn't because Jaquon appeared out of nowhere. He jabbed me in the side jokingly. I blocked his moves, hoping he didn't notice my erection from looking at Kea's smooth skin. I quickly played it off and placed both hands in my pocket.

"What up, Derrick?" asked Jaquon.

"What up with you?"

"I'm just enjoying this wedding. It almost gives me ideas of marrying this beautiful lady right here," he said looking at Kea whose smile disappeared.

"I was wondering where you were," he said to her.

"I needed some air."

"How much air do you need, baby? You've been gone for a while now."

"She was looking at the moon," I said pointing to it.

"Damn. I didn't notice it," Jaquon said.

"How could you not?" Kea retorted.

"It must be these drinks, baby. They never should have put a free bar in the same room with me because I have been making them bartenders earn their keep tonight."

"How many drinks have you had?" Kea asked, snatching the half-filled cup of liquid out of his hand.

"I've only had eight."

"Man, don't you think you need to cut yourself off?" I asked.

"This is my last one," he said giggling. He reached for the drink Kea took from him, but she moved it out of his reach.

"Maybe you need to stop drinking now, Jaquon," Kea suggested.

"Or maybe I should have one more for the road."

Kea was visibly irritated and tossed the drink in a nearby trash can. She then turned her full attention back to the moon.

"What's got your panties in a bunch?" Jaquon asked. "Oh, I forgot. Your dear old mother ruined your mood."

"And now you're picking up where she left off," Kea said furiously.

"Whatever," he replied, slurring his words. "So, Derrick, my man, what do you have planned for tonight? I thought we could hit the club later," he said.

"I got plans already. You're going to have to catch me another time."

"Please tell me your plans don't involve that whore, Zacariah. You just got that chickenhead outta your life."

"It's not Zacariah. I'm done with her for good," I said.

"That's what you said before and you took the trick back."

"I'm for real this time. She's outta my life. Plus, I've met someone else," I said.

I looked at Kea who never broke her concentration on the moon in the star-spattered sky. I knew she knew I was talking about her, but she played it off nicely. Jaquon was too drunk to notice.

"That's what I'm talking about," he said bumping chest with me. "You didn't waste any time getting back in the game. Who's ass you tapping tonight?"

Annoyed, Kea turned to Jaquon and told him she was ready to go home.

"But, baby, the night's still young."

"And I'm tired. I've been on my feet all day. I'm ready to go home and get comfortable."

"Then if that's what my baby wants, that's what my baby gets," he said still fumbling his words. "I have to find my keys," he said, patting his blazer to locate them.

"I hope you're not driving," I said to him.

"He's not driving me anywhere. I'll be doing the driving," Kea said.

"But, baby, I'm good."

"You are good, all right. Good and drunk."

Kea grabbed Jaquon by the hand and led him away. Before she completely disappeared out of my view, she looked back at me. The two-second stare was enough to let me know I would be seeing her later. Jaquon wanted to know who I was tapping tonight. Little did he know I hoped it would be Kea.

Kea

I didn't know why I was so nervous. My body trembled making my way to Derrick's door. Once there, I stood for a minute. Then that minute turned into several. I held up my hand balled into a fist and started to knock, but I didn't. What was I doing here? This wasn't right. How was I any better than Jaquon if I was doing the same thing he was doing to me? Yes, I felt like he needed to hurt, but I didn't need to stoop to his level and cheat in our relationship. Especially with his best friend. I could be overreacting for no reason though. Maybe Derrick and I would really talk this time and no repeat of our last encounter would happen. But a major part of me wanted something to happen. I wanted Derrick to take me into his arms again and love me as deep as his manhood could enter me.

Placing my hand on the door I closed my eyes, wanting to be with Derrick, but I couldn't. I had to leave before this thing went any further between us. We had already crossed a line with being with each other once before and this could not happen again. Turning to leave, I took two steps before the door swung open.

"Hey, Kea. Where are you going?"

"Derrick, I'm going to leave."

"Why?"

"This," I said pointing to the brick sidewalk, "can't happen again."

"What? You can't walk down my sidewalk again?"

I laughed at his humor before saying, "You know what I'm referring to."

"Kea, all we are going to do is talk. I'm not going to pressure you into anything you don't want to happen."

I turned my head sideways saying, "But what if our talk leads to something else?"

"And what if it does?"

"Derrick . . ."

"Kea, please come in so we can talk about this, okay?"

I looked into his eyes and immediately closed mine. Damn, this man was fine. I should have looked at his shoes, but then I would have thought about his size thirteen foot which would have led my mind to think about his long dick. I opened my eyes and looked at him again. This time I took all of him in. My heart fluttered looking at him in his baggy jeans and nice, white, button-down shirt which was open, revealing the white tank top underneath. Damn, this man was mesmerizing. I knew I was in trouble if I stepped foot in his house.

"Please," he said holding out his hand to me. I stared down at his hand before I took it into mine and entered his place.

"Come with me," he said, and I followed. We ended up in his living room where he had a picnic set up in front of his fireplace. The room was dark, only lit up by the blazing fire crackling in the fireplace. A fleece blanket was laid out for comfort. Hot wings with potato wedges and rolls were placed on it. He also thought to put ketchup, hot sauce, celery sticks, and ranch and blue cheese dressing in little bowls to dip the wings in. He even had hand towels for us to wipe our hands on.

He got down on the floor and held his hand out for me to join him.

"I thought you said talk, Derrick."

"We are going to talk, but I thought a midnight snack wouldn't hurt. I don't know about you, but I'm still hungry."

I smiled asking, "How did you know that this was one of my favorite foods."

"Because you are a woman after my own heart. I remember every time we, meaning me and the person I'm trying to forget, would go out with you and Jaquon, you would often order wings."

She nodded as if she remembered.

"Food isn't good unless you can eat it with your fingers. Most women order salads or things where their hands never have to touch their food, but not you," he said smiling.

"When it comes to getting my eat on, I don't try to be cute."

"Even when sauce was all over your face, you still looked as beautiful as ever."

"I never had sauce all over my face," I retorted.

Derrick dipped his finger into the ranch dressing and placed it on my face.

"You do now."

"Oh, it's like that?" I said doing the same.

"Okay. I quit. You win."

We laughed as I picked up one of the towels and wiped my face and hands off. He did the same.

"On a serious note, let's try to relax and enjoy the late-night snack. I picked this up on my way home, and I've been keeping it warm in the oven for us."

"I still can't believe you paid attention like this."

"I did. Now, get comfortable. Take your shoes off and let's dig in. And don't try to be cute either."

"Oh, I'm not. I'm going to lick my fingers and everything," I laughed.

"Please don't give me that visual," he snuck in slyly. "It will put other images into my head."

I smacked him on the knee and said, "Let's eat."

After downing the food, we sat there with our bellies full and toothpicks in our mouths trying to pick chicken from between our teeth. Both of us leaned back against the sofa watching the flames dance for us.

"Are you glad you came?" he asked.

"Yes, I am. I was against this, but I have enjoyed your company. Don't get me wrong, though, I still feel guilty being with you."

"I've thought about this too, and I know I have broken the ultimate rule of being with my best friend's girl, but ever since we got together, Kea, I can't stop thinking about you."

"I can't stop thinking about you either."

Derrick turned his body toward me saying, "That one night sparked more in me than I ever felt with Zacariah. Call it destiny. Call it infatuation. Maybe we can even call it love. I honestly don't know what this is, but I do know I want more of it. I want more of you."

I looked at the compassion in his face matching his tone as he talked with me. He put his hand on my thigh and instant tingles went through me. I wanted him to move his hand because being this close to him made me crave him more. But it also made me want to scurry out of his house to never return again.

I didn't know what to do. I didn't understand what I was feeling. All I knew was I wanted him just as bad as he wanted me. It scared me to think this was a man who could take the place of Jaquon. What would be the repercussion of what Derrick and I were doing? Did I even care? Was I coldhearted not to care what anybody thought about us? Did I want to ruin years' worth of friendship just to be with Derrick? Did I want to put him in that spot to choose between me and Jaquon? I didn't know.

"Kea, you're not saying anything."

"That's because I don't know what to say. I have a thousand thoughts running though my head right now. I know I need to walk away, but I can't will my body to do so."

"Then don't," he said softly.

"Who am I to ruin a friendship spanning over years?"

"I made this choice, Kea. You didn't. I did this, knowing what I was getting myself into," he said confidently.

"And if he finds out?"

"Then we'll cross that bridge when we get to it. Now I want to enjoy being with you. I don't want to think about anybody else. Right now, I want you."

He got on his knees and gently took my face into his hands, pulling my lips into his. The kiss was enough to make me want to tackle him to the floor and take him right where we were. When he pulled away, I almost pulled his lips back to mine because I didn't want it to end.

"Can I have you?" he asked tenderly.

"Yes."

He stood, taking me by the hand, and led me to his bedroom. Pieces of our clothing fell where they may, and Derrick and I reconnected a burning desire that was fulfilled to the utmost. Climbing on top of him, I slowly slid down his dick. Starting with a slow grind, I rotated my hips. Then I began to ride him vigorously. His hands gripped my waist, guiding me along his long piping as our bodies heated and glistened with sweat. I never wanted this moment to end. Whatever Derrick wanted I was willing to give wholeheartedly. Engrossed with one another, we somehow didn't hear the doorknob turn. Nor did we hear the footsteps that led drama into Derrick's bedroom.

Zacariah

I stood in the bedroom that used to be mine, watching Kea riding Derrick. At first I couldn't speak. Something had my voice, even though I opened and closed my mouth trying to speak. Still nothing would escape past my lips. I couldn't believe what I was seeing and watched in dismay as my mind tried to process the situation. This couldn't be my honest Derrick with little Ms. Princess herself. I couldn't understand how they came to be.

The scene burned into my mind. Neither of them noticed me standing and watching as they enveloped one another like it was their last time to ever make love again. But this couldn't be love. Derrick loved me.

Still not being able to utter a word, I managed to will my body to do what my mouth couldn't. I slammed the door shut, causing a loud boom to echo throughout the room.

Kea jumped off Derrick pulling covers around her naked body, and Derrick sat up pulling the sheets around his waist.

"Is this why you kicked me out, Derrick?" I asked, still in shock but now able to find words to spew. "Did you dump me for her?"

"How did you get in my house?"

"Answer the damn question and tell me, did you leave me for her?" I demanded.

"I left you because you cheated on me, Zacariah. Now how did you get in my house?"

"I have a key to our house," I said holding it up. "You never took it, which led me to believe you really didn't want me to leave, but I can see this time I was wrong."

"You have no right to be here," Derrick stated.

"Yet you think it's right for you to be screwing your best friend's girl?" I screamed. "It's a little too late to be talking about rights."

"You should know," he said throwing his leg over the side of the bed.

"I'm going to leave," Kea said, searching for her clothing scattered around the room. Derrick stood up holding the sheet around his midsection. Even with the drama going down, his erection still could be seen through the cotton material.

"Give me my key, Zacariah, and get the hell outta my house."

"Not before I beat her ass," I said removing my sterling silver hoops that dangled from my ears.

"There isn't going to be a confrontation up in here," he said. He slid his boxers on under the sheet like I hadn't seen what he had to offer before.

"She knew you were my man, and she still slept with you."

"I also know he left you," Kea said smartly.

"Oh, little Ms. Perfect got some guts. Maybe I need to stomp some of it out of you," I said bolting for her. Derrick got to me first, hooking me around the waist with his right arm pulling me away from Kea. She stood smiling and shaking her head as she put on her sneakers.

"You are not about to tear my house up because you mad you found me with somebody else. If you want to get mad at somebody, get mad at me," he said.

"You don't have to protect me, Derrick. I can handle myself," Kea said.

Derrick looked back at her like he was shocked to see little Ms. Kea stepping up.

"The beating I will put down on you will be one you haven't experienced before. I *guarantee* you that," I calmly said.

"You might get surprised and catch a beat down yourself," Kea retorted.

"You better tell her who I am, Derrick. I will hurt her up in here!"

Kea said, "All mouth but still standing across the room. The only thing that might be scared up in here is our eardrums from all your screaming."

Derrick shook his head laughing at everything Kea had to say, and that only made me angrier.

Kea walked toward the bedroom door to leave.

"You better run," I snarled.

"I'm not running. I'm trying to maintain my cool and not mess your face up," she boasted.

I escaped from Derrick's grip and went for Kea. I pushed her, causing her to lose her balance and fall against the door. She regained her footing and swung, hitting me in the mouth. Surprised, I went to swinging, but Kea stood there with fist firm and waited for an opening. She socked me in the mouth again, then swung the other fist connecting with my left cheek. Derrick jumped between the two of us, but I swung around him, clipping Kea on the shoulder. She stood looking unfazed.

"I'm going to get you," I spat as my fingers touched the blood that was now trickling from my mouth. "So help me, I'm going to make you pay," I screamed.

"I'll talk to you later, Derrick," Kea said, totally ignoring me.

She walked out the door, and I continued to scream, "No, you won't either, trick. I better not find out you talking, grinning, or even grinding up on my man."

Derrick remained standing in front of me until I pushed him away from me.

"You're protecting her now too."

"It didn't look like Kea was the one who needed to be protected. You never should have pushed her first."

"How can you do this to me?"

"Did anybody tell you to come over here, Zacariah? Now look at you. Face been worked over and you still trying to think of ways to get revenge. And you wonder why I don't want to be with you anymore. You full of drama, and I can name of couple of other things you full of too."

"Baby, I'm your woman. You were supposed to call and ask for me back."

"You got to be kidding me. Kea hit you too hard, didn't she? Right now you're delusional. I guess you expected me to take you back like the other time, huh?"

"Yes."

He laughed and grabbed a pair of gray jogging pants folded on his dresser, sliding them on.

"Not this time, Zacariah. You had your chance with me. I'm kind of glad you came by. Now you can see I have moved on to bigger and better things."

"You mean *her?*" I asked venomously, pointing at the door Kea walked out of.

"Maybe."

"It's not going to work."

"Oh, it will work if we want it to work," he replied.

"And is she worth throwing away years' worth of friendship with Jaquon?"

"Why do you care? You don't even like him."

"That's not the point. You broke the best friend code."

He ignored me, walking over to my keys that I attempted to throw at Kea's head as she walked out.
Derrick picked them off the floor and took all his keys
off and tossed the rest back to me.

"You can go now. I don't want to ever see you back
here again," he said coldly.

"You're going to throw our love away . . . just like
that?"

"You did," he said with his hands in his pockets.

"But I love you, Derrick."

"You love to play games. You thought your sex could
reel me back in, and that's why you came over tonight
thinking you would climb into bed with me like you did
before and work your evil on me. But you got fooled
this time. You walked up on a snag while I was making
love to Kea."

"You don't love her. You love me."

"I don't trust you, and I can't be with somebody I
don't have faith in. I'm finally done with you."

"But—"

"Please leave, Zacariah. I'm trying to be as nice as I
possibly can. I don't want to carry you out of here."

I couldn't believe he was treating me like this. After
all we'd been through, he was *dismissing* me.

"What if I tell Jaquon?" I asked trying to get the upper hand on this situation.

"Tell him. As many things as we know on him, what is
he going to say? He's just like you when it comes to re-
lationships, so maybe you should tell him so he can feel
like you do now. Hell, when he sees you coming, he'll
probably run the other way. Let's not forget, you two
don't like each other."

"Well, we liked each other enough to . . ." I began.

"Enough to what?" he asked accusingly.

"Nothing," I said trying to backpedal.

"Enough to what?" he screamed.

"Enough to sleep with him."

Kea

When I got home Jaquon was still asleep. It didn't look like he had moved much since I left him to go see Derrick. I was glad he was still here, but mad to see him too. Then Zacariah's face came into my mind, and I was reminded of the evening ending with me shutting her mouth with my fist. She deserved it. I should have hit her again for ruining me getting my nut with Derrick. He was so good, and I was so close. But when that door slammed, my heart damn near stopped. For a split second I thought it was Jaquon.

I knew it would be only a matter of time before big-mouthed Zacariah tells him. Now that I think about it, I didn't care about him finding out. What in the hell could he say anyway?

I was tired and wanted to close my eyes and go to sleep. Getting in bed next to Jaquon did feel good because he was here with me for a change. At the same time, I carried so much resentment at how he treated me. He was sleeping so peacefully. His small breaths put my heart at ease. His movement let me know he knew I was getting in next to him. I turned my back to him, hoping he would cuddle with me, but he turned his back to me. Seconds later, he was snoring. It was loud enough to wake the dead.

How could he sleep when our relationship was in turmoil? Not only was he cheating on me, but now I was cheating on him. Any moments together that didn't consist of us arguing was a winning situation. At least, then, I showed I cared. But now we weren't winning at all. How could sleeping be the only peace between us?

I closed my eyes hoping to go to sleep, but I was restless. I guess I was too tired to sleep. Or maybe my adrenaline was still pumping from the earlier events. The miniblinds were open, and the moon's luster peeked its way into the room. I opened my eyes to witness it. Everything around me was so quiet and dark. I took in the stillness and turned it into bitterness. How could he sleep?

I wanted to elbow him. Then he shifted to his back, which made his snoring worse. I considered smothering him with a pillow to shut him up. Then I thought maybe I should show him why he was with me in the first place.

I turned to face him. I positioned myself beside him with my arm under my head. He did look good. I loved watching him because this was the only time I could see his innocence. I imagined we were content like this all the time. His chest moved up and down, and I wanted to take my hand and rub him gently, but I didn't want to wake him. Looking down the covers, I saw his dick was erect from his night's sleep. I immediately got the urge to jump on it. I was becoming aroused. And since I didn't get what I needed earlier, I considered him the vessel to finish me off. At the same time, a part of me didn't want to give him something he didn't appreciate. Of course, as a man, he was going to enjoy our intimate moment, but what about after? Were we supposed to lie here and look up at the ceiling, trying to think of a conversation to have that wouldn't lead to another argument?

Then I thought about why we argued and anger consumed me again. Not knowing whether to jump on his dick or cut it off, I got out of bed and went to the kitchen to get a drink of water. While sipping the liquid, I realized I could do both. Retrieving a knife from the drawer, I went back to the bedroom putting the weapon on the nightstand.

Once back in bed, I knew what would wake him for sure. I pulled the covers back, knowing he wouldn't stop me. Jaquon was a heavy sleeper and still a little drunk, but he was familiar with this movement of the covers. Once he realized what I was trying to do, he would be all for it.

Reaching down into his boxers, I pulled out his erectness. As soon as my warm hand touched it, he sucked in a soothing breath, letting me know he liked what I was doing. He was slowly awakening, and his hand caressed my hair, further letting me know he anticipated my mouth coming in contact with him.

Brushing his tip against my lips, he lifted his hips to move his dick closer to the entry of my mouth. He gripped my hair tighter before I took him in completely. With each movement up and down, his other hand graced my head, helping me maneuver back and forth on his shaft.

He called out my name, and I became eager. The more excited he became, the more I enjoyed working him over. I thought about Derrick and thought this should have been him.

When he whispered he was about to explode, I pulled away. He released my head gently and looked at me with devotion. I gazed at him before climbing on top of him and taking him into my center. Slowly I slid down. His hands gripped my hips until I had all of him within me. He grinded beneath me, and we were making love. Rather, we were having sex.

I wanted to think this had something to do with love, but my anger only allowed me to see this as two individuals getting together to do something they both enjoyed.

With each stroke, I got closer to my peak and angrier at myself for doing this. He didn't deserve this. His hands didn't deserve to explore my body like this. I leaned forward, wrapping my hands around his throat. His head went deeper into the pillow, allowing me to grip him. I tightened my hold, steadily bouncing up and down on him. The harder I gripped, the harder his strokes deepened.

I knew what he was thinking. He wanted to release with me. This was something we both loved and being together as long as we were, we knew when the other was coming to that crest. With my body tightening, so did his. Harder! Faster! We moved rhythmically together until our bodies convulsed into ecstasy. I leaned forward letting my body rest on his as my inner walls quaked. I was exhausted and his hands rubbed my back welcoming me.

Realizing it was back to reality, I sat up looking down at Jaquon. Neither of us said a word. There was that awkwardness I dreaded. He brushed his finger on my face looking sincere, but I couldn't help but to think this was another one of his tricks. He didn't love me. I leaned forward and grabbed the knife off the headboard. Coming back up, he didn't know what was going on until I had the knife's blade at his dick. He winced at the weapon digging into his tender flesh.

"I could really hurt you right now," I said coldly.

"Kea, what are you doing? I thought—"

"You thought things were cool between us. No, it's not. I had the urge, and you were here to scratch it. That's it."

"Baby, please put the knife down," he pleaded, hoping I wouldn't cut his world off.

"Why do you insist in hurting me like you do, Jaquon? What have I ever done to make you hate me?"

"Baby, I don't hate you. I love you."

"Then why would you hurt the one you love? You keep breaking my heart, and I don't know how much more of this I can take," I said irately.

"Baby, we can get through this," he pleaded.

"Can we? Or will you go back to being Jaquon because that's who you are and you can do anything you want to do? Do you remember telling me that? 'I'm Jaquon, and I'm not changing for nobody.'"

"I remember, Kea," he said lying as still as possible so the blade wouldn't dig deeper into his precious manhood.

"You're listening. I'm proud of you."

"I do love you, baby."

"Actions speak louder than words. Didn't your mother ever tell you that?"

"Yes."

"And you still don't get it. It's not polite to play with people's hearts, Jaquon."

"I know my actions haven't shown my sincere love for you, Kea, but I do care about you."

I leaned back off of him. His manhood shriveled in fear in my hand, and I began to laugh. Then I pushed the knife deeper into his shaft, watching his face twitch in pain. I kept it there for a minute before lifting both of my hands in the air so he could see I was no longer a threat. Well, maybe I was since I still had the knife in my possession and his chest was fully exposed to possibly getting what was due him. But I smiled and dropped the knife. He jumped, thinking the blade was going to pierce his skin, but it didn't even prick him.

Once he saw it out of my hands, he tossed me off of him and jumped to his feet, throwing the knife as far away from me as possible. I sat there smiling.

"You're crazy, girl!" he screamed.

"You made me this way," I said with a twisted smile on my face.

"You could have hurt me for real."

"You're okay. There was no harm done," I said calmly, looking at him hold his dick like he was making sure it was still there.

"And you wonder why I do what I do."

"Watch what you say to me, Jaquon. You never know when I might want to go through with cutting your dick off."

Essence

When I went to retrieve my morning paper, I was greeted with another surprise. I picked it up thinking it was heavier than usual and opened it before taking it into the house. Hitting the ground was a dead rat the size of my hand, with blood covering its fur. I threw the paper on the ground and ran in the house screaming for Zacariah to wake up.

"Get up! Get up!" I shouted, shaking her as hard as I could. She was a deep sleeper, especially since she kept such late hours. For some reason, this morning, her mouth was swollen. Not worrying about her injuries, I shook her again until she woke up screaming, "What!"

"You got to get up. Somebody put a dead rat in my newspaper."

"Stop playing."

"I'm not playing, Zacariah. Get up now and come see this."

"I don't want to see a dead rat."

"Zacariah!" I screamed.

"All right. All right. Damn. You aren't going to let me sleep until I see what you're talking about," she grudgingly said, moving slowly, sliding on her slippers and throwing on her fluffy robe.

I was waiting outside when she came out there. Wiping the sleep from her eyes and yawning, she looked down.

"What the hell?"

"See what I'm saying. Who is doing this to me? First, it was my car, and now, this."

"Somebody doesn't like you."

"Duh," I said.

"Did this rat have a note?"

"I didn't think to check. Once I saw that rat fall out of the newspaper, I was no more good."

Zacariah squatted, rummaging through the bloody newspaper. "I don't see anything."

"Look," I said, pointing at the rat. "It looks like something's sticking out of its mouth."

"And I guess you want *me* to pull it out?"

"I can't do it. I can hardly look at it, let alone touch it."

"What makes you think *I* want to dig in its mouth?"

"Come on, Zacariah. You're not squeamish like me."

She sighed and with the tip of her fingernail, pulled out a rolled up piece of paper, opened it up, and read it to me.

"Since you like slumming, I thought I would bring something from home to you."

"What does that mean?" Zacariah asked.

"I don't know."

"You lived in the slums."

"If you want to call the projects the slums, then I did."

"Did you have rats?"

"What project didn't?"

"Then this is a piece of home," she said unfazed.

"I don't understand why someone is doing this to me."

"Somewhere down the line, Essence, you have pissed somebody off. Did you steal somebody's man? Wait a minute. You've done that a few times."

"So have you. Why isn't somebody threatening you?"

"I don't know. Maybe this stems from something that happened a long time ago. Essence, I have no clue. Maybe you should call the cops."

"Why? So they can do nothing?"

"It will at least be on record."

"That's true."

"And you did take pictures of your car before you got it repaired. Give them all that evidence too."

Between the questions and the neighbors looking in dismay, trying to figure out why cops would be questioning me, it only made me feel worse about the situation. Many preferred to find you guilty of a crime than to find out what was going on. Pictures were taken of the rat, and then it was removed from my driveway. I sat on the steps of my entryway and watched.

"Do you know who could be doing this to you?" the officer asked.

"No," I replied looking at him dumbfounded. "If I knew who it was, then I'd be telling you."

"Anybody looking to get even?"

You had to be kidding me. Was he not standing here ten minutes ago when I explained I didn't know any of these things?

"What type of questions are these, Officer? You already received the answers," Zacariah said perturbed at the tall muscular cop with black curly hair. He looked as though he had been on the force one day. You could clearly see he didn't know what the hell he was doing. I guess if this incident would have happened on the rich side of town, we might have received a seasoned cop who knew what he was doing.

"Ma'am, please don't get upset with me," he said trying to sound important.

"Why would this situation not warrant her being up-set, Officer Perez," Zacariah said, looking at his badge. "Somebody sent my friend a dead rat and covered her car in grease. Would *you* be happy about that?" she asked.

"No, ma'am, but—"

"But nothing. Are you done, because we got things to do?"

Officer Perez looked around at his partner who was waiting by his car. He closed his notepad and put it into his shirt pocket.

"Here's my card if you need to call. I hope this doesn't happen again, but in case it does, you'll have my number," he said now looking at me in an unprofessional manner.

Was this man trying to get with me? Is that why he was asking all these stupid questions? I looked at his card, and then looked at him. He walked to his patrol car opening the passenger door. Before climbing in, he turned to look at me one last time, waved, got into the squad car, and pulled off.

"I know he was *not* trying to hit on you," Zacariah said.

"You got that vibe too?"

"Yeah, you had his mind so scrambled, he couldn't do his damn job."

"Well, hopefully, I won't have to call him."

"I don't know, Essence. He might have been lacking in the job skills, but the man was fine. He looked Cuban, and boy, do I love my Cuban men."

"What type of man do you *not* like?"

"Shut up, Essence. I'm tired of dealing with you and your problems this morning. I'm going to fix me something to eat and get back in bed."

"Speaking of problems, by the look of your lip, you had some problems yourself. Who tried to shut your mouth?"

Zacariah

Breakfast took no time to throw together. Essence and I were sitting at the dinette table when I decided to explain what happened to me last night. She sat there looking at me with her hand over her mouth, no longer even eating her food.

She then said, "Kea and Derrick?"

"Yes," I said biting into a piece of bacon.

"They were having sex?"

"Yes."

"You mean buck-naked sex with penetration and everything?"

"Yes, Essence," I said almost losing my appetite.

"Yet *you* were the one who caught the beat down and not Kea," she said giggling.

"It isn't funny, Essence."

"Yes, it is. I can't believe you let that girl punch you in your face like that. Have you seen your face this morning?"

"It ain't nothing a little foundation and lipstick won't cover up."

"I guess you found somebody bigger and badder than you."

"Don't worry. Kea is gonna get what's coming to her if it's the last thing I do."

"I hope you aren't going to slash her tires or put sugar in her tank," she said, stuffing some eggs into her mouth.

"That's too simple for her. I'm going to hit her where it hurts."

"So . . . you and Derrick are officially over," Essence voiced.

"That's what he says."

"You know you deserved this, right?"

"How?"

"You cheated on Derrick. What better way for karma to come back than you finding him in bed with another woman?"

"I didn't deserve this," I replied sternly.

"Zacariah, all of this scheming we've been doing has finally caught up to both of us."

"Except mine is not as serious as yours. Granted, we both got some drama going on, but yours is a bit more serious since you don't know who's doing all these nasty things to you. I know who's making my life a living hell."

"True, but Zacariah, we need to stop playing games and grow up. We are getting too old to plot, scheme, and fight. We're almost thirty. We need to act like we have some sense."

"Speak for yourself. I'm still twenty-five."

"In your mind," Essence said.

"And my body. Look at me. I'm fine."

"You all right, but that fineness isn't going to last forever. You better think about getting a job or go to school or something, because those looks are going to disappear eventually."

"As long as I got beauty, I'm going to always snag the rich cuties. And once I have one of them in my life and in my bed, I will not have to want for anything."

"You never listen when somebody is trying to give you some sound advice."

"Okay Ms. Advice-Giver. How about taking some advice yourself? Leave that low-life Jaquon alone."

"I'm going to as soon as I sleep with him a couple more times."

"You have let him stimulate your mind to the point of infatuation."

"Enough of this playing tit for tat," she said getting up from the table with her plate and glass in hand.

"You're the one who wanted to talk. I guess my words are stepping on your toes."

"And I'm getting ready to move my feet," she said, putting her dishes in the sink and leaving the kitchen.

I finished my food and thought about how my life had changed so drastically in the past few days. What Essence didn't know was that no matter how hard I was trying to forget about the images of Derrick and Kea together, I couldn't. It was seared in my mind. I was hurting from what he did to me, even if I did act like it didn't bother me. I never thought he would allow another woman to come between us, let alone Kea. He had to really like her to risk his friendship with Jaquon. But after my little revelation, I guess if Jaquon found out about their tryst, it wouldn't matter since Jaquon had already crossed the line of sleeping with his best friend's girl too. I could still see the hurt look on Derrick's face when I told him.

"You slept with *Jaquon?*" he asked, stunned, and I wished I hadn't said anything. It was bad enough I had cheated on him, but to admit sleeping with his best friend was my biggest mistake.

"Derrick, I didn't mean to say that."

"But you did, and I can tell by the look on your face that it's true."

I looked down at my hand which started to tremble a bit.

"When?" he asked.

"Several months ago," I answered nervously.

"Where?"

I looked over at what used to be our bed, and his eyes followed them.

"My bed? You slept with him in *my* bed?" he exclaimed grabbing my shoulders, shaking me.

"Let me go," I said, struggling to get out of his grasp.

"Who the hell are you? What type of slut did I allow myself to get involved with?"

"I'm not a slut."

"Well, you damn sure haven't shown me anything different. How many more men have you spread your legs for?" he asked, pushing me backward into the wall.

"You did it too. I just caught you."

"But the difference between now and then, Zacariah, is now we are not together. Then you were living with me. Then you were driving the car I bought you. Then we were supposed to be the only ones sleeping in that bed," he said pointing at the mangled sheets he and Kea just came from up under.

"I'm sorry for my part in this."

"Your part *started* all this, Zacariah. If you would have just loved me truly like I loved you, then we would be lying there now. I would still be giving you everything I thought you deserved. But now I know you deserve nothing. You appreciate nothing. You spit on our relationship to whore around, and that's why we're over."

His words ripped through my heart like a bullet tearing through flesh. And this was all Kea's fault. She's the reason why we are not getting back together. That tramp is definitely going to get what's coming to her. I'm going to make sure I destroy her life.

Kea

I hadn't heard from Daddy since the night of the wedding. I wanted to know how he was doing. I tried calling him several times, but he didn't answer. This was unlike him. So I decided to drive over to see what was going on. When I entered my parents' house, stuff was everywhere. Someone had ransacked their home, and I began to worry. I wanted to run out and call the cops, but Daddy's car was in the driveway, so I knew he had to be here. Not wanting to panic before I had to, I called out to him. There was no answer. I called out again, but still, no one responded. My heart wanted to leap into my throat, but I tried hard to maintain my cool. This was a big house, so maybe they couldn't hear me.

I walked farther into the house looking at picture frames which had been shattered, broken vases, ripped down curtains, and even the flat-screen above the fireplace mantel in the den had been destroyed. I called out again, and finally, my mother walked down the spiral staircase with a glass in her hand.

"Well, well, well. Look at the trash in my home."

I wanted to believe she was talking about the destroyed items, but I knew she was referring to me.

"Hello, Mother."

"I didn't think I told you to come in."

"You forget I have a key."

"Remind me to get my locks changed because you are no longer welcomed here," she said through slurred speech. That meant Mother was on one of her drinking binges.

"Where's Daddy?"

"You mean that piece of crap I've been married to for all these years? He's around here somewhere."

No sooner than she said that, Daddy came walking down the stairs with two huge suitcases in his hands.

"Daddy, can you tell me what's going on here? I tried calling you, but you didn't answer," I said. "And why do you have those suitcases?"

"I'm leaving your mother, Kea. This is something I should have done a long time ago," he said glaring at her.

"Get the hell out then," she yelled throwing the glass at him. It missed him by miles.

"And the reason why you didn't get me is because Frances destroyed my cell phone along with all of this," he stated, looking around at the demolished space.

"And I would do it again," Mother said. "Most of my money paid for all of this anyway."

"Keep thinking you did this all by yourself," Daddy replied.

"I never should have married you, Joseph. You were the biggest mistake of my life. No. No," she said pointing at me.

"*She* was the biggest mistake of my life."

"Why do you insist on treating me like this, Mother? What have I ever done to you?"

"You were born," she spit out coldly.

"Enough," Daddy said. "Let's get out of here before your mother picks up something else to throw at us," he said hurrying to the door.

"You're just a coward," Mother bantered. "You thought you were helping me when you married me. All you did was burden my life," she yelled at Daddy.

"Let's go, Kea," Daddy urged.

The look on his face was one of fear. I knew Mother could be a scary lady, but I knew Daddy wasn't afraid of her either. Something else was making him act like this.

"Why are you rushing me, Daddy? What's going on?" I asked curiously.

"He just doesn't want me to tell you what I should have told you a long time ago," Mother smirked.

"Daddy, what is she talking about?" I asked confused, turning to him.

He lowered his head.

"Daddy, please talk to me."

"Tell her, Joseph. Tell her everything," Mother snickered evilly. She went to the bar and poured herself another generous drink.

"What type of hold does she have on you?" I asked Daddy compassionately.

"I'll tell you," came her cold reply as she walked closer to me, tripping over the broken items on the floor. Daddy stepped in front of me before Mother could get any closer.

"No, you won't. If anyone is going to tell her, it's going to be me."

She stepped back smiling deviously.

"Tell me what, Daddy? You're scaring me."

"Kea, maybe you should have a seat."

"I don't want to sit down. I want you to tell me what's going on!"

"Don't be afraid now," Mother sneered. "You acting like you scared to tell her. Enlighten her as to why I hate her so much."

Daddy looked at me through sorrowful eyes and said, "You know I love you. I love you more than life itself, and I hope you won't let this affect our life in the future. I'm going to always be here for you, no matter what, and I'm going to help you through this any way I can."

"Get on with it already," Mother bellowed.

Daddy looked at her to shut up, and then turned his attention back to me.

"Kea, the reason why . . ." he paused with his hands trembling.

"Kea, baby, I'm not your father."

His words stung like a thousand hornets attacking.

"Not my father?" I said, not understanding.

"Biologically, I'm not," he revealed with water forming in his eyes.

"I don't understand," I said shaking my head.

Out of nowhere, Mother pushed Daddy aside and said, "*You* are the product of a *rape*."

I looked back and forth from Daddy to Mother waiting for the punch line. I looked around for the *Candid Camera* crew to jump out and say you've been punked, but the looks on their faces with Mother glaring at me like I repulsed her and Daddy looking distressed let me know this had to be true.

"Rape?" was all I could manage to utter. "But you raised me," I said looking at Daddy.

"He raised you because I didn't want you," Mother said uncaringly. "I was a poor little girl who grew up with nothing. Half of the time there was no food in my house to eat. I had a mother who worked three jobs to support her children and a man who refused to get off his lazy behind and do anything for us," she fumed. "He would beat Mama until she gave him her check. Then he would go out and blow it on drinking, gambling, and other women. A lot of times we sat in the dark at night because my stepfather spent the electric bill money. He spent the grocery money. And all Mama could do was work to take care of a fool who didn't love her. I think she worked as much as she did to get away from him. But she failed to realize she left children at home to deal with him."

I listened intently. I never knew about any of my mother's past, and now I could see why she didn't want to disclose it.

"I felt alone as a child. I had no one to turn to. Yes, I had siblings, but they were trying to survive just like me. And in my loneliness, my stepfather took it upon himself to provide the companionship I needed. But I didn't want the type of companionship he was giving. I didn't want to play the game of touchy-feely," Mother said with tears now running down her cheeks.

"And this went on for years until I developed into a woman. By the age of thirteen, my stepfather was sleeping with me," she said through hot tears.

"He was raping me, and there wasn't anyone who came to my rescue," she screamed, turning around kicking the objects on the floor while Daddy stood looking at me as if he wanted to take me into his arms and shield me from all this ugliness.

"I was a child, dammit. How could my own mama not see what this man was doing to me? And when I finally got up the nerve to tell her, she didn't believe me," Mother said with more tears falling.

"But that didn't stop her from confronting him anyway about my accusation, and, of course, he denied it. Hell, the bastard beat Mama for asking, and she let it go after that. I didn't understand why she just didn't pack her children up and run. She could have taken us away from him. We could have lived in a car or something. Anything was better than what we were dealing with. But my mother chose to stay. She allowed him to continue to do what he was doing to me," Mother said, still crying.

"My stepfather didn't expect me to get pregnant because when he started having sex with me, I wasn't having my period. I didn't get that until I was almost fifteen years old. And that's when I got pregnant. He told Mama I was hot in the tail and I let some boy get me knocked up. I tried to tell Mama it was her husband's child I was carrying, but she wasn't trying to hear me," Mother screamed as loud as she could, releasing all that pent up anger. "And don't you know that time I lost the baby. I ended up miscarrying. My stepfather couldn't even wait for me to stop bleeding from losing the baby before he was climbing on top of me to . . . to . . . rape me again. Needless to say, it didn't take long before I was knocked up a second time," Mama said looking at me.

By now, I was in tears myself. This story was horrible, and to know my mother went through so much suffering disturbed me.

Daddy came closer to me saying, "That's when I met Frances. I fell head over heels in love with her the first time I saw her. I could see she was going through something, but I didn't care. I loved her. Eventually, she trusted me, letting me know she was carrying her stepfather's child," Daddy said.

"I wanted to lose this baby too. I thought about throwing myself down some steps. I drank. I smoked. I did everything I could to lose you, but you kept growing inside me," she said glaring at me.

"You kept moving and making me feel miserable. It was like you were fighting to live, and I didn't understand why I was being punished. And Joseph told me he would stay with me. He told me he would take me away from all of that and wanted me to stop what I was doing and that it wasn't the baby's fault. He begged me to keep you, but I didn't want to," Mother said despondently.

"I married your mother right before you were born," Daddy said.

"Mama couldn't wait to sign those papers giving me to someone else to handle. She saw me as a problem within our family and was more than happy to see me leave. Or maybe a small part of her knew what her man was doing to me and with me gone he would no longer be cheating on her."

She paused a second, getting choked up at the realization of her mother not wanting her.

"I had you when I was only sixteen years old," Mother said.

"And I thought you were the most beautiful baby I had ever seen," Daddy expressed. "I fell in love with you as soon as I laid my eyes on you. Your tiny hands gripped my finger, and I knew I was where I was supposed to be. I was supposed to raise you as my daughter."

"This is too much," I said backing away. "If I was your daughter, then why did you let Mother beat on me like she did?"

"I should have stopped her, and I will regret it for as long as I live, but Frances told me if I ever went against her when it pertained to you and Emory, she would send you to live with your real father," Daddy said dejectedly.

"You threatened to send me to the man who *raped* you?" I asked Mother.

"He was your father! I spent enough time raising you on my own. It was his turn."

"You were not raising her alone, Frances," Daddy yelled.

"I had to look into this child's face every day of my life. She was a constant reminder of a life I was trying to put in the past, but how could I when the past was staring me in the face," Mother said with hatred dripping off her words.

"Did you *ever* love me, Mother?" I asked, not wanting to give her the thrill of seeing my pain. It took everything I had in me to hold back tears. I felt like what I was hearing was changing my entire existence.

"Did you ever love me, Mother?" I asked again.

"No," she said, shooting me a poisoned look, not even blinking. She meant it too. I shuddered at her insensitive reaction to hurting me with just that one word, no.

"Baby girl, I loved you. Do you hear me? I said I love you. Look into my eyes," my father told me. I looked up at him.

"See the love I have for you. What I should've done was leave your Mother to live her life. I wanted to take you and Emory away from all of this, but I knew she would call the cops on me. She told me if I ever left with you girls, she would have me locked up for kidnapping and I would never see the two of you again. She told me she would send you to the man who raped her and raise Emory on her own. I couldn't let her do that to you. Regardless, the two of you were sisters. I felt like my hands were tied, and I didn't know what to do," he said crying. "I loved you both so much."

"But aren't you Emory's father? How could she lock you up if you were Emory's dad?" I asked, figuring if Daddy married Mama when she was pregnant with me, then Emory had to be his.

Daddy turned and looked at Mother saying, "Frances cheated on me numerous times. Emory is a product of her adulterous behavior in our marriage."

"What marriage?" Mama said acrimoniously. "You *really* think what we had was actually a real marriage?"

"I married you because I loved you, Frances," Daddy said sincerely.

"Well, too bad I never loved you," she threw back cruelly.

I went to Daddy and embraced him. I could feel his tears drip on me with my own, wetting his shirt.

"I love you, Daddy."

"I'm so glad you girls have turned out as well as you have and have grown into gorgeous, resilient young women. Today I take a stand for you, Emory, and my-self. I'm leaving Frances and starting a new life with you all. Frances is going to have to continue to live with the demons that have haunted her all these years without me there to help her," he said, looking over at Frances whose fangs were no longer visible. She looked like she felt bad for once.

In that moment, I felt sorry for her because she didn't have a Joseph any longer. All she had was her-self, and I thank God for blessing me with a man who stepped up and called me his own.

Daddy grabbed my shoulder and kissed me on the forehead.

"I love you, Kea. As long as I'm granted breath in my body, I'm going to continue to love you and Emory be-cause I'm your father."

"I love you too, Daddy."

"Now let's get out of here," he said moving toward the door.

"You'll be back," Mother yelled, but Daddy didn't respond.

"And Kea," she called. I turned to look at the woman who birthed me, thinking this may be the last time I would see her for a while.

She smiled cruelly and said, "Don't you want to know who your *real* daddy is?"

Zacariah

I knew this was underhanded, but I didn't care. I had to find a way to get Kea back, and this was the only way I could think of for that to happen. I searched high and low trying to find some nasty skeleton in the closet that would crush her, but I couldn't find anything on her. This girl was really Ms. Goody Two-shoes.

I knocked at the door. It took a minute for someone to finally answer.

"Can I help you?" the woman asked, opening the door.

"Yes. My name is Carolyn," I answered, intentionally giving her a false name. "I'm looking for Kea."

"She doesn't live here," she said unconcerned.

I pulled out a piece of paper with the address written on it. "This was the last known address I had for Kea. I went to school with her. I got back into town last night and was hoping I could catch up with her here."

"Well, she doesn't live here," came the frigid answer.

"Do you know where I can find her?"

"Come in and I'll get you her new address," she said, motioning me to enter.

I walked in and was amazed at how spectacular this house was. A huge foyer, crystal chandelier, and spiral mahogany staircase greeted my eyes. This house was amazing. I hoped to have something just like this one day.

Kea's mother walked over to a cherry oak desk reaching in the drawer and pulled out an address book. She wrote down the information on a slip of paper and brought it to me.

"Here it is," she said handing it to me.

"Thank you so much, and might I add your home is magnificent."

"Thank you."

"You and Kea's father have done an excellent job restoring this place."

"How do you know we've restored it, and how do you know if her father and I are together?" she asked distrustfully.

"I can tell by its architectural features and your style of dress that you are responsible for this fantastic décor. And to answer your second question, I saw a family portrait sitting on the table in the foyer. I figured it had to be your husband and Kea's father."

She smiled nodding her head but not too hard, still eyeing me suspiciously.

"Who are you really?" she asked crossing her arms.

"I said I was a friend—"

"Cut the crap. I know a liar when I see one. What's your purpose for coming over here, and what's your real name?"

I started to panic. Pulling out my Zacariah confidence I said, "Look, Mrs. Fields, my name is Zacariah."

"Go on."

"And I'm not looking for Kea. I know where she may be and that's with my man."

"You mean the wretched Jaquon."

"Hell, no. I'm talking about Derrick," I said frowning.

"So Kea did meet someone else new," she said smirking. "It sounded like she was hinting around about that at her sister's wedding."

"Yeah. She stole my man."

"Are you and this Derrick married," she said looking at my ring finger.

"No, but—"

"So how did she steal him away from you if you didn't even have legitimate papers linking you and Derrick together in holy matrimony?" she asked boldly.

"Papers or not, he's my man."

"So why are you knocking on my door, child?"

"Call me cold. Call me calculating, but I heard through the grapevine that you and Kea do not get along."

"This's true," she nodded.

"And I heard about what she did to you at your daughter Emory's wedding."

She frowned, not saying anything.

"If I'm a good judge of character, like I think I am, I know you are not the type of woman who lets anyone get the best of her," I said.

"This is true."

"I think this goes for your daughter also."

"Go on," she said.

"Your daughter slept with my man. I caught the two of them in bed together, and I was devastated."

"Sorry to hear that."

"We got into an altercation, and ever since then . . ."

"You want to get back at my daughter, and you want to use me to do it."

"Yes," I said.

"What makes you think I need you to get back at my own daughter?" Mrs. Fields asked finally sitting down on the plush white sofa. She didn't bother to offer me a seat so I continued to stand.

"I know you don't need me. I was hoping you would help me. You can get satisfaction in knowing I will do what I need to do to make her pay."

"You have completely lost your mind," she said wearing a mirthless grin.

"Yes, I have. I will not rest until I get your daughter back. You may want to protect her, but I don't get that vibe from you, Mrs. Fields. This is why I came to you."

"You do know you are asking me to take revenge out on my own daughter?"

"Yes, ma'am."

"This is bold of you to think I would."

"Again, I was hoping."

Mrs. Fields stood looking me up and down with her hand on her chin. Perhaps only a minute or two passed, but it felt like an eternity..

"What do you want to know?"

"Anything incriminating."

Zacariah

I only had to knock twice when this elderly man looking like he was damn near eighty answered the door. His appearance took me back for a minute because he was hunched over with a receding hairline meeting the patches of thin gray hair that still grew upon his head. He walked with a cane and looked like he couldn't stand straight up to save his life. It was probably all that excess weight he had around his belly.

"Can I help you?" his crackling voice greeted me, taking me aback.

"Yes. I'm here to see Mr. Hanks. Is he here?"

"You're looking at him," he said gazing at me through wrinkles but had the most alluring smoky-gray eyes.

"Hi. We haven't met, but I need to speak to you, if you don't mind."

"About what? I don't know you."

"I know, but it's very important. Can I come in please?"

He looked me up and down making me feel a little uneasy since Mrs. Fields let me know a little bit about his background.

"I only have a few minutes, and then you have to leave. My lunch will be here in a minute."

"Your lunch?"

"Yes. Meals on Wheels. I hope they have meat loaf with mash potatoes today."

"Sounds good," I said walking in and closing the door behind me. I slowly walked behind the elderly man noticing his place needed a good cleaning. By the looks of him, I knew he was not able to do this himself. Old drapes hung from the half windows that looked like they hadn't been cleaned in years. Cobwebs hung from corners in the ceiling.

"Have a seat, dear," he said sitting down in his recliner. "So tell me why you are here."

"I'm here to talk about your daughter."

"Which one?" He looked over at the bookcase filled with many pictures of children.

"How many do you have, if you don't mind me asking?"

"I have nine daughters that I know of and eight sons."

"You have a really big family," I said thinking, *What woman in her right mind would have any children by this man? Seventeen kids by numerous women, and he could have more. How crazy is this?*

"Yeah, I got around in my day," he said coughing. It was hard to get used to his cough. Every time he did it, I jumped, unable to brace myself from his outburst.

It looked like his wild living took a heavy toll on this man. Trying to feed into his ego I asked, "How old are you to have these many children, because you don't look a day over fifty-five."

"Now, come on, child. I may be old, but I'm not senile," he said chuckling. "Time has been hard on me."

"I'm sorry. I didn't mean to—"

"You don't have to apologize. I'm a little happy to hear a kind compliment now and then. I don't hear too many anymore."

Sarcastically I thought, *I wonder why.*

"So you said you are here to speak to me about my daughter. Which one are you referring to?"

"A girl who was born to Frances Fields."

His facial expression instantly changed from a smile to a frown. He lowered his head and rubbed his wrinkled hands together.

"I haven't heard that name in a long time. She . . . she . . . She hates me, and she has every right to."

I didn't know what to say so I just listened.

"Miss, I have done some horrible things in my day. When I say horrible, I feel like the Lord himself shouldn't forgive me for some of the sins I committed. I'm a changed man now and have repented, but I have to wonder if I'm paying for all my sins now being old and alone."

I still said nothing, listening intently and hoping this man would give me something more to work with.

"Frances was pregnant with my daughter. I lied to her mother and never once claimed the baby as my own. To this day, I don't know her name or even what she looks like. Frances hasn't had anything to do with me since the day she left, but I can't blame her. I hurt that girl something terrible and regret the things I did to her," he said starting to weep and cough at the same time.

"I hope one day I'll be able to apologize to Frances. I also hope the day will come when I get to meet the daughter we created. Honestly, I would love to see all my children. I slept with so many women, using them for what I could get from them, and then leaving them to raise these kids on their own. I never looked back because I only cared about myself. Now look at me. I'm old, decrepit, and sad. Nobody cares about me."

"You have to have someone," I said, trying to make him feel better but not really caring.

"There's one person who sees after me every now and then."

"See? You have someone."

"But I should have my children visiting me," he said wiping the tears away with the back of his hands. "Just look at them," he said pointing to the many pictures. "Some of the mothers were nice enough to keep in touch and send me pictures of my kids. I put them up there because this way, I get to see them every day. Take a look at them. They are some beautiful kids."

I got up and walked over to the shelves filled with pictures of smiling children. Some of the photos were really old and some were more recent. Each child looked as though nothing but happiness filled them. I scanned the photos until I came across one that reminded me of someone I knew. It was a young boy holding a basketball. I picked up the black-rimmed frame and asked him who he was.

"That's my boy. He used to play basketball in high school. His mother and I had a thing going on until I left her when she became pregnant with him. I have to say she was one of the ones who kept in touch, letting me know how he was doing. She sent me pictures every year. That one was from his senior year. I guess after that you can't make your grown son take photos because I haven't received one since."

"Do you talk to him or know where he lives?"

"He's doing well for himself."

"And that's all you know about him?"

"I was told he was getting married at one time, but his mother didn't approve. If she didn't think the marriage was going to work, it wasn't. But I haven't heard from his mother in quite sometime, so I'm not sure if he's married or not."

After speaking to Mr. Hanks a few minutes more, slipping the picture of the young boy into my purse, I left. The knock at the door gave me the opportunity to take the picture without him noticing. Lucky for me his food arrived right on time.

Entering the parking lot, I saw Kea pull up parking right next to me. I peered at her and watched her get out of her car. She looked a bit upset.

"What's wrong, Kea? Did somebody pee in your Kool-Aid?"

"What the hell are you doing here, Zacariah?" she said looking angry.

"Is there trouble in paradise?" I asked.

"Paradise is lovely with Derrick. I mean, Jaquon," she said smirking.

"Speaking of Jaquon, can you tell him I came by looking for him? I needed to talk to him about something," I said playing off why I was here. Kea knew what that meant, and I loved seeing the concerned look on her face.

I unlocked my car doors to get in and said, "It's so good to see you again, Kea."

"And look, I don't have to smack you in your face again. We can get along," she said smugly.

"Oh, I haven't forgotten about you putting your hands on me. You'll be seeing me again. I guarantee it."

"Aw, damn. Just when I thought I wouldn't have to see your face again," she came back.

I couldn't wait for the day when I was going to permanently wipe that smirk off of Kea's face. And as luck has it, I think I found the information I needed to tear her world apart.

Essence

When Jaquon called and asked if he could come over, I was more than happy to say yes. A few hours later he was walking through my door. I wanted to pull him straight to my bedroom and ride him to bliss all night long.

"It's good to see you looking fine as ever," he said, putting his feet up on my coffee table.

"Do you have any home training?" I asked.

"Oh, my bad. I was trying to get comfortable," he said.

"You mean you came over for some action?"

"That too, but I'm trying to be a decent enough brother to see how you're doing first before I go diving headfirst in them panties."

"How considerate of you, Jaquon. I guess I'm supposed to fall into your arms right now since we got the small talk out of the way."

"We can skip the logistics and get down to sex now," he agreed, reaching for my hand. "Now come over here and give me some loving."

I went to him, mesmerized by his come-hither eyes and climbed on top of him. Facing him, I gripped his face and said, "Thanks for checking up on me."

"Anytime," he responded, leaning in kissing me feverishly.

I thought I heard my door open but figured it was my imagination until I saw Zacariah walking in, and she was in one of her moods.

"Essence, I need to talk to you. Guess what happened to me—" She stopped in her tracks when she saw Jaquon and I meshed together. She crossed her arms smiling smugly.

"What do we have here?" she asked.

"Zacariah. What are you doing here?" Jaquon asked curiously.

"You didn't tell him, Essence?" she asked looking at the two of us.

"You know her?" Jaquon asked, pushing me off of him.

"Jaquon, Zacariah is my best friend."

"Get the hell out of here."

"You can go there," Zacariah interjected.

"Of all the women I had to get myself involved with, you had to be friends with that one over there," he said pointing at Zacariah.

"You *don't* want to go there, Jaquon, because this is a clash you will lose."

"Trick, I will go and do whatever I feel like doing."

"Essence, you better get your hound dog. I don't want to have him spayed and neutered."

"You didn't mind my reproductive organs when you had my balls in your mouth."

"Whoa! Whoa! Whoa! Hold up," I said holding my hands in the air like someone had a gun pointed at me saying, "Freeze."

"What did you just say?" I asked flabbergasted.

Zacariah turned like she was looking at a sculpture on my wall when nothing of interest was there.

"When did Zacariah have your balls in her mouth?"

"Girl, don't pay any attention to Jaquon. He's nothing but trouble."

"You knew I was seeing him. Why didn't you tell me the two of you had something going on?"

"We don't have anything going."

"But it looks like you did."

"I didn't think it was important," Zacariah said.

"You thought I would enjoy scrounging over your leftovers?" I asked angrily.

"By the time we got a chance to talk, the two of you had already done your thing. So, I figured, why say anything. I didn't want to bust up your groove. You thoroughly enjoyed him by the way you were walking around here like he could screw no wrong. Anyway, Jaquon and I don't get down like that anymore."

"Damn right we don't," Jaquon agreed. "Trick wasn't good anyway. Your girl did me better," he said to Zacariah.

"Jaquon, I'm not going to have you disrespect me like this. Don't be sitting here comparing me and Zacariah because I don't want to hear it."

"Essence, baby, come on. You know you are who I'm feeling."

"What about your girl?" I asked.

"Yeah, what about Kea?" Zacariah said making sure we both heard his girl's name. Jaquon seemed to be stunned by this and said nothing.

"You know what? The two of you got to step," I said wanting to be alone.

"But I live here," Zacariah said.

"You live here?" he asked. "So my boy Derrick finally got smart and kicked your ass to the curb."

"You don't want to go there, Jaquon," Zacariah said. "Anyway, Essence, I really need to talk to you. It's important," she said, whining like a child.

"We can talk in the morning."

"And I came over to spend some time with Essence," Jaquon said probably still aroused from me straddling him.

"She doesn't want you anymore. Get your trifling ass out of here before you get cut."

"Zacariah, shut up before I bash your face in," Jaquon threatened.

"Both of you shut up! You two are making my head hurt with this bickering back and forth!"

"Girl, I got some Motrin in my purse." She reached in searching for the pills to relieve my tension.

"Don't you mean crazy pills? We both know you don't have it all upstairs," Jaquon threw out.

"Look, I got my own pills. I want the two of you to leave please," I said rubbing my temples vigorously.

"You always know how to bust up somebody's groove," Jaquon said, pulling his buzzing cell phone out of his pocket.

"Is that Kea calling you to come home?"

"No, it's your mother begging for a shot at me too. Wait a minute. You don't know who your mother is since she chose a bottle of liquor over you."

Zacariah was on Jaquon with fist, teeth, knees, and fingernails. Any way she could get to him, she did, leaving her marks for sure. I tried to pull her off, but it was to no avail. I could tell Jaquon didn't want to hit her, but after a few seconds too long of him tolerating her abuse, he pushed her, causing me to fall to the floor. Zacariah, on the other hand, fell unto the couch.

"How dare you talk about my mother like that!" Zacariah screamed.

"Truth hurts, huh? Why don't you search the alleys to see if she's residing in some Dumpster?" Jaquon said crudely.

Zacariah tried to jump back on him, but Jaquon kept pushing her back down on the couch until she finally decided to give up. Then he reached down, offering me a hand off the floor.

"Essence, I'm sorry. I didn't mean for you to get caught up in all this. If I would've known she-wolf was your friend, I would have told you. I know you haven't known me long, but one thing you do know is I haven't lied to you, unlike your friend here." He pointed at a now-weeping Zacariah.

"You know about my girl so that wasn't a big revelation tonight. I enjoy your company and hope we can get together again."

"Jaquon, I need some time to evaluate this, okay?" I said, still turned on by this man.

"What is there to evaluate?" Zacariah yelled. "He's a cheat with a girl already. Dump him and find another man who can give it to you like you want."

"Trick, please," he said to her. "If time is what you want, Essence, then time is what I'll give you. But don't wait too long, okay, because I'm going to be knocking at your door."

"That smile isn't going to be on your face for long, Jaquon. You like calling me a trick; you better check your girl," Zacariah said spitefully.

Jaquon looked at Zacariah curiously. "Kea is a good girl, unlike yourself."

"Good girl?"

"Zacariah, let it go," I warned.

"Maybe you need to check in at home once in a while because you might not find her there."

"Zacariah, don't do this," I warned again.

When the words rolled out of her mouth, I knew this situation had just got worse.

Zacariah

It felt so good when Derrick's name rolled off my tongue, causing Jaquon's face to crash like his heart did. I almost saw a tear try to work its way out of the corner of his eye.

"The last time I saw your girl, she was riding my man's dick."

"What!" Jaquon yelled.

"That's right, Kea and Derrick are sleeping together."

Jaquon snatched me up off the sofa by my shirt. The material never ripped as he pulled me close enough to his face so that I could feel his warm breath.

"Kea would never cheat on me."

"And I'm telling you she did. I saw it with my own eyes."

"Let her go," Essence told Jaquon.

He let me go not having the energy to hold me anymore because all the strength he had just flew out the window at hearing his girl was sleeping with his best friend.

"You're lying," he screamed, causing Essence and I to jump.

"Why would I lie?"

"Because you don't like me or Kea. You would do anything to ruin our relationship since you and Derrick's no longer exists."

"Everything you said is true," I said nonchalantly, "but think about it, Jaquon. Why would I choose my man to have your girl to sleep with? I mean, come on. There's too many men out here for me to choose. Why would I choose Derrick?"

"You're jealous of us," he said unconvincingly.

"Please, be jealous of you who cheats all the time? I don't have to ruin y'alls relationship because you're doing a fine job of that yourself. And even if I wanted to, don't you think I could have ruined y'alls relationship a long time ago? All those nights you stayed with Derrick while you lied to Kea, I could have blown your spot months ago. Now don't get me wrong, I do enjoy seeing the pain in your face by this revelation. Look at you, looking like a sick puppy," I said smiling triumphantly.

"You have to be lying," he said pacing.

"Think about it, Jaquon. Kea has called our house asking about your whereabouts several times, and I never once told her what you were doing."

"That's because you would be implicating yourself since you slept with me too," he said.

"You think I would admit to that? Sleeping with you is nothing to brag about."

"Like I'm ready to stand on a mountaintop and shout I've been with a whore."

"You've been with many whores so why you perpetrating? You standing here thinking you had it all going on, smiling in your boy's face knowing good and damn well you had slept with me. What type of best friend are you?"

"And what type of woman are you? That's why he kicked you out."

"Is that all you can come with? You have been hiding behind lie after lie using your boy to do your dirt. As mad as you getting right now, you can't even confront him because you are guiltier than he is because you did it to him first, and Derrick still doesn't have a clue."

"This is all some sick, twisted lie you've come up with to get things started."

"You don't have to believe me. The proof is in Kea not caring what you doing right now because she's doing Derrick."

"I don't believe you."

"I'm pretty sure if you asked little Ms. Innocent Kea about her and Derrick, she's going to deny it. Then again, she may admit to it just to hurt you like you hurt her. I mean, she does have every right to since you've been cheating on her the duration of your relationship. Talk about things coming full circle."

Jaquon just paced, not knowing what to say, and I loved the destruction of his confidence. He was an arrogant bastard and deserved everything I was giving to him. The more he got upset, the more I got energized.

"You mean to tell me you haven't noticed a difference in Kea lately?" I asked.

Jaquon stood thinking for a minute while looking around the room. I guess he thought the answers were going to pop out somewhere.

"I bet she's happier. I bet you she acts like she doesn't care. Before, she was crying when you didn't come home. Now she's probably wishing you would leave so she could be with him."

Jaquon thought and I could tell he did realize Kea's mood had changed. She was basically brushing him off, but he was too busy to notice, just happy that she wasn't riding his back. But that was because she had an ace in her pocket too: Derrick.

Jaquon grinded his balled right fist into the palm of his left hand. He paced like a madman while Essence and I sat back watching. With each step taken, the carpet beneath his feet screamed in agony. Next thing we know, Jaquon bolted for the door running out like a madman. Essence went to the door calling out to him, but her cries went unanswered.

"That was foul, Zacariah," Essence said closing the door.

"He got what was coming to him."

"But ratting out his girl and best friend?"

"No one makes a fool of me and gets away with it."

"You do a good enough job looking like a fool by your damn self," Essence said.

Her words hurt.

"I caught Kea riding Derrick like a jockey on a race-horse. You think I'm just going to let that go? She's going to get hers, and if using Jaquon is what it took for her to possibly get her face bashed in, then so be it."

Essence shook her head. "You had a good man who mentally, physically, and financially took care of you, but you didn't want him because you were too busy sleeping with random men for money." She frowned.

I couldn't say anything because she was right. I messed up.

"Now, you're mad because he got with someone else, thinking he would never betray you when it was you who came home with your coochie filled with another man;s fluid."

"You make it sound so immoral."

"That's because it is," Essence said.

"I didn't want to see Derrick with anybody else. Especially Kea. I love him," I said angry at myself for wanting to cry.

"You had a funny way of showing him. And you know I know more about your little escapades than he does. Zacariah, come on. You cheated on him constantly. How is that love?"

"He was supposed to beg me to come back," I said forcefully.

"You can't expect that man to live the rest of his life being stupid in keeping you. You took him for granted when you had him. Don't be mad because he's moved on."

"I'm not letting him go that easily, Essence."

"Reach into the realm of your mind and find some common sense, please. You know good and damn well Derrick is never going to take you back after what you did. This game of revenge you are playing is going to catch up to you. Let it go and move on with your life. Remember, karma always comes back around."

"Then I'll deal with it if it comes, but for now, I'm going to get my revenge."

"I feel so sorry for you," Essence said shaking her head. "I'm trying to tell you some good stuff, and you too stubborn to listen. I'm the only friend you have, yet you even betrayed me."

"How?" I said as she raised her hand to shut me up.

"You were supposed to tell me about you and Jaquon no matter if I had been with him. What is it with you hurting the people closest to you? One day you are going to end up completely alone and my words will remind you that you could have stopped all of this before it blows up in your face. But again, I know I'm talking to a brick wall. Do what you think you need to do to feel better, but don't always expect me to be here to help you pick up your pieces."

And with that said, Essence went to her bedroom.

Kea

It had been so hard getting through these past few days having to deal with the bombshell my parents dropped on me. The past reared its ugly head and changed the dynamics of our family, mostly affecting me. Emory was gone. Daddy had moved out and got a place of his own. Mother wanted nothing to do with me, and I was the product of sexual abuse. My real father was a rapist. My face was what reminded her of a past that no child should have had to go through.

For some reason, the person's shoulders I could rely on to get me through all this was Jaquon. He saw me sad the other day when he came home and actually showed concern about what was going on with me. The puffy eyes and tearstained pillows might have given my sadness away. He climbed in bed with me, wrapping his arms around me and cuddled me. Lying on his chest, I tried to think back on the last time Jaquon had done this.

Even though I was lying in his arms, I couldn't help but to think about Derrick and the time I couldn't spend with him. A small part of me wished it was Derrick's arms wrapped around me. Then guilt came over me. Had I turned into the person I hated most? Was I becoming a Jaquon?

Here he was showing me more love than he had in a long time and I was thinking about his best friend. I was the variance which would separate their bond of friendship. Maybe Jaquon felt something was going on. Maybe his instinct was starting to talk to him, telling him I was cheating on him now. Whatever it was, it must have shaken him to his senses.

I didn't know what happened to change him all of a sudden, but I welcomed his open arms. The way he stormed in here the other day, I thought he had found out about Derrick and me. But he didn't mention anything about my affair. He saw my sorrow and immediately started to comfort me.

Yes, I knew it was just a matter of time before bigmouthed Zacariah was going to say something. She couldn't keep anything to herself. Plus, I was number one on her hit list of individuals to get back at since I took her man. But now it was time to figure out which man I would call mine now.

As time passed with Jaquon and I spending more time together and him actually staying home at night, I was still surprised. Derrick had been calling the house I knew to hopefully speak to me, but most times Jaquon was answering the phone to speak with him. I couldn't say let me talk to him when I really never carried on a conversation like that with Derrick before. So I had to play faithful mate and be true to Jaquon since it seemed like he had made an effort to remain true to me.

Jaquon came up with a suggestion that we have a get-together with friends and family. I tried to figure out what the catch was. The only get-together he was ever down for was with him and his whores.

"I talked it over with Derrick, and he said we could do it at his house."

"And he doesn't mind?"

"Not at all. He thought it was a great idea."

"And you sure you want to do this?" I said with raised eyebrows.

"Yes. Why you looking like that?"

"I'm just surprised, that's all."

"We haven't had anything like this in a while. I would have liked to do it here, but our place it too small. Derrick has the yard space and that huge deck for an event like this."

"And when is this supposed to happen?"

"Saturday."

"This Saturday?" I asked.

"Yeah," he said excitedly. "I can't wait for us to have some fun."

"Why does it have to be so soon?"

"The sooner the better," he said.

"What has gotten into you?" I asked curiously.

"What?"

"You being here with me and wanting to cuddle and watch TV together and go places together. Now, you're planning this get-together with me being involved. What has sparked this flame in you?"

"Baby, I know I haven't been here for you like I should. I've done a lot of bad things in our relationship, and I finally came to the conclusion I don't want to lose you," he said, looking at me with the most sincerity I had ever seen coming from him.

"You have to know this is freaking me out. I'm waiting for you to tell me you got some chickenhead pregnant or something, and that's the reason why you've been sugaring me up."

"Nobody is pregnant, Kea, unless . . ." he smiled, rubbing my stomach.

"No. Nothing is in there," I said pushing his hand away as he laughed.

"I can't wait until you have my babies," he said.

"Who says I want any?"

"You did, remember? You said you wanted three."

"That was before a lot of unnecessary pain dropped in and destroyed what I thought was special in my life. I can't bring a child into this confusion."

"You shouldn't be confused about me loving you."

I sat up out of his embrace and said, "Jaquon, what is really going on? Be serious with me."

Sitting up to face me, taking my hands into his, he said, "Nothing. I can't show my girl some affection?"

"Not when the affection came out of nowhere."

"Before you complained about me not showing enough affection and now that I am, you're still complaining. I don't understand."

"I did want it," I said.

"Did? Has something changed that you haven't made me aware of?" he asked suspiciously.

"No. What I meant to say was I do. For so long I have begged for your attention. As soon as I stopped begging and let you be you, you give me what I've asked for. I have to wonder, is it too little too late?"

"You don't love me anymore?" Jaquon asked with a frown on his face.

I pondered that question before I answered, "Yes, I love you. I will always love you."

"You say that like you want us to be just friends."

"I need some time to think about this whole thing."

"Kea, I don't see what there is to think about. You wanted me; you got me. I'm not the same person I was."

"And when did this new Jaquon emerge? How do I know he will stay around or whether he will get bored with me and want to see what's out there again?"

"Baby, I love you," he said gripping my hand.

"Jaquon, you hurt me. My emotional scars haven't been erased because you have wrapped your arms around me and said you've changed. The way I'm thinking right now, no amount of hugs from you can take away all the hurt you have done to me."

"I'm willing to try. Kea, don't give up on me. Give us a chance. Please."

"This is going to take some time."

"That's all I ask for. In time, I will prove I've changed."

"I hope so, Jaquon. I hope you are not messing with my emotions because if one more thing is revealed to me, I swear our relationship is over."

Essence

I couldn't believe Jaquon called to invite me to a get-together at Derrick's place. I hadn't heard from him since he stormed out of my place, and now he's calling me for this. Was he trying to set me up or what? As far as I knew, he was still with Kea. I didn't know if he had confronted her about sleeping with his best friend. Was he taking her too? I knew nothing and was torn. In a way, I wanted to go because I was curious to see this woman who had his heart. I felt like I knew her already, even though I had yet to lay eyes on her. And then again, I didn't want to go because I didn't know if anything was going to happen.

Finishing up the fourth slice of pizza, I had to relieve myself. The doctors tried to warn me, but my problem wasn't as simple as quitting the next day. I was addicted to the high of puking and couldn't stop. I knew I needed professional help, but didn't want it now. I was fine the way I was.

After relieving myself, I opened the door to my bathroom to leave. To my surprise, Zacariah was standing on the other side of the door.

"So, you haven't learned your lesson yet?"

"What are you talking about?" I said still trying to wipe my mouth.

"Come on, Essence. I thought you had quit."

"I did, for a while."

"What? Two hours? One day? Three days? What?" she asked holding out her hands. "I don't understand. You could die from doing this."

"I'll be fine."

"Okay, Ms. Fine, I'm done talking to you about it. Maybe you need to collapse and get admitted into the hospital again before you realize how dangerous this condition is. Evidently you dead set on something more serious happening to you in order for you to wise up."

"Damn, Zacariah, when did you become a psychiatrist?"

"Yesterday. I received my master's from a place called I Give A Damn. I finally found that place called Common Sense that you didn't think I had so I could talk to you."

"Did Common Sense wise you up to let this revenge thing go with Kea?" I asked, pushing her out of my way as I walked toward the kitchen to get me something to drink.

Zacariah followed saying, "I only pulled it out to use it against you."

"Figures."

"Essence, your condition isn't a joke, but since you act like you getting an attitude, I'm going to leave you alone."

"Good. Why are you stalking me anyway?"

"Well, I was coming to tell you I know how I'm going to get Kea back."

"I don't want to hear it," I said throwing my hand up.

"But I may need you."

"How?"

"I heard about the get-together Derrick and Jaquon are having. I still don't understand why neither of them have ripped each other to bits since both of them know the other has slept with their girl. They're acting like things are still cool. What the hell is going on with them two? By the way, I heard you talking to Jaquon earlier and . . ."

"Why you eavesdropping on my conversations? You need to hurry up and get up out of my house so I can finally have some privacy."

"Essence, please. Are you going to hear me out?"

"No. I don't want any part of this."

"I know he invited you."

"And?"

"Just take me with you," Zacariah pleaded.

"Absolutely not!"

"Essence, please."

"I don't even know if I'm going."

"Please go and take me."

"If they wanted you there, then they would have invited you. You with Derrick, Jaquon, and possibly Kea in the same room is the makings for a disaster."

"Not for me."

"Something is wrong with you."

"That may be so, but I got some information I need to drop. I think the heavens are opening up for me to do this. What better place than at this get-together? I might get a two-for-one deal here," she said.

"Who?" I asked.

"You'll see when you take me."

I sighed.

"You know you're curious."

"I'll think about it."

"We only have a couple of days, so think fast."

"I said I'll think about it."

"Thanks, Essence. I know you're going so why don't we go to the mall and buy the sexiest outfits we can?"

The look on Zacariah's face was one of euphoria. I knew it had to do with this retaliation she was plotting. I swear I wanted no part of this, but this situation was like watching a bad movie you just paid for. You make yourself go through it anyway just to see how it's going to end.

Derrick

Mama was here and had taken over the cooking of the seafood. She had already fried some catfish and clams, and the lobsters were being steamed. Not only was she putting a hurting on the food, she brought homemade coleslaw and hush puppies, which I requested. She also made baked beans, corn bread, four sweet potato pies, and a pineapple upside-down cake. Mama looked for any excuse to cook, and I took advantage of her expertise in her cuisine. This event was the perfect opportunity to get my mama to come visit me. She didn't live too far away from me, but she didn't drop by as much as I would have liked either. But I knew that had a lot to do with Zacariah.

Most of the men pitched in purchasing the seafood with me. It was a BYOB event, so they also brought their own alcoholic beverages. The ladies brought additional side dishes. I provided hamburgers, hot dogs, and some alcohol too.

My house was full to capacity. Most of the crowd was outside and not trampling through my house, which is the way I liked it. I didn't want anyone getting stupid and start tearing up my stuff because if they did, there was going to be a problem.

When Jaquon came up with the idea, I wanted to reach through the phone and choke him to death. He had slept with Zacariah and acted like nothing had ever happened between the two of them. I wanted to confront him so bad my body ached, but Mama told me to "Leave it alone. You are not with Zacariah any more, so let things be. Yes, Jaquon was wrong, but you two are like brothers, and you should never let a woman come between you."

It was true. We had been friends for so many years. But I had to wonder whether Zacariah was the only girl of mine he had slept with. Doubts about our friendship started to surface, and I didn't know how to handle it. I didn't know how I was going to act when I saw him. But when I did, he acted like the same old crazy Jaquon, which, in a way, made it a lot easier to deal with. That was, until I saw Kea linked arm in arm with him. She was looking so damn sexy. I tried to play it off, but her beauty made it hard for me to concentrate. A part of me wanted to tear her away from him, punch him in his face, and take her away to be with me forever. But I maintained. Maybe this was also due to Mama standing right there watching me. She kept giving me the eye to let sleeping dogs lie. Little did she know how bad I wanted to lie with Kea.

Jaquon took off to the back to help with the setup while Kea joined Mama in the kitchen helping her with peeling the shells off the already deveined shrimp to be dropped into the deep fryer outside on the patio. The two of them hit it off immediately. Once Mama walked back outside to drop some shrimp, I walked behind Kea gripping her hips, pulling her body to mine.

"What do you think you are doing?" she asked.

"I've wanted to do this since you got here."

"We're going to get caught, Derrick. Move back," she said sticking her butt out, bumping me away.

"You know that's making me want you more," I said pulling her closer, making the space between us disappear. I knew she had to feel the growth forming underneath my jeans with each pulsation of my heart.

"Derrick, please stop," she asked seductively.

"Do you *really* want me to, or do you want me as bad as I want you?"

"This isn't right," she said.

"Neither is your man cheating on you, but it doesn't stop his flow."

She turned in anger pushing me away. "You supposed to be his friend."

"And you supposed to be his girl. Come on, Kea. You know I speak nothing but the truth," I said holding up my hand like I was being sworn in to testify.

"Don't get mad with me because you have feelings for me. I'm innocent," I said shrinking the space between us again. The heat emitting off her body made my manhood stretch out to reach her.

I leaned my body against hers, pushing her against the counter. She held her hands up, trying not to get shrimp juice on us. I leaned in and kissed her. Her lips were supple and tongue-inviting. I couldn't bring myself to break away, but hearing voices made Kea break free and walk out of the kitchen. Mama opened the door to find me standing at the sink pretending to finish shelling the remaining shrimp left in the bowl. No matter how much I didn't want to get caught, my extension would have drawn enough attention to itself to give me away. I hid it by leaning against the counter pretending to be helping.

"Derrick, what are you doing in here?"

"I'm finishing the shrimp. I have a couple more, and then you can have it," I tried to say calmly.

"Are you okay, son, because you look a little flushed in the face? What's going on with you?"

"I'm just tired, and you know it's hot as hell." I tried to stop the words from rolling off my tongue but couldn't take them back. "I mean heck."

"Boy, I was getting ready to say, you know better."

"I know, Mama. I'm sorry."

"That's fine. I come to see where you were and to soak up some of this cool air. That heat is something else. To be October, it's hot for this time of year," she said pulling up a chair at the kitchen table. "Seasons mixing like this can't be good. The Lord is on His way back. People better start paying attention to these signs. Everybody needs to get their souls right with God because when He cracks this sky, it's going to be too late for many. And that's including you, Derrick."

There was nothing like a good sermon from Mama to bring a man's erection down, literally. I loved Mama and knew she was telling the truth, but sometimes her preaching did get to me. I grew up in the church. I sang on the choir. I ushered and everything because that's what Mama had me do when I was coming up. Now I understand why she did what she did because I am aware where all my blessings come from. But she needed to understand it's a process for me, just like it was for her. It took time.

"Baby, you hear what I'm telling you?" she asked.

"Yes, ma'am," I replied rinsing the last of the shrimp.

"I wish everybody knew God like I know Him," she said fanning herself with a newspaper I had on the table.

"Are you all right, Mama? I hope you haven't overdone it out there. You were supposed to come over here and let us do all the work."

"Son, I'm good. I'm just trying to cool myself down. And you know I don't eat everybody's cooking. I can't stand to see too many hands handling the food."

Kea walked into the room wiping her hands on a towel.

"Honey, what did you say your name was again?" Mama asked.

"Mama, this is Kea."

"Jaquon's girlfriend, right?" Mama asked.

"Yes, ma'am."

"Oh, so you the girl dumb enough to get yourself wrapped up in that man."

"Yes, ma'am," Kea said looking staggered.

"I'm sorry, baby. I didn't mean for it to come out of my mouth like that."

"Mama speaks her mind," I said softly to Kea, knowing Mama heard me.

"Boy, step back and let the girl breathe."

I laughed along with Kea.

"Are you having a good time, Mrs.—"

"Call me Ms. Shirley, and yes, this is really nice. I better get back out there and check on the food. I don't trust Jaquon or your daddy to be handling anything," Mama said getting up. "Pass me those shrimp so I can finish cooking. I hope we don't have burnt fish," she said walking out.

Kea

Almost getting caught earlier made me try to stay away from Derrick as much as possible. Every now and then I would look around and catch him watching me, but I played it off. I kept hoping Jaquon wouldn't notice. Yes, a small part of me wanted to be with Derrick, but not here and not now. Jaquon was who I came with, and he is who I had to show the majority of my affection to. I have to say he made sure to pay more attention to me, which was a total turnaround from the last get-together we attended. The last cookout consisted of Jaquon smiling all up in some woman's face and whispering in another one's ear, but I couldn't think about the past now. I had to concentrate on our future, but did we have one together?

We ate and we drank until we couldn't eat anymore. Ms. Shirley put a hurting on the food, and we broke one of the commandments, and that was the sin of gluttony. Everybody sat back with their bellies tight, and now it was time for the men to get caught up in their card games, Jaquon being one of them.

People were quick to eat, but no one was quick to clean up after themselves. Ms. Shirley attempted to tackle some of the mess, but I made her sit down. She had done enough with the cooking. Now it was time for her to sit back and relax.

I picked up where she left off by throwing all the used paper plates in the trash can. I dumped drinks out of cups and picked up paper off the ground. I swear some people just didn't have any home training.

One of the trash cans was running over with garbage. I tried to lift the industrial-size black plastic bag, but it was too heavy for me to pick up. Derrick showed up out of nowhere to help me.

"I got it," he said brushing his hand across mine. Instantly tingles surged throughout my body. "I wouldn't want you to hurt yourself," he said.

I couldn't do anything but smile and get away from him. The only thing left to do was to store the leftover food and wash the dishes. Derrick had a dishwasher, so it made that easy.

Derrick kept looking at me with a passion hot enough to ignite us both into flames. Finally he got his chance again to be with me alone when I was loading the dishwasher.

"Meet me later," he whispered to me.

"We can't do this. Not tonight," I said.

"I need to be with you, Kea."

"How is it going to look when both of us disappear?"

"Who's going to notice? Everybody is dancing and playing cards. No one will miss us," he said grabbing my hand and kissing the back of it gently.

"You are really not making this easy," I said.

"Dip out in twenty minutes and meet me at the cut overlooking the city. I'm going to leave now."

"And you think your mother won't notice?"

"I'll tell her I have to dip out for a minute if that will make you feel better."

It didn't make me feel better. Twenty minutes went by, and Derrick still hadn't left. I figured out later he was trying to see his parents off. They were ready to go home. Once he got them on their way, he mingled a bit, and then disappeared.

Watching the digits on my watch move at a snail's pace, I longed for that time when I could make my grand exit. What was I thinking, though? I couldn't go be with Derrick after uncurling myself out of the arms of Jaquon earlier. What does that say about me? And wouldn't Jaquon get curious about my sudden departure? Wouldn't he wonder why he doesn't see Derrick either? I would have to think of something. The guilt of the entire thing was killing me. Why was I worried about what Jaquon thought? He disappeared on me all the time. Why was it I was always thinking about our relationship when he never once considered me when it came to him doing what he wanted to do? I know he claimed to have changed, but why should I believe him? Or was I making excuses to justify me doing my dirt now?

I needed to do this. Maybe we could make this our last time together. Tonight I was going to step outside the box and do the unexpected. I was going to play Jaquon's game and be with the person I wanted to be with, Derrick. Whatever happens, happens.

Grabbing my car keys, I left without saying a word. Luck was with me because Jaquon was too busy playing cards to even notice. I was also glad no one screamed, "Where you going?" since a beer run needed to happen every hour and any car moving was responsible for the next run.

Arriving at the location Derrick specified, I saw him sitting in his car. The neon lights from his stereo glowed brightly. I let down the automatic window and cut my car off, and he did the same.

"Get out and get into my car," he said. I didn't hesitate doing what he asked. Once in, I enjoyed the new car scent as the black leather seats welcomed me into his new ride.

"You like?" he asked.

"I do."

"I have been wanting this SUV for a while now, and I finally got it," he said, brushing his hand across the steering wheel.

Not meaning to change the subject I asked, "Derrick, what are we doing?"

"Honestly, I don't know. The one thing I do know is I want you. I know you feel a connection between us, Kea. When I saw you standing alone earlier, my mind led me to embrace you. Your body fits like a glove against mine, and I knew then that maybe what we got going on is not just an ordinary fling."

"So you want me for my body?" I questioned jokingly.

"No. I love your mind too," he said smiling. "I love your eyes, your scent, and your smile. I just love being in your presence."

"But . . ." I said.

"I know what you're going to say. What about Jaquon?"

"And your crazy ex-girl, Zacariah," I added.

"Zacariah and I are over. There's no going back. I'm only looking forward. I'm driving blindly, but I clearly see I want you. When I saw you walk in with Jaquon, my heart skipped some beats."

"I was nervous about coming because I was scared someone would figure out we've had something going on."

Derrick reached for my hand.

I said, "You know, Jaquon told me he's going to change, and lately he's been showing me a different side of him."

"But for how long?" Derrick asked.

"I don't know, but he hasn't been going out, and he's been spending more time with me."

"Do you trust him?"

"Of course not. I'm still leery. I'm wondering where all of this newfound devotion is coming from all of a sudden."

"Maybe he's starting to realize it's too late for him. He had his chance, and he blew it. Maybe I'm the man you need in your life right now."

"And you're willing to lose your friendship with him?"

"Yes."

The truth was in Derrick's eyes. I looked intently into them, searching for something that would let me know this wasn't meant to be. But the longer I stared, the more I could see his affection for me wasn't wavering.

"I don't know," I said cautiously.

"Aren't you tired of getting walked on all the time? I know I am."

"I am too, but—"

"Kea, I know all of this sneaking around isn't right, but we walked around looking like fools with people who openly cheated on us."

"I know, but—"

"Baby, let's do this. Let's be together. I know I don't know your entire story, but I'm willing to convert this tragedy into a love story with a happy ending. And if you didn't know it already, Kea, I've fallen in love with you."

If there ever were words a woman wanted to hear, here was Derrick telling them to me.

"Let me make love to you again."

"Derrick," I said before feeling the tip of his finger on my lips.

"Shhhh, just kiss me."

He leaned over the console and planted his lips on mine.

"I want you so bad," he whispered reaching under my shirt, taking my right breast in his hands. His thumb came in contact with my nipple, sending quivers through me.

"What do you want from me?" I said, then immediately thought it was a dumb question.

"I want you, baby."

He leaned his seat all the way back to the reclining position and asked me to get on top. I crawled over and straddled him as my legs gripped both sides of him, fitting perfectly. I was happy I was wearing a short denim mini. Feeling his hardness beneath me, I leaned down and kissed him some more. His hands explored my body while I unbuckled his belt and jeans. He eased them down, exposing his immense manhood.

"Come on, baby, give it to me," he whispered, ripping my G-string off. For a minute I thought how in the world was I going to explain to Jaquon not having on panties, but I figured when that time came, I could lie like he did.

Pulling Derrick's python free, I lifted myself upward, positioning his dick at the exact spot to enter me. Coming down slowly, we both sucked in sighs of pleasure. Mine was coming from this massiveness, and his from my warmth and wetness. And I was wet, dripping from the excitement of feeling this man inside me. My womanhood throbbed for him as I moved my hips in a circular motion while I watched the bliss all over his face.

"Oh, baby, you feel so good," he said, sending my body to elevations never experienced with Jaquon.

"You feel good too, baby," I murmured.

"I want to be in control," he said sitting upward with his mouth connecting to my breast. "Let me be on top," he said.

He maneuvered us to a comfortable position within the confined space of his new SUV. With one leg on the driver-side window and another on the dash on the passenger side, my body invited him in, and, boy, did he knock hard. He made love to me with a dynamism that sent my body into compound explosions. I believed if I would have asked him to keep going, he would have, but we had to get back to reality. Our lovemaking lasted a lot longer than it should have, and I hoped I wouldn't have to explain why I was gone for so long. But, boy, was it worth it.

After we were done, we fixed ourselves, not saying anything. We both looked into the darkness as the moon shined bright. We seemed to do this every time we were together. With us both spent and me now tired and sleepy, I closed my eyes, wishing I could doze off right here. Opening my eyes before I did fall into a deep slumber, I looked over at Derrick who was gazing at me.

"What? Why are you looking at me like that?" I said softly.

"You look so beautiful."

"You full of compliments tonight, aren't you?"

"I mean it too."

"You don't look bad yourself."

"I hope you have no regrets."

"Not a-one. I'm glad I came. And, boy, did I ever." We both laughed.

"Happy I could assist," he said.

"Glad you could please," I smiled.

"I guess we should head back to the peeps," Derrick said.

"Do we have to?"

"Not if you don't want to."

"I don't, but I guess we should."

"Where do we go from here?" he asked brushing the hair from my face. "Are we going to be together?"

"Derrick, I don't know how we're going to do this, but I want nothing more than to be with you. I've fallen in love with you too and hope you will be a part of my future."

Derrick

When I got back to the house, there were still quite a few people congregated in the backyard. When I left, there was one table set up for cards and now there were three. By the looks of the intense faces examining the cards in their hands, I don't think anyone noticed me being gone.

On cloud nine, I walked into the backyard with the intentions of mingling a bit when I was stopped dead in my tracks. Was I seeing this for real, or was this my imagination? Zacariah was looking at me, and she was sitting with Essence and Jaquon. I couldn't believe it. The fact Zacariah was bold enough to show her face back here and Jaquon arrogant enough to be sitting beside some female who was a little bit too close to him made me want to fly into a rage.

Zacariah waved, smiling that devilish grin of hers with her hair pulled up into a silver clip exposing her neck and silver hoop earrings. I turned with my hands balled into fists, wanting to snatch all three of them up, removing them from the premises, but I managed to maintain my composure.

I went into the house to clear my head a bit. I paced, wondering what I should do next. I felt like fighting. I had been letting these feelings fester way too long, and I was about to snap. Should I go out there and confront Jaquon now in front of everybody, not caring about my affair with Kea coming out, or should I just leave this situation alone?

I needed a drink. I went into the fridge to get a beer but when I went to reach for one, I was surprised to find none. These freeloaders had drunk up all my damn beer. I put what I wanted them to have in the coolers positioned near the table. Who the hell told them they could have my stash, and why in the hell were they in my refrigerator? I slammed the door shut, madder than I was when I walked in.

Kea entered trying to look inconspicuous. She must have seen the distressed look on my face because she came over to me asking, "What's wrong, Derrick?"

Before I could open my mouth to answer, Zacariah walked in.

"Hello, lovebirds. Where have y'all been?" she asked holding one of my beers that had been in my fridge.

Kea and I looked at each other and didn't say anything. Kea knew now why I was upset. I couldn't do anything but turn my back to Zacariah because if I kept facing her, I might slap the hell out of her.

"Oh, y'all don't want to answer me. I understand. You might incriminate yourselves."

"I thought I told you to never step foot back in my house," I said, snapping back around to address her.

"I was invited, Derrick," she said fearlessly.

"By who, because I sure as hell didn't invite you?" I said raging.

"I accompanied Essence," she said looking out the patio door at her girl smiling up in Jaquon's face.

"Who is Essence?" Kea asked.

"Oh, you don't know who she is," Zacariah said slyly. "She's the one with the off-the-shoulder floral print number sitting beside Jaquon. Don't they look nice together?"

I wanted to smack that grin off her face. I knew what she was trying to do. I walked over to her, grabbing her by the arm and telling her, "You need to leave now."

Zacariah snatched her arm away from me, and we both watched as Kea peered out into the backyard. I knew her mind was calculating things, and Zacariah was eating it up. She glanced back at me, and then at Kea who, by now, was opening the door to enter the backyard.

Kea

I went over to Jaquon who was raking the stack of money over to himself smiling because he had won big. When he saw me, he looked at the girl sitting next to him, and then back at me. She looked at him, and then at me, and the smile dissipated from her face.

Walking up to him, I crossed my arms and asked, "Who's your friend, Jaquon?"

"What are you talking about?" he asked, stacking the twenties he had just won.

"Oh, so you going to sit here and act like I don't see this female all close and personal with you? Who the hell is she?" I asked pointing at her.

"This somebody I met here at the cookout."

I looked at her and saw her twist awkwardly in her seat.

"Who invited her, because Derrick doesn't remember inviting her or Zacariah?" I asked, pointing at the house where Zacariah was now walking out, beaming.

"Maybe somebody else invited her, but it wasn't me."

Essence stood up to leave, but I stopped her saying, "Please don't go."

She paused, looking in Zacariah's direction.

"If you don't mind me asking, who invited you?" I asked the woman.

She didn't answer. All she did was look around at the individuals who were now concentrating on us. Jaquon didn't give her a chance to answer, standing and holding up his hands, saying, "You need to chill out, Kea."

"And you need to sit down so she can answer."

"You're making a scene."

"I feel like you're stalling. Are you attempting to take up for her now?"

"No. I'm trying to stop an altercation."

"Why would there be an altercation, Jaquon? Do I have a reason to start one?" I asked angrily.

"You came over here starting problems. We were playing cards. That's it."

"I don't believe you. I think you invited her."

"Think what you want to think, Kea. I know what I've done. And since you want to start problems, maybe I should be asking you where the hell you been. You've been missing for a hot minute."

I paused.

"Cat got your tongue? You can't answer me now?" he said confidently like he had scored a winning point.

"I went to get some more beer."

"Where is it? I didn't see it in your hands when you came in," he countered.

"It's in the car. I was coming to get you to help me bring it in until I found you all snuggled up with *her*."

Jaquon looked around, knowing if he went to that car and saw I had beer in it, he would look like an idiot. Most of the people here could care less about his embarrassment because I had some free beer for them to drink up.

One guy said, "You drive the gray car, right? I'll go get it," and left to retrieve it without me saying a word.

"Let me take you home," Jaquon said, picking up the money on the table. A few guys made remarks not wanting him to leave because they wanted a chance to win back some, if not all, of their money.

"I'm not leaving until you fess up and admit you have been sleeping with her," I stated, pointing at the frozen woman watching.

Jaquon looked at Essence, and then me.

"Okay, then," he said, "if that's the way you want this to go down. I'll tell you what you want to know. I have been sleeping with Essence."

My reaction was to smack the hell out of him. His head whipped around as ooooohhhhhhhhs from the crowd rang out.

Jaquon grabbed his cheek, rubbing it and asking, "What the hell is wrong with you?"

"How could you do this to me again, Jaquon? You told me you changed."

"I have. When I told you I was devoted to you, Kea, it was after we had our fling. I haven't slept with Essence since I told you I wanted us to work on our relationship. You can ask her for yourself."

I looked at Essence, and she nodded saying, "Kea, I'm sorry about all this. I was invited to come, and I did, knowing Jaquon was going to be here. My curiosity got the best of me because I wanted to see the woman who had his heart. Jaquon did let me know tonight that we could no longer see one another. He said he was cleaning up his act and wanted to be strictly with you."

I looked at Jaquon who looked like a kid who finally tried to do the right thing but was scolded anyway because all I saw was all the wrong he did. I didn't know what do and how to act at this point. I could see both were genuine in what they were saying, but was this another trick to make me stay with him?

"Baby, I told you I love you. I want you," he said walking up to me wrapping his arms around me.

"It looked like the two of you were—"

"I know, Kea, but, baby, that was not the case this time."

"I'm so sorry," I said.

"Hold up! Wait a minute!" a voice screeched. "I know you are not going to believe this bull," Zacariah said.

"I do believe him," I replied, looking her up and down.

"I'm not talking to you, trick. I'm talking to Jaquon."

"What you talking about, Zacariah?" he asked.

"You believe she went for a beer run?"

That's when the guy who went to get the beer out of my car entered the backyard with his hands full of cases of beer. Jaquon and I looked at her, then Jaquon said, "Now what?"

"That's just an alibi for Kea to cover her behind because she and Derrick were creeping," she smirked.

"What?" Jaquon said.

"Don't act like you surprised. I told you the other week I caught them two in bed together."

More Ooooohhhhhhhhs rang out. I almost expected to look around and see everybody eating popcorn as they gleefully watched the drama unfold.

I looked at Jaquon, Essence, Zacariah, and then Derrick whose facial expressions were all different. I saw the "what the hell" look. I saw the "not here" look. And I saw the "let's handle this" look.

I turned to Jaquon and asked, "She told you?"

"Yes, but—"

"And you didn't confront me on it. Is that why you've been acting all lovey-dovey with me because you knew?"

"When she told me, Kea, I was going to go over and stomp a hole in Derrick," he replied, pointing at him.

"You were going to *try*," Derrick shot back.

"Shut up, Derrick."

"No, you shut up, Jaquon. You're standing here acting innocent when everybody knows you ain't nothing but a dog."

"That's true, but that still didn't give you the right to sleep with my woman. I confessed everything to her so we could start things with a clean slate. How could I be angry with her for sleeping with you when she was paying me back for all I did to her? I sat and thought about all of that and came to the conclusion I wanted my baby back. If giving up the streets is what it's going to take to make us work, then that's what I'm willing to do. Now you, on the other hand, that's a different story because you were my best friend. How could you betray our friendship?" Jaquon asked.

Derrick clapped his hands as everybody watched intently. "Bravo, Jaquon. That was good. I'm glad you 'confessed,' as you say. But did you tell Kea about you and Zacariah sleeping together?"

Derrick

Jaquon's eyes closed, and Kea turned to look at him. I immediately wished I hadn't said it when it escaped my lips. Kea gasped, putting her hand up to her mouth looking at all of us. I shouldn't have said it. I could have waited to handle Jaquon once we got alone, but I didn't. This news was hurting Kea, and that was not my intention. I could see the surprise and hurt written all over her face. I knew how she felt because I felt her pain too.

"You slept with Zacariah?" Kea asked Jaquon.

"Yes, but it was a long time ago."

She turned to look at me. "And you knew?" she asked me bitterly. "When did you find out, Derrick?"

"Zacariah told me the night she caught us together."

"And you couldn't tell me?"

"I didn't want to hurt you like that, Kea."

"And you think dropping this bomb right now in front of all these damn people isn't hurting me?" she said coldly.

"If you cared for her like you think you do, you would have told her," Zacariah smirked. She was gloating at the situation. I wanted to strangle her, but I continued to restrain myself.

"Derrick and I have always been Jaquon's alibi when he was sleeping around," Zacariah said to Kea. "He was never with Derrick all those times he called you up and said he was over our house. Those were just the lies he told you. And if he did come over, it was so early in the morning that he might as well stayed where he was because the sun was coming up. I think Derrick even considered giving him a key because he got tired of getting out of our warm bed to open the door for him."

Kea looked confused, turning around looking at everyone listening to Zacariah's ranting.

"Baby, everything is over with now. I want to be with you," Jaquon pleaded.

"But she doesn't want you. She needs me now," I said walking closer to Kea who was weeping silently. The tears meeting at her chin were an indication of her grief.

"I can't believe I have been surrounded by individuals who do nothing but lie to me."

"Come on, Ms. Perfect Kea," Zacariah said sarcastically, "I didn't see you confessing your affair with Derrick to me or Jaquon. So don't stand here and act like you innocent in this whole thing. I mean, think about it. You were with Derrick tonight, and you standing here pretending like nothing happened when I know it did. The nerve of you to come out here and go off on us like you so righteous! You can't be mad at us when you've been doing the same thing," she said.

"Shut up, Zacariah! Haven't you and Essence done enough?"

"Hold up, Derrick. I haven't done anything," Essence retorted.

"You came knowing Jaquon and Kea were going to be here," I said.

"No, Kea was here with you," she countered, pointing at me. "And like I explained to Kea, I was curious. By the looks of everything, I'm the only honest one among the bunch."

"Derrick, it was time for all this to come out in the open," Zacariah said, coming to the rescue of her friend.

"But it could have been handled better than this," I said waving my arms.

"Who says? No matter where this would have went down, somebody's feelings would have gotten hurt. Look at me. I caught the two of you twisted up together," Zacariah declared.

"You deserved what you got."

"That may be true, but look at the mess the two of you have weaved also," she retaliated.

"Us? Us?" Kea said irately. "Derrick and I didn't start this! It was you and Jaquon! Both of you have been screwing around from the beginning! Not only did you sleep with each other, you slept with others too. Did either of you stop to think about how you were risking our lives?" Kea said turning to Jaquon. "I could have a disease because of you," she said jabbing her finger into his chest. "I stay in the doctor's office because I'm afraid you're going to bring me something I won't be able to get rid of."

"So you were willing to risk Derrick's life?" Zacariah laughed. "See? There goes that selfishness. And this coming from the most stupid girl I have ever met."

"Stupid?" Kea asked.

"Yeah, stupid. You chose to stay with Jaquon. So you don't have anyone else to blame but yourself. You could have dumped him a long time ago. All the evidence was dropping right there in your lap letting you know he wasn't faithful, but you stayed anyway. Pat yourself on the back for that one because none of us standing here had a damn thing to do with your decision."

"You know what? We've had enough of the drama, and it's time for everybody to leave," I said to the remaining people, hoping I could get this situation under control. I could tell by the looks on each of the ladies' faces this was not going to turn out well. Everybody started moving toward the door until Zacariah spoke out again.

"Don't anybody go anywhere. This party's just getting started."

Zacariah

Derrick held himself up with an empty chair as he leaned into it, clenching it in frustration. I couldn't let him kick me out yet. Not until I handled some unfinished business. I reached into my purse and pulled out the picture I stole from Mr. Hanks. I held it out for Derrick to take, but he stared at me without budging.

"Take it, Derrick."

"What is this, Zacariah? My patience is wearing thin with you."

"Just take the picture and tell me who that is."

Derrick took the picture and looked at it for a minute.

"Well? Who is it?"

"It's me, when I was in high school. Where did you get it from?"

"I got it from your father's place," I said smugly.

"My father?" Derrick said frowning.

"Yep. He and I had a nice little visit. I actually went over to talk to him about Kea," I beamed, turning to look at her.

"Me? Why are you talking about me? You can't find anything better to do?"

"Oh, I found something to do. I even took it upon myself to go visit your mother."

Kea looked stunned and didn't say anything. It was like I smacked her in the face without using my hand to do it.

"I knew that would get your attention. I found out that your mother hates you. She hates you because you are the product of her getting raped as a child by your dirty old father."

"Stop this, Zacariah! You shouldn't be doing this here," Jaquon said.

"There's no better time like the present."

I walked closer to Kea so she could see the glee in my face.

"Your mother told me who your real daddy is. Did she bother to tell you?"

Kea didn't say anything. She stood motionless, unable to move.

"She told me your father's name is Otis Hanks."

Kea's face dropped. She looked back at Jaquon who seemed to be shocked also.

"Mr. Hanks is my father?" she said not asking anyone in particular.

"Yep."

"That man is just our neighbor who lives downstairs," Jaquon replied.

"Your mother gave me his name, and I found him living in the same building you do. How ironic is that," I sneered, feeling like I was a trial lawyer revealing the facts in a case.

"I told him I was a good friend of yours, and he welcomed me in with open arms. I was a little leery at first because he is a rapist, of course, but I had to do what I had to do for your own good," I said pacing and laughing.

"He talked with me about his philandering back in the day and all the children he had. But how shocked was I when I looked at his wall of shame with pictures of children he had collected over the years and came across the one Derrick is holding now."

Derrick and Kea looked at me, and then each other. The blood seemed to drain from their faces, and I was eating this up.

"Enough, Zacariah!" Jaquon said walking up to me, grabbing me by the arm to pull me out of the backyard. I snatched my arm from him.

"You better not put your hands on me again or so help me, I'm going to have you arrested for assault," I blurted.

"I think you need to stop before this goes too far," Essence warned.

"I got this, girl. Let me do me. I've been waiting for this moment for so long. So don't spoil it for me, okay?" I told Essence.

"I mean, look at their faces. I know they should have figured out what I'm trying to tell them by now." I turned in Kea's direction, and then in Derrick's so I could look back and forth at their stunned expressions and not miss anything.

"I hate to be the bearer of bad news . . ."

"Don't do this here," Essence pleaded, but I ignored her.

". . . but the two of you are brother and sister."

Essence

I couldn't move. I watched in shocked disgust as Zacariah stood there laughing and clapping her hands like she was standing on the stage in a comedy club telling the funniest joke. But this wasn't a joke, and no one else was laughing. She was playing with people's lives. If she was right, this meant that Derrick and Kea were siblings that had slept with each other.

Neither of them moved. No one moved. You could have heard a pin drop at that moment with no one reacting to what Zacariah had said. Everyone was stunned. The only thing heard was Zacariah's evil laughter. I walked up to her, grabbing her by the shoulders, saying, "You need to stop. What's wrong with you?"

"Nothing is wrong with me. You should be asking the two of them what's wrong with them. I mean, they didn't know they were brother and sister? How nasty is that?"

"We need to leave," I said, gathering my things, but Zacariah refused.

"No one has anything to say?" Zacariah asked, still beaming.

"This is not funny," I said.

"Yes, it is. Derrick and Kea have been committing incest. How sick and twisted is that?"

"You shouldn't have done this," I warned.

"I told them I would get them back. They thought I was a joke, and now look at them. Who's laughing now? They deserve what they get. Little Ms. High and Mighty over here," she said looking at Kea who stood with no tears, no expression, just shock plastered on her face.

"And you," Zacariah said, sneering at Derrick. "I was your woman. I loved you, and you cheated on me with her. This serves you right. I bet you wish you would have kept your dick in your pants now. You wouldn't have had to worry about something as sick as this happening. Karma, baby, karma."

"Shut up, Zacariah," I said putting my hand over her mouth. She snatched my hand from her face. I tried to pull her by the arm to leave, but she kept resisting.

"This can't be true," Derrick said sadly looking at the picture of himself, and then at Kea. "I don't believe it, Zacariah," he said, shaking his head in denial.

"I don't believe you either," Kea finally spoke.

"Okay, then, ask your parents. Derrick, you don't have to wait. Look at what's written on the back of the picture," Zacariah instructed.

Derrick hesitated. He hit the frame against the table beside him, shattering it. His hand was cut by the broken glass, but he seemed unfazed by the blood trickling from it. He pulled the picture out, looking at himself before flipping it over.

"Read it out loud for the world to hear," Zacariah encouraged him.

For some reason, Derrick did. It was as if he were a zombie. He murmured the words,

"This is a picture of your son. Isn't he handsome? I'm so proud of him, and I know he's not a part of your life, but I wanted you to have this so you could see how

*well I did raising him despite you not being here. He's
a grown man now. This will be the last picture I send
you. Take care and I hope one day you will be man
enough to contact your son. Sincerely, Shirley.*"

Derrick's hands started to tremble. He dropped the
picture. He turned and walked into the house without
saying a word to anyone.

"You aren't happy until you have made everybody's
life a living hell," Kea said in a quiet rage. "Are you
happy now?"

"As a matter of fact, I am," Zacariah said flippantly
with her hands on her hips.

"You didn't have to do this to him. Derrick has always been there for you."

"The bastard shouldn't have cheated on me."

"You cheated first," Kea said accusingly. "Blame
yourself for losing your man. Maybe if you would have
kept your legs closed, you would still have him, you
trifling whore."

"And you were more than eager to step in where I
left off. Oh, how quickly did your legs open up for *your
own damn brother*. I may be considered a whore, but I
wasn't trifling enough to sleep with a family member."

Kea bolted toward Zacariah. Before Zacariah had a
chance to react, Kea was on her, punching her in the
face. Zacariah hit the ground, and Kea pounced on
her, sitting across her chest, punching her repeatedly
in the face. Zacariah tried to fight back, but Kea's rage
wouldn't allow her to even get a hit in. Kea grabbed
Zacariah by the hair and began pounding her head into
the ground over and over again. Zacariah screamed,
but no one would do anything. Everybody stood
around and watched the assault take place. I wanted

to help, but a part of me wouldn't budge. I guess a part of me thought Kea's rage would turn to me since I was one of the women Jaquon had slept with. And maybe a part of me thought Zacariah deserved this. It was a long time coming. She always thought she was invincible, and now she was being taught a lesson.

When Zacariah looked like she was losing consciousness, Jaquon jumped in and grabbed Kea off her. Kea was screaming and reaching to get back at Zacariah who was not moving.

I ran over to her and called out, "Zacariah," but she didn't say anything. I palmed her cheeks and gently tapped her right cheek, but she still didn't respond.

"Somebody call an ambulance," I yelled. "Call 911 now!"

Zacariah

When I woke up I was lying in a hospital bed. My head felt like I had been hit with a baseball bat or something. I touched my head thinking I could push the pain back but felt only bandages. I felt my face, and it was swollen. I looked around for a mirror and didn't see one. Looking over at the sink where the nurses washed their hands, I saw a large mirror. Slowly, I got up feeling sore and battered. Placing my feet on the cold tile, I walked over to the sink, clicked the light on which blinked twice before coming on completely. The brightness caused me to cover my eyes until they adjusted to it. When things came into focus, I didn't recognize the person staring back at me.

White bandages were wrapped around my head like a cocoon. Both eyes were black, and my lip was split. The left side of my cheek was swollen, and scratches were everywhere. I started to cry, quickly clicked the light off, and climbed back into bed.

I wanted to close my eyes and pretend like this hadn't happened to me. I was hoping this was only a nightmare, but when I opened my eyes, I realized I was still in the same place.

I turned to the large window covered with vertical blinds which happened to be open and looked out at the murky sky sprinkled with a few stars. The dark night replicated my spirit.

Tears continued to run down my temples, hitting the pillow. The television was playing TV Land's best when the door to my room opened. A nurse walked in, and it happened to be the same nurse I had a confrontation with weeks back when I came to pick up Essence.

"You've finally woke up. How are you feeling?" she asked. She was wearing a top printed with SpongeBob SquarePants and solid blue bottoms.

"I feel . . . I feel . . ." I stopped. I couldn't answer her. How ironic to have the same woman I was so rude to be the same person who was here to take care of me.

"You'll be fine. It's okay to cry. You've suffered a minor concussion and have a few bruises here and there. Other than that, you'll be fine," she said, giving me a smile that actually comforted me.

"How long have I been here?" I asked.

"Not long. A few hours maybe. Your friend Essence was here with you for a little while, but she had to leave. She told me to tell you she would be back to see you tomorrow."

I smiled happy I still had one friend in my life.

"You have yourself a great friend," the nurse told me.

"I know," I agreed. "Look, Nurse, I'm sorry about—"

"There's no need to apologize. It's okay."

"I guess you're thinking I got what I deserved," I said, touching the bandages wrapped around my head.

"I never wish harm upon no one. I do believe in a higher power, though. Sometimes things have to happen in order for us realize certain things," she said putting the blood pressure wrap around my arm.

"Call it a wake-up call," she said smiling. She hit a button on the machine, and in seconds it had my reading.

"Your blood pressure is perfect. But like I was saying," she said as she took off the contraption, "we cannot go through this world thinking we can treat anybody any type of way. Eventually, all the ugly things we do to other people catch up with us. Open your mouth," she told me, putting the thermometer under my tongue, waiting for another reading. The machine beeped. "Your temperature is a little high, but not enough to worry," she said patting my arm.

"Why are you so nice to me?" I asked.

She smiled and said, "Now don't get me wrong. I don't know why you ended up here, and I'm not saying you did something to have this happen to you. I'm going on my experience with you, and you were not a nice individual from what I saw. Still, I couldn't allow you to bring me down. I'm too blessed to get upset over nonsense like that, sugar," she said confidently. "I could never hate you or anyone else."

"How do you do this? You seem so positive."

"It's called faith. Honey, I prayed for you when you left this facility that day. I knew there had to be something in your past that made you the way you are. I prayed that God would see you through this. I knew, and still know, He's wrapping His loving arms around you."

"But look what happened. I'm in a hospital," I said through more tears.

"God didn't do this, baby. Please don't ever think that. He may allow situations to happen in order for us to realize we need Him, but punish us—never. He wants us to realize He should come first before all things. This situation might not have been the work of the devil, either. We always want to blame one force or another for things that happen, but sometimes we cause a lot of these traumatic events to happen to ourselves."

I nodded listening intently. This was probably the first time ever I took the time to pay attention to what someone was telling me. She picked my hand up with her left hand and patted it.

"It's going to be okay. It's never too late to change. It's never too late to pray either. I can see you are not a bad person. There's some good under that hard exterior, but it's up to you to want to bring that forth. No one can do that for you," the nurse said sincerely.

"I don't know if I can change."

"Then try praying. Ask God to order your steps. Talk to Him like you're talking to me now. He'll hear you. The more you do it, the easier it gets."

"Talk to Him just like I'm talking to you?" I questioned.

"Yes, and watch how things change for you. But I have to say this. When you do get to the point in your life when you want to make this change, don't think that bad things will never happen to you again because that's when more things seem to fall out of the sky. Now *that's* the devil trying to stop you from accepting God into your life. Don't let him steal your joy. Claim your joy, baby. Claim your happiness. Claim your life back."

"I understand," I said tearfully.

"If you ever want to talk, you know where to find me," she said letting my hand go, giving me the most heavenly smile. "I'll continue to pray for you."

The nurse went to leave the room. But she stopped and turned to look at me and said, "When you pick up the Bible next time, turn to Psalms, chapter thirty-seven, verse eight."

Her eyes went from looking at me to looking at the nightstand in the room. She looked back at me, smiled, and left.

I pulled the top drawer open to find a Bible inside. I picked it up and held it for a minute, then finally opened it looking for the scripture she suggested.

Cease from anger, and forsake wrath: fret not thyself in any wise to do evil.

Essence

This evening had been way too much for me. I needed to relax and try to forget about all the drama that happened. I tried to tell Zacariah, but she wouldn't listen to me. She opened up that big mouth and outed as many people as she could, which landed her behind in the hospital. I sat with her for a while until I decided to do what I do best. Mingle.

Needing to feel wanted again, I set out to get back into the game. Sitting alone, I sipped on my drink and listened to the smooth sounds of the music relaxing me. A tall and sexy gentleman approached me.

"Is this seat taken?" he asked.

"No, it's not," I smiled, scanning over him quickly. This man was fine. Dressed in blue denim jeans and a chocolate suede jacket over a black tunic, he was dressed to impress. A ring accented his pinky finger, and his watch blinded me. The old me would be trying to get this man for his money, but I decided if anything went down tonight, I was going to do this because I wanted to and for free.

Tall and Sexy looked at me like I was the only woman around, even though we were surrounded by the sounds of people talking.

"My name is Tony, and you are . . .?" Tall and Sexy said, speaking with a voice seductive enough to do phone sex.

"Jasmine," I said, holding out my hand to shake his.
"Are you enjoying yourself this evening?"

"I'm doing much better now," I said smiling and that's when I saw him. Jaquon was peering at me, and seeing him caused me to stammer for a minute.

"Are you okay?"

I tried to play it off, saying, "I'm okay. Just thought I saw someone I knew."

I had. Jaquon was sitting at the bar drinking. He put down the glass and stood to come my way. Part of me wanted him to come over and take me into his arms, but the other part wanted him to deal with his home life first before he ever tried to talk to me again.

Jaquon took a few steps in my direction. I continued to talk with the gentleman, focusing my attention on him, all the while trying to figure out what Jaquon was going to do next. Jaquon paused. He didn't move any closer to me. He glared at me, and then he nodded, turning away from me and leaving the bar. I guess that meant we were done for good.

My night wasn't ruined because I still had Tony. It wasn't long before we were in a hotel room ripping each other's clothes off. This man didn't play around. He tossed me to the bed and proceeded to please me. I thought I was going to lose it when he introduced his tongue to my wetness before his muscle broke up the engagement and wanted to join the party. He was doing things to me that made me want to climb the walls. He was so good I was ready to swing from the vines in a jungle in Africa screaming like Tarzan. Just when I thought no one could do me like Jaquon, another man had stepped up to the plate and proven me wrong.

I dug my nails into his chest, causing him to sigh, but it never stopped him from lifting his hips off the bed to meet my inner sweetness. Each pound jolted me closer to an orgasmic state.

I moved back and forth using my inner walls to suck him inward, pulling when I came up off him, which probably felt like my hand was stroking him. I threw it to him, back and forth, knowing it didn't matter how hard this man tried to last and make himself look like "The Man," he couldn't handle me. He was reaching unfathomable depths and began to lose it just like I thought he would. I watched as his body tightened with each thrust, and I got excited knowing our moment was coming. The stronger he became, the more I grinded my hips into him. One thrust . . . two, and then several before both of us let out an orgasmic scream together.

Tall and Sexy wanted me to stay all night so we could do it again, but I decided to make my way home. He seemed disappointed but didn't push the issue. Taking a quick shower and throwing my clothes on, I was out the door leaving him knocked out.

I looked at my cell to see if anyone had called me, and no one had. I was disappointed to see Jaquon hadn't called. I also wondered if Zacariah had awakened yet and considered going back over to the hospital to sit with her for a bit.

Getting closer to my car, I reached into my purse searching for my keys. I knew better, especially being a woman by herself at night, that I should have had my keys in my hand when I walked out of the hotel, but I wasn't thinking. I had too many other things on my mind. I did search the area like I always did to make sure no one was looking at me or following me, and no one was. So I proceeded with caution.

Reaching my car I still hadn't found my keys and wondered if I left them in the room. Not finding them, I turned around to find someone standing directly behind me. Before I could say anything, a hand with some type of cloth covered my mouth. The person turned me around quickly to get a better grip while holding the cloth over my nose and mouth. I twisted my ankle trying to free myself. My purse dropped to the ground. I was scared out of my mind and tried to fight hard, but seconds later, my strength began to diminish. Everything around me blurred, and then went black.

Kea

As soon as I got home, I knocked at his door waiting for him to open it. I knew it was late, but I didn't care. I had to speak with him. I was excited and saddened. Mr. Hanks was a wonderful man from what I could see, but to know I was a product of him raping my mother was a bit hard for me to swallow. I knocked and knocked, but he never came to answer the door so I went home. I figured I would wait until morning to speak with him.

Secrets from my mother's past continued to destroy me. Derrick was my brother. He was my brother. How was that? I mean, out of all the men I had to get involved with, I had to choose the one who was my blood sibling. I guess that was my punishment for stooping to the level everyone else did.

And to think the man I had been talking and drinking coffee with and living in the same building with was my father.

A knock at my door scared me half to death. It was the way the knuckles thudded against the door. It was urgent. I knew it was a matter of time before the police would come to arrest me. Beating Zacariah like I did, I knew she was going to press charges on me for aggravated assault. No matter how you looked at the situation, she was in the hospital and I was the one who put her there.

The knocks persisted. The person on the other side of the door was not going to go away, even though I wished they would leave me alone.

"Who is it?" I screamed.

"It's your neighbor."

Great. It was Freak-a-Leak from across the way.

"Go away!"

She knocked again saying, "Girl, you better open this door. I'm not going anywhere."

"I'm coming," I shouted wishing she would leave me the hell alone. I peeped to make sure it was her, and sure enough, it was. Blowing all the air out of my lungs, I unlocked the door and swung it open. I know she could tell by my facial expression I was not pleased to see her.

"Ew, why you looking like that for?" she asked, smacking and popping her gum. For a change, she actually looked decent. Decent in the sense of having on more clothes than I was used to seeing her in. Her hair was dyed a darker blond and cut into layers, making her look like she had some sophistication.

"What do you want, Fr—" Catching myself, I said, "I mean, Shelia."

Holding a cup in her hand, she said, "Can I get some sugar? I was getting ready to make me some red Kool-Aid when I saw I didn't have any. I can't eat my chicken wings until I have some Kool-Aid, unless you got some already made. If so, you can pour me a glass and I'll bring your glass back later."

Was she serious? She banged on my door like she was the police all because she wanted some damn sugar? I was even more pissed off. Not long ago my night had been ruined; now, she's going to come over and disturb me for a no good reason. I almost slammed the door in her face.

"You okay, because you staring at me like you want to hurt me? Did I catch you at a bad time? I ain't disturbed nothing, did I?" she asked looking around me, I guess, to see who I was with. I was by myself.

My body language shouted, "Hell, yeah," but my mouth said, "No, Sheila."

"It don't matter what you give me. Sugar or a tall glass of Kool-Aid would do. I would appreciate it."

I thought any glass I would let her use would be kept once it crossed her door into her place.

"I can give you some sugar, Sheila," I replied, grabbing the cup and walking into my kitchen. She came in and shut the door behind her. I went into the cabinet and pulled out the bag of sugar located on the top shelf. I poured it into her glass with her popping gum behind me.

"Girl, did you hear what happened to Mr. Hanks earlier?"

I turned abruptly spilling sugar all over my counter, asking, "No, what happened?"

"He got himself shot. Some young boy shot him in the head. You weren't here when all those ambulances and cops were out here acting like they were doing their job."

"Is he okay?" I asked, thinking this really couldn't be happening to me right now.

"Did you not hear me say he was shot in the head? Don't nobody come back from that. They pronounced him dead at the scene," she said unfazed, like she had seen plenty of homicides in her life. Knowing Freak-a-Leak, she probably had.

I couldn't say anything. Could this day get any worse? I tried to pick up the glass of sugar, but my hands wouldn't stop shaking.

"You didn't see all that blood on the stoop?"

"No, I didn't notice," I said glumly trying not to cry.

"Well, they must have sprayed if off then. Girl, blood was everywhere. His brains were splattered against the building and everything. And all because the boy thought Mr. Hanks had a lot of money on him. He even took the man's keys and ransacked his place searching for this mysterious hidden stash he won in the lottery."

"He was shot over money?"

"Isn't that usually the reason why people get shot? Especially around here. Either it's over money, over a relationship, or over a drug deal gone bad."

I finally picked the sugar off the counter and handed it to her.

"I can pay you for this if you want. I got a dollar."

"That's okay, Sheila," I said, walking her to the door trying to get her out of my place. You could hear a guy yelling as soon as we opened the door. The voice was coming from the other side of her door.

"I'm coming!" she screamed. "The nerve of some people. He's calling me like he ain't got any sense. And he better not have eaten all my wings up too or you might be calling 911 on his behind. This will be a relationship gone bad. Girl, you welcome to some. I got thirty of them things. I haven't even put hot sauce on them yet."

"No, thank you, Sheila," I said still trying to hold back the tears aching to escape my eyes.

"Suit yourself. More for me and Junebug. Thanks again for the sugar," Sheila said, swishing away, entering her place of freakiness.

I shut the door and let the tears fall as I leaned my back against it. Mr. Hanks was gone. All of the questions I wanted to ask him would never get answered. He wouldn't ever know that I was his daughter. He wouldn't know that one of his children did care about him, regardless of his past. The man I came to know as Mr. Hanks was a great man in my eyes, and he was my biological father. I just wished he didn't have to die alone.

Derrick

Mama was stroking the back of my head as I looked at the floor. Ever since Zacariah told me Kea was my sister, I had been mentally destroyed. My running joke of asking a female who her father was ended up being a joke turned on me in the end. I told Mama everything. I relinquished this catastrophe that had unfolded before my own eyes. Mama said nothing. She just looked at me with pained eyes. And part of me wanted her to feel the agony I was feeling. Why hadn't she told me about keeping in touch with my real father? I wanted to question her too, but I couldn't do this right now. All I could do was soak in the misery as my mind tried to piece together this uncertainty. My biological father's whoring created children none of us knew about, and the one woman I fell for ended up being my sister. I still couldn't believe it. And to make matters worse, Kea called to inform me he had been killed. Just hearing her voice broke me down, but to hear this man that was supposedly my father had been shot was icing on top of an already rotten cake.

"Baby, it's okay," Mama said.

"Mama, it's not okay. I was with my . . ." I paused, not able to bring myself to say those words. It was bad enough with it replaying over and over again in my mind.

"You didn't know."

"But I should have known," I said sadly.

"How? Is there some type of sign indicating brother and sister status?" Mother argued.

"No, Mama, but it still doesn't help me in knowing what I've done. And now with him dying on me, I'll never get a chance to confront him. I'll never get a chance to approach him as a man and let him have it. I can't yell at him and ask him why he wasn't there for me. Why he left me. Why he thought it was okay to use women and create all of these children he had no intention of taking care of. I want to know if he ever considered us in this process of him scamming and whoring around. I want to know if he ever loved me."

"I truly believed he loved you and all his children, Derrick. I feel as though in his last days he knew he had done a lot of bad things in his life. I believe he was also ashamed of those things."

"And I guess that's why he got shot in the head. Payback, huh?"

"Derrick!"

"Mama, I'm sorry. I'm just so . . . so . . . angry right now," I said gripping my hands tightly.

"It's okay to be angry, but don't let this anger consume you."

I chuckled, saying, "And the father who raised me is sitting in the living room right now smoking on his cancer sticks."

Mama laughed.

"Have you spoken with Kea since she called about your father?"

"No. When she called to tell me about *him,* I couldn't find any words to say to her. I still don't know what to say. I can't even imagine myself looking into her face again."

"Son, you need to talk to her."

"About what?"

"Don't you think she's feeling the same way you are?"

My cell phone began to vibrate in my pocket. I pulled it out and looked at the caller ID screen to see it was Kea. I sat up and turned to Mama.

"Well, who is it?" she asked.

"It's Kea," I said, not flipping my phone open. I just watched it buzz in my hand.

"Answer it, Derrick."

"But what—"

"Answer the phone," she said sternly getting up and exiting the room.

I opened the phone, put it to my ear, and hesitated to speak.

"Derrick," she called out.

"Yes, Kea," I said nervously.

"How have you been doing?"

"Not too good."

Kea

Derrick's and my last conversation was so awkward, even though I loved hearing his voice. His tone let me know he was not doing well at all, and I was in the same boat with him. Not wanting to face the world, I stayed locked in my apartment until the day came I had to pay my last respects to Mr. Hanks.

It was so hard seeing Derrick again. I wanted to go over and put my arms around him, but I held myself back. As he and I stood by the casket at the graveside, I looked around at the mere handful of individuals who decided to show. Derrick stood by his mother's side in a black suit and shades shielding his eyes as he clasped his mother's hand. In that moment, I wished I had my mother here with me too. Even though she was one of the most evil women I have ever known, she was still my mother. But I was lucky to have the support of my father whose hand embraced mine.

I looked at the ground that was wet from the rain earlier. I guess the old folks' saying was true, because the clouds did open up and shed a bucket of tears for Mr. Hanks. I just hoped his soul was right and that he asked for forgiveness for all his wrongdoings so his soul could be accepted into heaven.

I turned and looked at the pile of dirt that would cover Mr. Hanks in a little while, which represented the end of his life. Even though he had been gone for four days, it never seemed final for me until I saw the newly dug dirt in front of the tombstone.

When it was over, I was unsure of whether I should approach Derrick. What would I say? How would I act? Do I now treat him like a stranger? Will my heart still feel the love I have for him? This was too hard, but I felt like I was handling it well. I didn't understand why. He was my brother. A man I loved deeply but not in the brotherly sense. It was in the sense of me living my life forever with him. I got the courage and approached him and his mother.

"It's good seeing you again, Ms. Shirley," I said giving her a hug.

"Good to see you too, Kea," she said.

"This is my father," I said pointing to the man standing behind me.

"I know who he is. We went to school together. It's been a long time, Joseph."

"Yes, it has. You looking good though," my father said, smiling. If I didn't know any better, I could have sworn he was trying to flirt with her.

"Thank you. You don't look too bad yourself," she replied.

While they carried on their conversation, I gripped Derrick around the arm and pulled him to the side. I could feel him tense up with my touch and quickly let go.

"How are you doing?" I asked.

"Not good. You know . . ." he said still shielding his eyes from me. I couldn't tell if he was looking at me.

"So, is this how it's going to be from now on? Both of us are going to walk around like we never met?"

"Kea, it's hard for me to look at you, let alone have a conversation and pretend like everything's okay," he said sincerely.

"I understand, but we can't just leave it like this. How do we even know if Zacariah is telling the truth?

We can't go on her words alone. We were hit with devastating information that can ruin us if we let it."

"I know. What do you suggest we do, because right now, I don't have the answers?"

"I think to be sure if all of this is true, maybe we need to have a blood test done to see if we are indeed brother and sister."

"Are you serious?" Derrick asked.

"Yes, I am," I said nodding.

"And if it comes back that we are blood related, then what? I don't want to get my hopes up on something as serious as this, Kea. If you are my sister—"

"Then don't get your hopes up. Let's just have the test done and worry about crossing that bridge when we get to it, okay?"

"When do you want to do this?"

"I can call tomorrow and see about scheduling the test," I told him.

"Are you sure you want to do this?"

"We have to know for sure, or we're going to drive ourselves crazy wondering."

Derrick

Three days had passed, and today was going to be the day I would find out whether Kea was my sister. I lay across my bed thinking back to us going to the facility to have the test done.

When the technician swabbed my inner jaw, and then did the same to Kea, my heart was about to jump out of my chest. The all-white walls in the room, with the technician wearing a white jacket with lettering engraved with the name Susan, and her white gloved hands seemed to be too much for me to handle. Mama was by my side as was Kea's dad by hers during the process. No one said anything. The only one who did any talking was the technician explaining about the test. I had to admit I was staring the woman down. Her name kept catching my eye, and I hoped she didn't think I was looking at her breast because I wasn't. I felt like I knew her from somewhere, but I couldn't remember where I had seen her before. I gave up trying to recall and figured it would come to me sooner or later.

"It's going to take two weeks," she said when I asked her how long it was going to take to get the results.

"Two weeks?" I repeated.

"Yes. That's the average time for our facility to get this information to you."

"Is there any way we can get those results sooner?"

"There is but . . ."

"But what?" I asked eagerly.

"There is an additional cost involved in wanting re-sults quickly," the technician said.

"How soon can I get it?"

"Within three business days," she said smiling. Her demeanor was so calm it put me at ease more than I would have been if I had someone who was uptight.

"Okay, I'm willing to pay," I told her. I needed to know as soon as possible.

Now we were here to get the results. I sat up thinking how I wanted everything to be all right. I wished my life would go back to normal. My state of mind lately was not good. I wasn't sleeping or eating. I didn't go out. I was becoming lax in my grooming, which was some-thing I never allowed to happen. I did manage to work, but I had to push myself to do that. I couldn't bring myself to admit this fiasco ever occurred, but when I thought about Kea, she was a reminder that it did. Every time I thought about the get-together where the news was revealed which ripped our world apart, my stomach churned. I began to throw up often.

Mom's words resonated in my mind as she told me, "Baby, the only way to get through anything is to turn it over to God. The Bible says, 'Be still, and know that I am God.'" She smiled as she quoted Psalms forty-six, verse ten.

"Don't let the devil win this. You may have lost some-one you loved dearly, baby, but you can possibly gain a sister. I know you didn't want it to happen like this, and I know it's hard to get through what the two of you have done, but both of you will get past this. If she is your sister, it was God's will. Everything happens for a reason, son, and regardless of anything that happens in your life, know that I am here for you always."

I smiled, and for an inkling of a moment, I did have some peace.

When the pleasant technician called us to the back, I tried to stand, but my legs were shaking uncontrollably. Mama grabbed me by the hand, then patting it, said, "Regardless of the results, baby, you're going to be fine."

I nodded in agreement, hoping she was right. Kea and her father followed closely behind. I hadn't made eye contact since I arrived, but entering the room which would determine our destiny, I finally got the courage to look back at her. Our eyes met immediately. She looked just as nervous as I was, but her smile eased me. I smiled back, hoping mine did the same for her.

"This is it," she said.

"Are you ready?" I asked.

"Yes. No," she giggled nervously. "But it's something we have to know. And, Derrick, regardless of the results, I'm going to still love you. Whether it's in the partner form or family form, we'll always have a connection."

I nodded, taking her hand into mine, and we both entered the room to hear the results.

Kea

The ringing of her words were deafening as I looked around at the stunned faces. Derrick stood, allowing his shock to be visible to us all. Then his shock turned into rage. He started punching the wall over and over again. My head fell into my daddy's open arms as he whispered, "I'm sorry, baby girl."

Ms. Shirley ran over to Derrick to stop him.

"I can't believe this is happening!" Derrick roared.

Ms. Shirley turned back to the doctor and asked, "Are you sure these results are correct?"

"The test proved by an average of 99.9 percent that Kea and Derrick are brother and sister."

"Are you absolutely sure?" Daddy asked again, hugging me as he tried to absorb some of my pain.

"Yes."

"I don't believe this. I don't believe this. I cannot believe this," Derrick kept repeating as he held his head like a child, not wanting to hear any more scary stories. He was hurt. He was angry. He was traumatized just like I was.

"Can they take the test again?" Ms. Shirley asked.

"Of course, they can. If that's what they want, we will run the test again."

"I can't do this today, Mama. I just can't do this," Derrick uttered.

"Okay, baby. We can come back and do it another time," she said rubbing his back.

"I got to get out of here," Derrick said, holding back the tears that wanted to fall. I watched him, thinking this man I loved so much was now my brother.

"We'll leave," Ms. Shirley said looking at the doctor and the nurse.

"It's okay. Just contact us when you're ready to have another test done," the doctor said.

Ms. Shirley nodded, and Derrick walked out of the room without saying a word. Ms. Shirley came over to Daddy looking at him with sadness in her eyes.

"Take good care of her, Joseph," she said.

"I will. And you do the same for Derrick."

When Daddy got me home, he took me as far as my couch. All I could do was lie down. This had been the worst day of my life. Mother treating me like dirt for years was better than what happened today. I'd rather get a thousand whips across my back than to deal with the realization that the man I cared for and have been sleeping with was my brother.

Daddy sat down in the chair and stared at me.

"Baby girl, I'm going to stay here with you tonight."

"No, Daddy, I want you to go home. I'll be okay," I said with a weak voice.

"You don't look okay."

When he said those words, pressure pushed up from the pit of my soul, and my eyes reflected the pain threatening to get out. Hot tears streamed down my cheeks.

"I'm here for you," Daddy said.

"I know, Daddy, but I'll be okay. I promise," I said sitting up to absorb his loving gaze as I wiped the wetness from my cheeks.

"I can cook your favorite tonight," he said smiling.

"Jambalaya," I said like I was a kid again. In this moment, I almost wished I was. Then I wouldn't have to deal with the hardships of everyday living in my now-grown-up world.

Daddy said, "I'll even put some extra shrimp in it for you."

"Another time, okay? I just need some time to myself."

Defeated breaths escaped his lips, and he stood to his feet.

"I wish you would let me stay to comfort you, but I understand."

I stood, walking over to him and wrapping my arms around his waist, burying my face in his chest.

"I love you so much, baby girl," he said softly. "I don't like seeing you like this. You've been through so much lately. I don't understand why all of these bad things keep happening to you. You deserve so much better."

I looked up at him saying, "I can't explain it either, Daddy, but what I want you to remember about me is that I'm a fighter. And I have you to fight with me too."

He kissed me on the forehead saying, "I'm going to be calling to check up on you."

"Okay."

"And I want to take you out for your birthday this week. I haven't forgotten," he said walking to the door.

"Okay, Daddy."

"I love you, Kea."

"I love you too."

I watched as Daddy walked out the door. Breathing deeply, I stood looking around the empty space. Derrick was my brother, and there was nothing I could do about it. For some reason I could not convince myself that those results were correct. I knew I could be in denial. This could be my way of finding a reason to be with him. I missed him so much. I missed his touch. I missed his kisses. I missed his body being next to mine, and then the image of him being my brother shattered those imageries because now, my thoughts were considered to be incest.

Something had to change. I didn't know what that was yet, but our situation had to get better than this. Taking another test was a good idea. I needed another one to believe he was my brother. I had to convince Derrick we should do this, just to make sure it was right. We had to do something because I knew the love Derrick and I had for each other couldn't be wrong. Our world couldn't be this cruel to make me fall in love with my very own brother . . . could it?

Coming Soon

My Man's Best Friend 2: Damaged Relations

Jaquon

My world came crumbling down in front of a yard full of people when I got flashbacks of Zacariah's rapid decent down the road of destroying as many lives as she could. She annihilated everybody tonight and stepped beyond the line of merely tampering with my life. Not only my life, but she destroyed Kea, Derrick, and possibly their families' lives. All because she wanted revenge. All because her world wasn't going according to the way she wanted it to go. So the beat down Kea gave her was well deserved. She deserved a hell of a lot more done to her as well. I wish I would have got a kick or swing in during the altercation.

I knew when I saw Zacariah there was going to be a problem. I knew I had to do everything in my power to stay as far away from her as possible. The woman came stepping up in the cookout with a gray tank top, black skinny jeans, and gray stilettos. Who comes to a cookout in stilettos? Regardless, she looked nice. I might not like her, but Zacariah always had it together wherever she went. I think tonight she was dressed to impress to get Derrick back, but I don't think he even noticed her. Why would he when he had his eyes on my woman?

When I was sitting at the game table pulling my money with Essence by my side seeing Kea walk my way, I knew things were about to be on and poppin'. I wanted to snap my fingers and be somewhere else. I wanted Essence to disappear into another realm while my life with Kea remained intact. But that was all wishful thinking as Kea approached me and the woman I had been sleeping with for weeks. Kea didn't know this, but she knew my past history in our relationship. I wasn't the most trustworthy companion to her. So like I expected, Kea went the hell off. One for disrespecting her, and two for having the audacity to have my fling there to flaunt in her face. Of course, I denied it, but after Kea kept pushing, I confessed my involvement with Essence.

Kea finding out through others about my adulterous behavior was one thing, but to see me chilling with the woman I had been sleeping with behind her back was another. It was innocent enough because Essence and I were basically done at that point. I was ready to try to make it work with Kea, especially since it seemed like I was losing her to my best friend. But as fate would have it, as soon as I was ready to turn my life around, I got hit with a cataclysm that ended everything for me.

The expression on Kea's face was seared into my heart forever. The anger and hurt that consumed her delicate features stared back at me with a vengeance I knew was getting ready to be rectified. So her smacking the hell out of me was only the beginning of what I knew was the end of our relationship.

I was busted plain and simple. There was nothing I could do at this point but deal with the repercussions. You would think I would have learned my lesson when she threw that brick through the window of the other woman she caught me with, but the dog in me kept humpin' around.

"Would you like another drink?" the bartender asked me, and I nodded. Minutes later, another rum and Coke was placed before me. It was my sixth drink, and

I still didn't have so much as a buzz. I guess sadness fought against intoxication.

I don't know what I was thinking when I invited Essence to that cookout. Was I smoking something that clouded my judgment to think it would be okay to have my girlfriend and the girl I was sleeping with in the same vicinity? I mean, I have dabbled with weed in the past but this time, I hated to say, this decision was done with a sober mind. Essence not being there would not only eliminate my own breakup, but it would have also eliminated Zacariah from coming, thus preventing her destructive behavior that she put into our lives.

I wanted so much to blame that selfish, conniving tramp Zacariah for everything that happened tonight, but I knew she couldn't take all the blame. Yes, she put everybody's business on front street, but I played a part of this debacle too. If I would have stayed faithful, this incident never would have happened.

Sipping on my drink, I watched the bartender mix a blue liquid into two tall glasses. He then put a slice of orange on the rim and set the glasses in front of two attractive women at the other end of the bar. One was a redbone with long, curly, auburn hair, and the other was a deep mocha chick with a short cut. The mocha chick was more attractive than her acquaintance. She must've felt me staring because she made eye contact with me. A smile crept across her face, but I just looked with not so much as a smirk on mine. Women and cheating was what had me sitting here drinking alone with my girlfriend ready to leave me. Yeah, I could accept Kea and I were over and go holla at mocha, but I really wasn't in the mood. It was time to go pay the piper and face Kea like a man. I needed to go home, but I think I needed another drink first just to deal with what was to come.

Gulping down the last of my drink, I gestured for the bartender to bring me another. Scanning the room, my eyes fell upon someone I was not expecting to see. It was Essence. It didn't take her long to jump back into another man's arms. She was just with me hours ago, and now she was sitting with some punk grinning all up in her face. Seeing this guy with her actually ticked me off. I stood to my feet to go over and ask her what the hell she was doing. I was going to snatch her up and try my best not to shake the hell out of her. Then I halted. She was not my woman. How could I flip out when she was not the one I had a commitment with? Kea was my main priority.

Essence looked my way. The look she gave me wounded my already sunken spirit. She gritted hard on me, but why? What did I do to her? Our little fling was just that, a fling. She knew my situation and didn't care, and now she was looking at me like I better leave her the hell alone. I guess she knew what she wanted, and I was not it. I was not about to stand in the way of her getting her game on. So I bucked the fresh drink the bartender placed before me, tossed three twenty-dollar bills on the bar, and left.

Driving around for a while, I finally decided to go home and face my demons. I didn't know what I was going to hear once I got there, and I guess driving around was helping me avoid the inevitable. I considered buying flowers, candy, and even a diamond ring, but I knew that wouldn't work right now. It was sort of like buying my way back into her heart instead of being a man and facing my mistakes. But still, anything to make Kea forgive me I was willing to do.

When I pulled up into a parking space in front of our apartment building, Kea's madness was evident. I pulled up to find all my belongings scattered about. I got out of my car looking at how Kea made it rain with my clothes, shoes, CDs, and game systems. She flung all of it over the balcony. To make matters worse, Kea had sliced and bleached some of my clothes. When I saw my new Jordan's I had just purchased days ago soaked in the destructive liquid with slashes all over them I really became angry. I knew I had broken Kea's heart, and, yes, tonight was the straw that broke the camel's back, but come on. She didn't have to stoop to the level of destroying my property. I'd expect something like this from Zacariah because she was trifling, but Kea? I knew Zacariah was down and dirty. When she came swinging, her blows felt like gut-wrenching punches being thrown by cement-filled gloves knocking everybody out, and now Kea had adapted to this same method of revenge.

Scooping up what wasn't destroyed, I tossed what I could salvage into my car. I then headed upstairs, putting my key in the lock to enter. Before I could turn the key, however, the door behind me opened. I turned to see Sheila standing there half-naked in a two-piece black lace nightie. Now was not the time.

"Hey, Jaquon," she said seductively as I thought about Sheila's attempts that did work on me in the past and landed me in her bed.

She was always good for coming to the door in something skanky, but I ignored her attempts until one day I was too weak to resist. I went over and did what I did best. I tore that ass up and not just one time, several different times until my cockiness almost got me caught by Kea. This particular day I was bangin' Sheila down from the back when someone knocked on her door. I snatched my Johnson from her and went to the bathroom while she got rid of whoever it was at the door. To my dismay, it was Kea, asking Sheila to turn down the music which was blasting to mask the moans and groans we both were making.

"I know you and your men like to have sex with the music blasting, but do you think you can turn it down please? Some of us are getting ready to go to sleep."

"Okay. My bad. I'll turn it down," Sheila said. As soon as that door closed I came from the bathroom knowing this could never happen again. I was playing with fire for sure cheating so close to my home with Kea sometimes sitting in our apartment while I screwed Sheila. In the beginning, it never occurred to me that the neighbors would talk if they saw me constantly coming from Sheila's place, but the dog in me didn't care because my Johnson overpowered my common sense.

I eventually put a stop to it. I hated to because Sheila was gifted in the bedroom. Hell, she was gifted wherever we decided to do it. She was the type of chick that sucked toes and licked balls. She even did this thing with pop rocks one night that made me consider leaving Kea for good. But she was a straight up whore. You couldn't turn a whore into a housewife, and Kea was housewife material so Shelia had to go.

Seeing Shelia standing in her doorway half-naked scared the hell out of me because I was afraid Kea was looking through the peephole watching this freak attempt to lure me back into her corrupted lair.

"You can't speak?" she said smiling at me, posing like she was doing a shoot for *Playboy* magazine.

"What's up?" I said turning back to the door I was about to walk through.

"You look a little stressed."

"I have some things going on right now."

"You need some help with relieving some pressure?" she said sucking on her index finger.

"No. I'm good," I replied turning the knob opening the door to enter.

"Holla at me later, boo. I'm here if you need me."

I turned to look at her before shutting the door in her face. I hoped Kea didn't hear what she said because she damn sure said it loud enough for the people on the basement floor to hear. If I didn't know any better, I'd think Shelia was attempting to break me and Kea up. I was surprised her trifling behind hadn't told Kea already. Maybe I should tell her before Sheila does, but right now that would only add gasoline to this inferno.

The apartment was dark and quiet. I clicked the light only to find it didn't work. With the light from the moon giving me enough illumination to maneuver, I made my way to the bedroom. I clicked the light on in there and it too didn't come on. Did Kea pay the electric bill I wondered. I looked at the DVD player in our room to see the time showing 2:19, which meant we had electricity. I walked over to the television and turned it on. Finally something worked. The TV lit the room and once it did, I saw Kea standing beside me. I jumped halfway across the room.

"Damn, Kea, you scared the hell out of me," I said with my heart beating rapidly. I wasn't expecting her to be all up on me like she was. I could tell she had been crying from her swollen eyes. She looked disheveled but through her madness, I couldn't help but to bask in her beauty. I looked her up and down until my eyes fell upon what she was holding.

"What are you going to do with that?" I asked cautiously.

"I'm getting ready to whoop your . . ." she said not even finishing her sentence as she swung the bat at me.

"You bastard. I'm sick and tired," she swung again, "of you cheating" *another swing*, "on me. I want you to pay," *swinging*, "for hurting me."

I jumped back with the bat barely missing me a few times. She swung again hitting the lamp this time, smashing it into pieces.

"Put the bat down before you hurt somebody," I yelled, trying to escape the path of the bat.

She swung again, but this time, I didn't get out of the way quick enough. The bat smacked in my lower back causing pain to shoot through my body. Again she swung, hitting me on my upper bicep this time. Her next swing was aimed for my head, but I turned quick enough to put my arm up to block the bat from making contact. Pain shot through my arm. Thinking quickly, I grabbed the bat before she could take it back to swing at me again. I made sure not to let go of it as Kea struggled to try to gain control of the weapon.

"Let go!" she screamed.

"Not until you calm down."

We played tug-of-war before I jerked it hard, snatching it from her grip. This made her angrier. She charged at me and began kicking and punching me. It was hard to block with one hand since I was holding the bat with the other. The beast in her was unleashing its rage which had been festering for years. Finally, I threw the bat across the room. Kea never noticed, still trying to beat me to no end. I went low scooping her off her feet and throwing her over my shoulders.

"Let me go," she said punching my back. I took her over to the bed slamming her down on her back. Before she had a chance to get up, I straddled her, pinning her arms down, making it impossible for her to move or swing at me again.

"Calm down, Kea!" I yelled.

"Let me go! Get off me!" she screamed.

"Not until you calm down."

"I hate you. I wish I never met you. How could you do this to me again?" she said as she began to sob.

"Baby, I'm sorry," I pleaded.

"I loved you, Jaquon," she said with tears streaming down the sides of her face. "Why? Why didn't you just love me back?"

"Baby, I do love you," I said feeling her pain in its intensity for the first time.

"You couldn't have," she said through a cracking voice. I could feel her body lose its strength as her struggling arms became limp and her outburst turned into uncontrollable sobs. I slowly let go of her arms. She didn't swing again.

"Baby, I'm sorry," I tried to say as sincerely as I could.

"All I ever asked was for you to love me, for you to stay true to me, Jaquon, and you couldn't even do that," she said.

I crawled from on top of her and sat next to her on the bed watching her anguish release itself. She placed her hands over her face and continued to cry. I placed my hand on her shoulder, but she shook it off. I wanted to wrap my arms around her letting her know it was going to be okay, but I knew she wouldn't allow it.

"Baby, talk to me, please," I begged trying hard not to lose it myself.

"What is there to talk about?" she said sadly.

"Us."

She sat up abruptly, and I leaned back a bit thinking she was going to start swinging at me again, but she didn't.

She said, "There is no us. I'm not even sure if there ever was an us," she said despondently.

"Don't say that," I said looking at her.

"I mean it this time, Jaquon," she said sniffling. "I'm done being your doormat."

"Baby, we have both done some wrong things here."

Her expression spoke volumes. She didn't have to say a word, and I knew what I said never should have come out of my mouth. How dare I throw up her indiscretions when I was doing wrong all during our relationship together? Fury invaded her, and I knew my words were not sanctioned here.

"You have some nerve bringing Derrick up right now," she said furiously.

"I didn't say his name."

"You didn't have to. It was insinuated."

I couldn't say anything because she was right.

"I had every right to cheat on you," she said.

"But how was that going to solve our issues?"

"Now you want us to resolve things. Now that I have slept with your best friend, that's when you want to make things work."

She got up off the bed and walked over to the closet.

"You know the reason why I slept with Derrick in the first place was because you weren't here. You were never here. You were always making excuses about why you were sleeping over at his house. So when he came over here to see you because he was upset about Zacariah and you weren't here, our emotions got caught up. He needed somebody, and I needed him."

Her words were cutting me deep. I didn't ask for particulars, nor did I care to know, but that didn't stop her from spewing the gory details.

"The next morning you come up in here saying you were with him. I knew you were lying because Derrick was screwing me. He lay next to me most of the night. And you know what? It felt good. He felt good," she said with a coldness I had never seen. "Your friend worked my body like it's never been worked before, but it could have been because he was releasing the pain he was dealing with too. Both of our grief integrated into a night of steamy passion I will never regret."

I couldn't say anything. All the conversations I had with myself didn't prepare me for Kea telling me, in detail, how she enjoyed getting it on with Derrick.

"I wanted to see for once what it felt like to be you. I wondered what had you out in the streets at all times of the night. But I guess in the end, the joke was still on me," Kea said.

I lowered my head saying the only thing I could. "Baby, I'm sorry."

She ignored my apology and said, "I only slept with Derrick because he was there for me. He listened to me. He gave me what I couldn't get from you because you were too busy giving it to other women."

I went to stand but a twinge of pain shot through my side, reminding me of what a scorned woman could do with a bat.

"Baby, I want us to work. I love you, and I don't want to lose you. I will forgive you for everything if you promise not to leave me."

"I could care less whether you forgive me or not. The fact of the matter is, I can't forgive you. I gave you way too many chances with my heart, Jaquon, and you stomped on it. For goodness' sake, you slept with the enemy."

I forgot about that. Zacariah was once my past sexual encounter.

"You did her *and* her best friend. I don't know what you got. Hell, I don't know what you could have given me," Kea said.

"Baby, please," I pleaded walking toward her, but she held her hand up for me to stay away.

"I need you to leave. Pack your belongings and get the hell out."

"Is there something left to pack? You threw everything off the balcony, didn't you?" I said laughing, trying to lighten the mood. It didn't work.

"Then go outside with your crap, Jaquon. I don't want you here."

"When can I come back?"

"Never," she said.

"This is my place too, Kea."

"I don't care. You're leaving here tonight. Go to Zacariah or Essence or whoever else you've screwed. Just leave me the hell alone," she said going into our master bathroom.

I sat back down on the bed looking in the direction where she left. I knew this was the end of us. I didn't realize how much I loved this woman until now. I was mad at myself for ruining such a good thing.

I stood back up and walked in the restroom to find Kea standing in front of the mirror. I walked up behind her looking at her reflection. She didn't make me move. She didn't scream at me to get out. She just looked at me with such sadness. I ran my finger across her cheek, almost whispering in a sympathetic tone, "Do you really want me to leave?"

The conclusion to our relationship abducted my voice. I couldn't speak any louder because the wind was being taken out of my sail.

"Yes," she said looking into my eyes through the reflection in the mirror.

I was choked up. I knew she could see how much I agonized over her decision and wished she would change her mind. Tears were on the verge of falling, but I tried my best to hold them back. I guess that was the man in me. Maybe if I dropped down this masculine wall and let the pressure of losing her spew from every inch of me, she would consider taking me back.

She would see she's won this battle and I'm waving a white towel in surrender because I want to make this relationship work. But I couldn't.

I stood nodding my head as I cleared my throat of any emotion wanting to escape me. I wrapped my arms around her for the last time, making our bodies into a solitary cell. I wanted our molecular components to transform into something beautiful. As many times as Kea played the song, "No Air" by Jordin Sparks, which I couldn't stand to hear before, now I understood what that song meant. Kea was my air. And no one could ever fill the span of my heart which belonged solely to her.

I let Kea go and walked back into what had been our bedroom. I looked around at the space surrounding me. We did have some wonderful times here. I placed my hands in my pocket, bending my head toward the floor. I looked back at Kea one last time, and I watched as tears streamed down her cheeks. This was really it. I had finally pushed the woman I loved away and right now, the only thing I could do was abide by her wishes and leave.

Zacariah

My stint in the hospital was a short one. I actually got out the next morning with no one to pick me up. For some reason, Essence didn't bother to call or come by to see me today. I kept calling her, but she never picked up. That ticked me off because I was there for her when she passed out while she was screwing Jaquon, but then, she do me like this. I swear if she was with Jaquon while I had to try to find a way home, I was going to go off.

Taking a cab home, I expected to see her car sitting in the driveway, but it wasn't. Once inside, I saw that the house was empty. I went to her bedroom to see her bed had not been slept in. I was ready to cuss her out if she was still sleeping, but she wasn't here. That was odd. Essence used Sunday as her relaxation day. I didn't think she got the spirit and decided to go to church because she really never went to church. I didn't know whether to be happy she wasn't here or mad. Where was she?

I picked up the phone sitting on the console table behind the couch and dialed her number again.

"Hi, you've reached Essence. Leave me a message and I'll get back to you when I get a chance. Later." *Beep.*

"Essence, this is Zacariah. Where are you, and why haven't you returned my calls? Look, I've made it home now, so when you get this message, please give me call. And I will try not to lay your behind out when you do."

I hung up the phone and looked around the space, a little worried about where she was. Then I thought about how nice it was to have the place to myself. The quiet was very much needed so I walked around the table and sat down on the sofa. Laying my head back, I looked up at the ceiling and replayed the events that landed me in the position I was in.

I told them I would get them back. They thought I was a joke, and now look at them. Who's laughing now? They deserve what they get. "Little Ms. High and Mighty over here," I said looking at Kea who stood with no tears, no expression, just shock plastered on her face.

"And you," I said sneering at Derrick. "I was your woman. I loved you, and you cheated on me with her. This serves you right. I bet you wish you would have kept your dick in your pants now. You wouldn't have had to worry about something as sick as this happening. Karma, baby, karma."

Snapping back into the now, I sat forward on the sofa, then stood up. I felt sore, like I had been in a battle. Well, I had been in a battle. I was just on the losing end of this one.

Walking into the bathroom, I looked into the mirror at my reflection. With black eyes and a busted lip, anger came over me again. I wanted to go looking for Kea to whoop her for what she did to me.

Yes, I had just opened up the Bible and read a verse the nurse recommended to me.

Cease from anger, and forsake wrath: fret not thyself in any wise to do evil.

But how do I do that? It's not in my nature to turn the other cheek. All my life people have never cared about me, so I don't care about anybody else. I'm the only person I can trust in this life. Not Mama and Daddy. Not any of my aunts and uncles. Not Derrick. And today, not even Essence. All I had was me. Who in the hell was doing anything for me?

Tired of wallowing in self-pity I decided I was going to order some takeout and chill for a little while. Deciding to wait and see if Essence contacted me, I took this time to get to know television again. Too bad the first bit of news I heard was the tragic death of Derrick's biological father.

"An elderly man by the name of Otis Hanks was shot and killed late last night at an apartment complex in a robbery gone bad," the anchorwoman said. *"Sources say the gunman was an African American male who appeared to be in his late teens. He was wearing black jeans and a jacket with green lettering on the back. If you have any information regarding this murder, please call your local police."*

I was shocked. Derrick's father was dead. I wanted to go over to Derrick's house to see him, but thought better of it. Not after what I had put him through. I did decide to do the next best thing and that was to call him. I knew once his caller ID showed it was Essence's house, he wouldn't answer, but to my surprise, he did.

"Hello."

"Hey, Derrick. It's me, Zacariah."

When he heard my voice, he said nothing.

"Derrick, are you there?"

"I'm here."

"I didn't know whether you hung up on me."

"I have every right to, don't you think?" he said impassively.

"Yes, you do, but, Derrick, please hear me out. I just want to apologize," I said, thinking this may smooth things over a bit.

"I think it's too late for that."

"Please, Derrick. I'm really sorry. I didn't mean for things to turn out like they have."

"It went exactly like you wanted it to go, Zacariah," he said loudly.

"Yes. No. Derrick, look, baby, I never wanted us to end up where we are now."

"You can't blame any of this on me."

"I know if I never cheated on you, we would still be living in bliss."

"I doubt that," he said coldly.

"Well, I think so. I love you."

"You love me so much you were determined to ruin my life. I'm sitting here unhappier today than I've ever been in my entire life, and it's all because you couldn't leave well enough alone. All you had to do was let me go on with my life, but because I wanted my future to be with Kea, you couldn't let that happen."

"You're right, but, Derrick, I didn't lead you to believe your father was your biological dad. That was your mother. And I didn't rape Kea's mom to produce Kea. That was your biological father," I said defensively.

The next thing I heard was a dial tone. I dialed his number back, but he never picked up the phone again.

I was so mad at myself as I wondered why I went there with him. I was getting aggressive because he was trying to blame all of this on me, but he couldn't. Why couldn't he see his mother, Kea's mother, their dad, and other family members let these lies consume a past all of them were trying to conceal, which eventually turned his world upside down? I was just the one who brought things to the light.

Four days would pass before I decided to leave Essence's house. And still, she hadn't shown up. I thought maybe she had gone to visit her parents. I was supposed to go with her, but if she needed to do this on her own, then more power to her. Right now, I had Derrick to worry about.

Since he decided to ignore my numerous attempts to talk with him again, I decided to call him from a local pay phone. It was difficult to find one since cell phones had taken over, but lucky me, I managed to find one. As soon as Derrick heard my voice, he hung up. I knew he was mad, but I thought he had to be over it by now. Maybe he was acting like this because he was grieving. I knew my boo needed me, and I wanted to go to him. I really was regretting I never told him how sorry I was about him losing his biological dad. And since he stopped accepting my calls, I decided to go to the funeral and pay my last respects.

While the service was going on, I made sure to remain in the background where no one could see me. The funeral was graveside so I stood in the very back. I had on an all-black dress with a hat and black shades to help hide my healing bruises. I felt like I should be sitting with Derrick and his family. Hell, I was practically family as long as Derrick and I were in our relationship. What we were going through right now was only temporary. I knew eventually we would be together and would get on with our life loving each other.

Once the service was over I watched as everyone greeted one another. Individuals lined up to express their condolences to Derrick and other family members. I could tell he didn't like this portion of the service. How could he when he stood in front of a casket holding a father he never knew. The pain was evident on his face, and for a split second, I regretted that I played a part in his pain.

As the crowd thinned out, it was then that Derrick saw me. The expression on his face was one I wasn't familiar with. It wasn't one of happiness or anger. It was as if he were an empty shell of a man going through the motions just so he could get home. I hoped when he saw my dependability he would see how sorry I was and would let me help him get through everything he was experiencing.

When I made my mind up to approach Derrick, Kea stepped to him. She caressed his arm gently and a bit of jealousy shot through me. Then anger crept in, and again, I tried to remember the words my nurse said to me. This was when I realized my anger was a part of me and so was revenge. I wanted to beat Kea down right here in this graveyard, burying her under one of these tombstones. But I had to maintain my composure. I had to do it for Derrick. My body trembled as I fought the urge to lay hands on this trick, but I held strong and remembered I was here for my boo.

I walked over to the two of them carrying on a conversation. I overheard something about getting paternity test results in a couple of days. Then Derrick nudged Kea, who turned her attention from him to me as I stepped to them. All conversation ceased when I approached. I was hoping Derrick would be the first one to speak, and he was, but I didn't like what came out of his mouth.

"What the hell are you doing here?" he said angrily through clenched teeth.

"Derrick, I wanted to come and show my support. I heard about what happened and—"

"And what? You came to gloat?" he said.

"No."

"You have some nerve showing your face here today."

"I came here for you."

"I didn't ask you to come. Never once did I pick up a phone and say, 'Zacariah, I need you.'"

"But I knew you would," I said, watching Kea smirk and shake her head in dismay.

"Are you happy that the man I never got to know is dead? Or is this some sick way of you seeing Kea and me together, knowing we can never be lovers . . .?"

Just him saying the words "Kea" and "lovers" in the same sentence made me cringe. But I held my ground.

"No. Please. Just hear me out, Derrick," I pleaded trying to look sincere, but it was hard seeing Kea getting some satisfaction out of Derrick embarrassing me in front of everybody.

"Why should I listen to anything you have to say? You have been the worst thing that has ever happened in my life. I don't even want to look at you right now," he said walking away. I watched him head in the direction of his mother who was glaring at me with undisguised disdain. That woman never liked me.

"You really got some nerve showing your face here," Kea said with her black clutch in her hand. With a black suit on, hair pulled back, and shades shielding her eyes, I still thought I was better looking than she was. I still didn't see what Derrick ever saw in her.

"I didn't come here for any drama, Kea."

"That's all you're full of, Zacariah. Everywhere you go there is a theatrical performance with you playing the leading role as queen bitch."

I smiled smugly trying not to reach out and smack the hell out of this trick.

"And here you are proving my point by reveling in our sorrow at our dad's funeral. Just when I thought you couldn't sink any lower, you somehow find new depths of dirt to throw in our faces. But I guess I shouldn't be surprised since low-down is your customary ranking."

My heart was beating so fast. I felt sweat beads building underneath my clothes, and one of my hands balled into a fist.

I said, "I didn't come here in triumph. Does it look like I have a victorious expression on my face? I'm saddened by what has happened, and I came here to support Derrick."

"Well, how did that work out for you? As you can see, he still wants nothing to do with you."

"I completely understand that, but I won't stop trying to be there for him. I love him."

Kea removed her shades and looked at me through squinted eyes. I didn't care if she saw how genuine I was or not because I wasn't here for her. I was here for Derrick. And since she couldn't comfort him like she used to, I knew he needed me back in his life. If he just gave me a chance, I could show him how right we were for each other.

"Leave Derrick alone," Kea said slowly like I was dense and couldn't comprehend her words.

"Excuse me?"

"You heard me. Stay away from him."

"And who the hell are you?" I questioned with attitude wondering why this female always had to test me.

"Just because you think I'm his sister doesn't mean I will not be in his life. If anything, I'm going to be there for him even more."

"Too bad it won't be in his bed again," I retorted.

"It doesn't have to be his bed when I got his heart," she said causing me to breathe deeply.

His heart. I had his heart . . . I thought.

"I'm going to be there to tell him to stay as far away from you as he possibly can. You are a manipulative, trifling little whore. If you ever come near him, I will beat you down like I did before. I warned you, and you crossed me. I showed what I'm made of too, so please try me again. I dare you."

No, this trick wasn't threatening me on the sacred ground of souls resting. The pastor who gave the eulogy stood several feet away chatting to some of the mourners but still managed to cast some worried stares in our direction. I took a deep breath clasping my hands in front of me. I was trying to play it cool, and she's the one getting ignorant with me. I swear I saw her neck roll and her pointing her little finger at me like I'm her child or something. I nodded, smiling slyly.

"You caught me off guard before, Kea, but don't think I'm going to ever let you get me like that again. You better be glad I'm not sweeping the ground with you right now. And some words of advice. Don't you ever threaten me again," I said like nothing was going on between us. Just a little friendly conversation was what we were having in everyone else's eyes.

"Oh, it wasn't a threat, Zacariah. It's a *promise*," Kea said before walking away.

A promise? Didn't I just tell her to not threaten me again? I chuckled as she made her way back to Derrick and his mom. All of them walked toward the waiting limousines. I smiled at the pastor who was still staring me down. Then I brushed my suit, tucked my purse under my arm, and proceeded to my car all the while wishing I had jerked Kea by her ponytail and slammed her face into these granite headstones. But I shook the thoughts off and thought of other ways to get her back.

Taking out my cell phone I found the number to my cousin.

"Hey, girl. Do you think you can stop by and see me today . . . For what? Don't be questioning me. Just come over as soon as possible. I need a huge favor from you, and I can guarantee I will make it worth your while."

About the Author

Tresser Henderson was raised in the small town of Skipwith, Virginia. Brought up by both her mother and father, she was the oldest of three siblings. At the age of fifteen, she realized writing a book was something she wanted to do. This was ironic since she didn't like to read. Never pursuing this, she went on to graduate from high school and college, getting an associate's degree in computer medical administration. Then Tresser worked for a major health insurance company. It wasn't until she was brought to a crossroad in her life that someone helped her realize writing was her God-given talent that she was supposed to be doing. Not letting this opportunity slip away again, she followed her dream. At this point in her life, Tresser developed her latent passion—reading. This, along with life's challenges, helped fuel Tresser's passion for the art of writing fictional stories. Getting married and having her children rank at the top of her life's blessings. Having the courage to step out in faith and accomplish her dreams comes in second. Tresser is currently working on the sequel to her novel.

Notes